Crossing The Lough Between

No Frills
<<<>>>
Buffalo
Buffalo NY

No Frills Buffalo Press
119 Dorchester
Buffalo, New York 14213
For more information visit Nofrillsbuffalo.com

To Joyce, thank you for the blessings of your friendship
and your daily example of faith.

Crossing The Lough Between

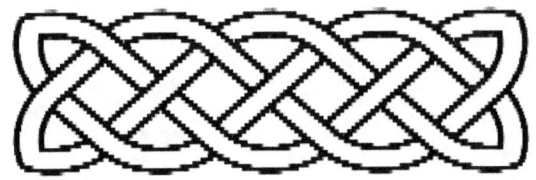

Sinéad Tyrone

Also by Sinéad Tyrone

Fiction:
Walking Through The Mist

Poetry:
Fragility

1

Spread between the A5, A6 and A505 motorways, where the lands of County Londonderry and County Tyrone blend, some of the most verdant, fertile farmland in all of the Emerald Isle forms a natural patchwork quilt of light greens, dark greens, tans and browns. The Sperrin Mountains run through the patchwork fields, lifting and lowering them in pleasant rolls, sun and cloud throwing alternating light and dark against the hillsides. The Glenelly and Owenkillew Rivers, rich with salmon, grilse and trout, flow past sheep and cattle dotted pastures. Among the network of minor roads, small towns rise against the backdrop of lush green fields, some with no more than a church, general store and pub, others with schools and expanding, pleasant housing tracts.

Nestled among the narrow roads, meandering streams that stretch their fingers out from flowing rivers, and multicolored fields that form this picturesque countryside, lay a midsize farm and large estate, with a small blue lough separating the two.

The farm consisted of an old weatherworn house, a shed, and a barn set in the midst of pastures of light, dark and medium shades of green, two of which were dotted with cream colored, black-faced sheep. From the barn, a young man stepped out and finished hosing down the barn floor and cement pad leading into the barn. He shut the water off, coiled the hose on the metal holder next to the faucet, then picked up a broom to sweep off any excess water that remained on the barn floor. As he worked, an older man checked an outdoor fuel tank for its level of oil, the winter heating source that supplemented their supply of turf, and made a notation in a small notebook he carried that he needed to order more. A woman removed clean, dry sheets and towels from a clothesline near the garden to the right.

The older man, Will Donoghue, glanced at the sun slipping closer to the crest of the mountains in the distance, gathered the tools he'd used earlier to replace worn belts on his truck's engine and set his toolbox inside the storage shed next to the barn. Peering inside the barn, he called to his son, "You best go bring our sheep home, lad."

"Aye, Da." Niall hung his broom back on its hook near the door and whistled once. The Donoghue's border collie rounded the corner into the barn, eyes so bright with excitement Niall had to laugh. "Farley, I swear you can tell time! Come on, boy, let's go gather our flock."

As Niall crossed from the barn to the house to grab his jacket, his mother called out, "Is our Aidan coming over for dinner tonight? You best call and remind him. Your father's setting steaks on the grill soon; it would be a shame for Aidan to show up late with nothing but a cold piece of meat to be had."

Niall buttoned his jacket and nodded to his mother. "I'll ring him, Mam."

Farley raced ahead, anxious to perform the job he'd been bred for, while Niall, walking slower, rang Aidan's number. "My mam wants to know if you're joining us for dinner."

Aidan O'Connell set his paint brush down, wiped his hands on a rag and glanced out the windows at the fading daylight. "I lost track of time. How soon will you be eating?"

"About fifteen, twenty minutes. My dad's grilling steaks. We're eating out on the patio."

Aidan pictured the patio trellis and rose bushes he and Niall had helped Mr. Donoghue set in place several weeks earlier. "You won't be eating there much longer. The weather's going to turn soon enough."

"It will indeed. You'll join us tonight though, won't you?"

"Sure. I'll be over as soon as I clean up here."

By the time he finished his call to Aidan, Niall had reached the pastures where his family's sheep grazed. Farley pawed at the gate, dashed through like lightning once Niall unlatched it, and ran several quick circles, each one smaller and tighter, until all the sheep were gathered and heading toward the gate. As the border collie worked Niall watched, amazed as always at Farley's inherent skills in herding and directing their flock of stubborn sheep.

As he and Farley guided their charges home, Niall looked out over his farm, the lough, and the estate house on the other side of the water. The contrast between the two properties could not have been any more vivid. Compared to the massive estate house Aidan now occupied, Niall's family's farm looked like a run down, dilapidated relic of the past. Oh, he harboured no envy or jealousy as he viewed the grand home his best friend now owned; in fact, he felt the opposite. The great house, in need of repair after years of abandonment, had given Aidan a new vision and purpose after he'd lost his family, and along with them his passion for life. Now Aidan's days were full of excitement as he planned and worked on repairs to the house; and living next door to each other had deepened the strong friendship that had developed between them both since they'd joined Macready's Bridge, the group of musicians they worked with.

Still, as Niall drew close to the farm he surveyed it with fresh eyes. The stone house stood firm through rain and wind, her roof showed wear but still kept them dry, her windows shone bright gold in the setting sun. A vegetable garden to the right of the house had fed them well all summer and would continue to through winter as his mother had preserved tomatoes, beans, carrots and potatoes. Her roses and other flowers, now fading as autumn set in, had graced the farm with bold colors and beauty. His parents had worked hard over the years to maintain their farm, but Niall had long thought, and thought again now, a bit of modernization would give their home a much needed lift.

Niall viewed the fields they owned surrounding the farm. Someday, when he was married, he'd build a house on the next field over. He had dreams of expanding their operations, increasing the number of sheep his parents tended, and updating their equipment and methods as well. He envisioned working side by side with his father, when breaks from his music career allowed; and dreamed someday he'd have a son of his own to carry on the tradition.

By now he'd reached the house, where his mother was busy setting dishes on their patio table and his father turning steaks on the grill. Pushing his thoughts aside he called to them both, "I'll be right there. Mam, set a place for Aidan as well. He should be here any time now."

South of Sligo, inside their small cottage near the sea, Patrick Leahy and his eight year-old twins, Conor and Caitlyn, sat at table, their breakfast on hold. From the bathroom where she'd dashed off to, they could hear the sound of Moira being sick, then flushing the toilet and running water to wash her hands and rinse her mouth out. She returned, flushed, with a smile Patrick could tell was forced.

"Are you okay Mum?" Caitlyn asked, eyes wide with worry.

"Aye, love, I'm fine." Moira set orange juice in front of the twins. "You best hurry and eat your breakfast so your father can get you to school on time."

She turned to the stove then and started to fry eggs and bacon for Patrick. Halfway through, she dashed into the bathroom again.

"Is our mum very sick?" Conor asked a few minutes later as Patrick drove him and his sister to school.

Patrick shook his head. "No. She'll be fine. She's just got an upset stomach." He wished he could tell them what was making their mother sick, that their mum was expecting, that in six months' time they'd have a baby brother or sister. Moira had insisted they wait until they'd had the scan and knew the baby was healthy before telling anyone though. Today was their scan appointment; by dinnertime they'd be able to tell Conor and Caitlyn the good news and relieve their worries.

Two hours later they sat in the examining room waiting for the doctor to confirm the scan results. They'd seen the shadow that had flickered across the technician's face, followed by her quick departure from the room.

"I wonder what's up?"

Moira placed a reassuring hand on Patrick's arm. He felt the trembling in her own hand even as she told him, "I'm sure everything's fine."

Dr. Madeleine McAfee entered the room, studied the monitor screen as she repeated scanning across Moira's exposed belly, then turned to the couple before her.

"Moira, Patrick, it's good to see you again. How are those twins of yours doing?"

"They're fine," Moira answered, studying the doctor's face for any clues as to what the scan had revealed.

"Let's see, they would be eight now, correct? I'll bet they're quite helpful around the house."

Patrick managed a light laugh. "Yes, when they want something they can be helpful indeed."

Dr. McAfee looked straight at Moira now. "Did you find having twins hard?"

Moira shook her head, growing more nervous. "In the beginning yes, but Pat was a wonderful help, and our parents as well. Of course, my mother is our only parent left, the others have passed on. She helps when she can, though. At this age the twins are easy, almost take care of themselves."

Dr. McAfee smiled at them both. "You might want to move your mother in for a while. You're expecting twins again."

Patrick and Moira stared at the doctor, stunned. She laughed, turned the monitor their way, and repeated the scan. "See? There's the first heartbeat, and the second. Here's a right foot, and another wee right foot." She continued, showing them two sets of everything decipherable.

"Can you tell if they're boys or girls?" Moira asked, peering hard at the screen, trying to determine for herself what the babies' sexes were.

Dr. McAfee shook her head. "They're not cooperating on that score. They seem to enjoy a good mystery!" She ended the scan then rose, shook Patrick's hand and helped Moira sit upright again. "Moira, you know carrying twins comes with a few extra risks. I'm sure everything will go fine, but look after yourself. Eat well, get plenty of rest, and if you have any concerns at all call my office straight away."

"Twins!" Patrick remarked, still stunned, as they drove home. "Can you believe that?"

Moira shook her head. "No, I can't!"

Sure he'd heard a twinge of nervousness in her voice, Patrick cast a sideways glance at Moira. "Do you think you're up to two babies again? Maybe we can call one of the neighbors in to help once they're born, or check around for a girl to come in after school."

"We've got time to sort that out."

"Still, something's on your mind. What is it?"

Moira hesitated, eyes straight ahead yet focused on nothing in particular before her. After a long minute's silence, she blurted out, "What if something goes wrong this time? I'm that much older now. What if I can't carry the babies to term? What if I have problems? Twins, Patrick! There are so many things that could go wrong."

Patrick recognized the panic in Moira's voice. He pulled their car to the side of the road, shut the engine off, and placed his free arm around her shoulders. "Let's not borrow trouble, Moira. God's given us the blessing of twins again. Not many people get two sets of them. Sure God wouldn't give us this blessing only to pull it away from us. Just do what Dr. McAfee says starting with a proper rest when you get home."

"You're right. I'm gathering worries best left to float away on their own." Moira settled back against the seat of their car and tried to relax. If Patrick said the new babies would be okay, then they would be. He was a good husband and a wonderful father. He'd see to whatever they needed.

Patrick watched Moira lean back and close her eyes, one hand placed as a protective shield over the babies she carried. Thankful her concerns had been relieved, at least for the moment, he wondered how he'd calm his own fears. As they neared home and their small cottage came into view, he wondered how they'd manage to squeeze another set of twins into already tight quarters. They could expand, but where would he find the money for materials and labour? Even without expansion, how would they make ends meet? Macready's Bridge, the band of musicians he was part of, had been successful enough; but he and Moira had still found their budget tight with the prolonged furlough they'd all agreed to while Aidan sorted his life out after the loss of his family a few months earlier. They'd be back to work soon enough, which would help, but they'd have to watch every Euro now.

Patrick pulled the car to a stop in their driveway. "Alright, love, let's get you into the house for a wee nap before Conor and Caitlyn rush in full of their usual chaos."

"I don't need a nap yet," Moira protested. "There's laundry to take down outside and tonight's dinner still to be sorted."

Patrick gave her a gentle push towards their bedroom. "You lie down. I'll see to the laundry." As he turned to head outside, his eyes fell on the photo collage frame on their hallway wall. Among the photos were Conor and Caitlyn's first baby pictures.

Seeing their innocent newborn faces, Patrick felt all over again the thrill of fatherhood. Twins, he thought again. We're having twins! His fears faded as he wondered what the new babies would be like, what sexes they would be, whether their looks would favor Moira or himself. He could almost hear their newborn coos and cries, and laughed to himself as he hurried outside.

Michael Sullivan glanced at the number he was about to ring on his phone, and sent a reluctant look across the living room of his Dublin apartment to the dining room table where his fiancé, Susannah sat, laptop opened and papers spread around her. "Are you sure you want me to do this?"

"We have to! Our wedding's two months away and our parents haven't even met each other yet. We have to have them over for dinner."

"We could go to a restaurant," Michael suggested thinking his father, at least, would be much less tempted to throw harsh words around in a public setting.

Susannah looked shattered. "Do you not trust my cooking?"

"Oh no! It's not that at all. It's just, well . . ." Michael paused. How did he explain a man he understood so little himself? If he said his father was a shrewd businessman, so what? So was Susannah's. If he told her his father was an angry, bitter man whose only son was a colossal disappointment to him, she would protest he exaggerated the truth, his father couldn't be all that bad. In the end, he chose to tell her part of the truth. "My father can have a terrible temper. I don't mind him being angry towards me, but I'll not have him treat you that way. If we eat out, he'd be more inclined to keep peace."

"He can't be all that bad," Susannah countered. "He raised you, and you don't have a hot temper."

"That's more down to my mother."

"Fine. We'll do whatever you want. We can eat out at a restaurant."

The way she said it, with a monotone voice and the spark gone out of her eyes, convinced Michael she'd had her heart set on cooking and hosting dinner for their parents. He couldn't bear seeing her eyes so dull, so disappointed, like some corner of her heart had been crushed.

"Alright," he relented. "We'll do it your way; we'll have dinner here. Now, let's get these calls over with."

"Next Friday?" Susannah's father studied his calendar. "We've got dinner with the Morrisseys. Can you change to the Friday after?"

She mouthed the silent question to Michael, who shook his head and mouthed back "My father's away. The Friday after?"

"Dinner with clients." Mr. Tierney replied. "Friday after that?"

When Edward Sullivan responded with a quick no, Michael couldn't hold his frustrations back. "Are you even trying, Dad, or will you say no to every date we suggest?"

"You know how busy I am," his father retorted. "I don't just leave my calendar open in the hopes of getting together with you."

Michael recognized an explosion about to erupt and eased off. "Sorry. Let's try it this way. What Fridays are you free? Or are Saturdays better?"

Ignorant of Michael's frustrations, but well aware that his wife, standing by his side, was desperate to meet Michael's fiancé, and knowing he'd been much too harsh with her the past few weeks as one of his real estate deals fell through, Mr. Sullivan studied his calendar once more and suggested, "Next Saturday or the Saturday after would work."

"Next Saturday?" Susannah asked her father, holding her breath and crossing her fingers.

Mr. Tierney realized how important this dinner was to his daughter, ignored the notation "dinner with Ashfords" on that date and told Susannah, "Yes, next Saturday is fine."

"Thank God that's over." Michael set his phone on the coffee table and leaned back against the sofa. "I was afraid we'd never get that date sorted."

Susannah's eyes glowed with excitement now that a date had been set. "What should we have for dinner?" She started searching her favorite recipe websites for options. "Steaks? Roast beef? No, I want something more special for this."

"Keep it simple," Michael cautioned. "You'll be nervous enough as it is; don't add to your stress by choosing a complicated dinner. Why don't you make your lemon chicken? I love that."

Susannah shook her head, golden hair shimmering, green eyes serious. "No, I want to impress your parents. Here, salmon! Does your father like salmon? This looks like a perfect choice."

Michael wanted to tell her it didn't matter what she served, she could choose caviar and lobster or pheasant under glass and his father still would not be impressed. He wanted to say the fault was not in her, but all down to him, that he never pleased his father. He wanted to tell her she could shine like the brightest star in the night sky, which no doubt she would, she already did, and his father would still be difficult. He chose to say none of these, though;

instead he watched and listened as she planned the menu for the biggest dinner in her life, and hoped, just this once, his father would choose to be gracious that night, for Susannah and her family's sake if for nothing else.

Mack Macready sat at the desk in the office of his large house on the Antrim coast, browsed websites for four more potential bookings for Macready's Bridge, phoned and left voicemail messages for each of the four clubs, then updated the contact information for each in his master log. He reviewed his chart for the twelfth time to confirm the status of each of the potential songs the boys would soon record and the copyright status for each, still debating the playlist, which songs seemed strongest, which ones might not make the final cut. He pulled his laptop calendar up and checked to see he had entered all of the possible club dates, rehearsal dates and potential recording dates that had swirled around his mind since waking up. Then he spent a half hour reviewing trade journals, reading industry blogs, noting which online ticket outlets artists were using this month, the newest technology trends in recording, and which music festivals he wanted to book Macready's Bridge into in the coming year. When he glanced at the time at last, he was shocked to see how late the day had grown.

In a hurry now, Mack powered his laptop down and filed his various charts and notes in the "pending matters" tray on his desk. He had planned tenderloin for dinner; if he didn't start soon it wouldn't be ready when Kate arrived home from work. As he cleared the top of his desk, his hand felt the smooth brochure he'd received the day before from the travel agency. He pulled it out now and studied the cover picture.

Belize. The word sounded like a whisper on a warm Carribean breeze. Images of turquoise water, white sand beaches, and thatched roof huts drew him like a magnet. Part of him wanted to turn his computer on, book reservations now and surprise Kate with an exotic tropical vacation far away from the rain that had fallen the better part of the past week.

The larger part of him held back. What would Kate think? Would the surprise thrill her? Or would she hesitate, and in so doing throw cold water on his plans?

Mack had thought his dream was complete when Kate moved back in eight years after they'd divorced. The past several weeks had been pure bliss, going to bed every night with Kate, the feel of her beside him, the sound of her gentle sleeping breaths, her soft stirrings in the middle of the night, then waking each morning to her smile, her light perfume. In between, their lovemaking had been as passionate as when they'd first married, offering a deeper sense of satisfaction than he'd experienced with any other girl in that long interim between when she'd left and when she'd returned. Now, though, a larger dream stirred in Mack's heart. He didn't want Kate just living with him. He wanted their reunion to be fully restored.

Belize would be a perfect second honeymoon destination. First, though, he would have to propose to her.

As he slid the tenderloin into the oven to roast, scrubbed and sliced potatoes and set them in a glass dish with butter and seasonings and slipped that in the oven as well, and started pulling together his classic garden salad, Mack surveyed the kitchen where he worked and the dining and living room beyond. The rooms were different, transformed since Kate had moved back in. She'd made her changes in small, subtle ways, a bowl of flowers here, framed photos there, throw pillows on the sofa, soft light on the hallway table. All of her touches combined to add a warmth and ambiance he'd missed for years without knowing it.

Mack's thoughts returned to Belize, to visions of Kate and himself walking a sandy beach along turquoise waters while a soft breeze cooled their sun baked skin. The sun shining down on them in his vision seemed to him the same as the sun that shone on his world whenever Kate stepped inside it. Without her, the house was once again cold and dark, no matter the weather outside. The contrast between his days with Kate and his days without her was so sharp, so painful, Mack knew he had to take the risk. Tonight, he thought. After dinner I'll make my move.

A half hour later, Kate burst through the front door, dropped her coat and bag on a living room chair, and sank onto the sofa.

"What a terrible day! One wrong shipment received, our checkout machine crashed, and if Mrs. Garvey ever sets foot in my shop again I swear I'll call the Gardai!"

"That bad, was it?" Mack poured a glass of Chablis, handed it to Kate, and sat down across from her. "What did Mrs. Garvey do?"

"Oh, that woman's a right pain!" As Kate described a mid-thirties woman with exclusive tastes and impossible demands, Mack felt all his hopes for the evening fall flat on the floor. Oh, someday he would propose to Kate and book their trip to Belize, but tonight, as she poured out her frustrations over wine, over dinner, and during their dessert, Mack couldn't bring himself to change the topic. She needed to let all her stress out, and he'd let her have her space to do so. When all her frustrations were spent, he started a fire in their fireplace, set the television up with one of her favorite romantic comedy movies, brought over the cream colored wool afghan she liked best and wrapped her in it, then sat in a chair next to the sofa watching her relax and before long fall asleep.

Aidan set his fork down next to his empty dessert plate, drank the last of his tea and sat back in his patio chair. "Mrs. Donoghue, that was the best peach pie I've ever had."

Mrs. Donoghue shook her head. "I'm sure back in her day your grandmother made better."

Aidan thought back to his grandmother and her legendary baking skills. It still hurt to think of her gone, but the pain had less of a sharp edge as time had begun to soften his memories.

"No, Mrs. Donoghue, for all her skills I don't believe she ever made a peach pie this good." He turned to Niall's father. "Thanks for letting me join you all for dinner. Your steaks were perfect."

Mr. Donoghue brushed Aidan's compliment aside. "No thanks necessary, lad. You know you're as good as family now, and always welcome to join us." He nodded toward the large estate on the other side of the lough behind the farm. "How is your house coming along?"

"I have a roofer coming by tomorrow for an estimate, and I think I've settled on the downstairs paint colors."

"You haven't had any new roof leaks have you?"

"No, thank God, but I don't dare delay getting the roof work going."

"Will you be ready for us to rehearse at your place next week?" Niall wondered.

Aidan teased, "I may have to pull you away from sheep duty an afternoon or two to help." He yawned and stretched. "I best get back now, though. I do have to make a little more progress painting the kitchen before I hit bed."

Niall rose. "I'll walk you part way."

Aidan laughed as he stood up. "It's only the other side of your yard. Pretty sure I can make it on my own."

"I know where all the low spots in the yard are. If you fall and break your leg on your own land that's one thing; I don't want to worry about you suing us if you fall and hurt yourself on our land!"

"As if!" Aidan teased back. "Okay, come along, walk your date halfway home."

When they were out of earshot of the patio, Aidan asked Niall, "Is your father okay?"

"I think so. Why?"

"His color seemed a bit off, and he didn't eat much."

Niall hadn't noticed any signs of his father not feeling well. "I'm sure he's okay, but I'll keep a closer eye on him the next few days."

"Good enough. Hey, let's hit a pub tomorrow night. We haven't been out since I moved here."

Niall hesitated. He dreaded running into Mary and Gary, his former girlfriend and best friend, now boyfriend-girlfriend themselves, at the pub in town that had long been his favorite watering hole. Aidan read his thoughts. "We don't have to go to Rafferty's. There must be another pub nearby."

Niall nodded, relieved. "Aye, I think there's something the next town over."

"Fine. How about eight tomorrow night?"

"It's a date." Niall laughed at Aidan's grimace. "Call if you need any help tomorrow."

They parted at the line near the lough where their two properties met. As Niall returned to his family's house to help clear things away from dinner and then settle their farm for the night, Aidan continued across the field to the house he'd bought a few weeks earlier.

In the gloaming, the dusky light before the dark of night set in, Aidan could trace the outline of the grand estate house. Three chimneys rose against the skyline, outlets for smoke that would rise from the house's seven fireplaces once he restored them. The broad, straight roofline from which the chimneys rose slanted down at their sides to a great stone structure both tall and wide. By day the stones showed soft grey against the green and tan fields surrounding it; now it blended into the dusk, only one or two shades lighter, more defined by outline than by substance. Light shone from the kitchen and through the dining room windows, tall, multi-paned walls of glass that provided a stunning panoramic view of the landscape by day, and now let the living room light he'd left on penetrate the encroaching darkness.

Stepping into the house through the back door next to the kitchen pantry, Aidan was glad he'd forgotten to turn the radio off. It felt less like walking into an empty house with the voices of singers filling the space around him. He surveyed the kitchen walls he'd spent most of the day painting, noted where he'd left off, fresh white paint contrasting the yellowed, water stained paint of old, saw how little work was left to complete the job, and headed upstairs to change his clothes. If he could finish the white walls tonight, he might complete the blue accents he'd planned before his Macready's Bridge bandmates came out for rehearsals in a week. They would recognize the color combination as the tribute to his grandmother he planned it to be, the kitchen she'd always dreamed of; perhaps they'd find reassurance in seeing he could pay tribute to memories and still move forward.

Aidan exchanged his clean clothes for paint stained work ones, and returned to the kitchen. As he repositioned his ladder, he glanced out the bank of windows over the sink. Lights from the Donoghue's home comforted him as they always did when night closed in around him.

Just as he turned back to his work, a moving shadow caught his eye. At first he thought it was an animal, a fox perhaps, running along the hedge that marked the right boundary line of his property. He peered into the dark to discern the figure further.

No, he thought, stunned. It was a man or, rather, more shadow than man, stealing along the hedges in the dark then disappearing between the hedge and the carriage house.

"What the hell?" Aidan spoke out loud. Curious, he grabbed the keys to the carriage house and stepped outside with cautious, quiet movements meant to catch the stranger rather than scare him off.

No shadow of man appeared around the perimeter of the carriage house, or anywhere else along the hedge or on his property. Aidan's heart pounded several hard, loud beats as he slipped the key into the lock and opened the carriage house door, not sure whether he wanted to find the man inside.

Throwing the switch on for the lighting he'd just had restored the week before, Aidan ran his eyes around the building. Stacks of old chairs and tables filled the center of the room; piled in corners and around the walls were worn garden tools, rags and old paint cans, cans of lubricants and auto care products and an assortment of auto repair and hardware tools. In one corner, wrought iron patio furniture stood piled up, waiting to be cleaned and put to use again.

Aidan looked to the top of the patio furniture and froze.

On top of the stack was a black wrought iron chair tipped at an odd angle. Perched on top of the chair was the same shadowy figure Aidan had spotted running along the hedge line. The figure wore long brown trousers, a long sleeved, faded navy blue shirt and tan vest, loose style clothing Aidan recalled seeing in a painting of farmers from centuries back. The man's image appeared translucent, ghostlike; Aidan thought he could see the back stone wall of the carriage house through the man's clothing.

The man raised a hand and tipped his tweed cap. "Dia dhuit," he called out in a voice both strong and thin. "Hello, young Aidan."

Before Aidan could reply, the man evaporated into the carriage house air.

2

Aidan rose early after a night of tossing and turning, each interval of sleep interrupted by visions of ghosts, some with familiar faces, some complete strangers. Upon rising he threw his jeans and shirt on and, determined to make sense of what he'd seen the night before, hurried out to the carriage house.

In daylight, the only footprints he found around the low building or hedges near it were his own. He slid open the wide front door where carriages and cars, in their day, had gained access. In the bright light the open doors afforded, no footsteps but his own crossed the dust covered floor. By the corner where the patio furniture had been stacked so many years earlier, none of the thick cobwebs had been disturbed and the top chair still stood perched on its precarious angle. If any human had touched it the night before, Aidan was sure it would have fallen.

Finding no clues or evidence of the figure he'd seen the night before, Aidan sat on an old wooden chair in the center of the long-abandoned room, puzzling over the apparition. Had he really seen it? Or had he just imagined it? Maybe the paint fumes had caused him to hallucinate; or perhaps too much time and work on his own had caused his mind to start playing tricks on him.

Then he recalled the words the ghost-like figure had spoken. "Young Aidan," he'd said. The ghost knew his name. Had his mind been playing tricks on him then as well? No. The voice had been real, clear and strong.

With no answers to the puzzling vision he could think of, Aidan decided he might as well clean out the building he'd already opened and save the kitchen painting for days when rain was forecast. He worked in a slow, careful manner, searching each piece he moved for any clues to the ghost-like figure he'd seen the night before as if searching for clues to a homicide.

Aidan was well into his cleaning when he heard a vehicle pull into the driveway. He looked up to see Barry Patterson, the roofer, step out of his van and gaze skyward, studying the roof of Aidan's house.

"Good to see someone taking this beauty on." Mr. Patterson called out as Aidan approached the van.

"She's a treasure," Aidan agreed. "She needs a fair bit of work though, and I best start with the roof."

"Aye. A leaky roof will ruin any repairs you make inside."

"That's what I thought as well. From the water stains I'm seeing inside, I'm sure the roof has some problems. I just hope it's not too far gone."

"I see you have a tile roof. They're famous for leaks and breaks over time. I'll get my ladder and check her out."

Aidan watched as Mr. Patterson climbed his ladder and walked various sections of the roof, praying the roofer wouldn't find any catastrophic damage there. He expected there wouldn't be, the pre-purchase inspection would have uncovered anything severe. Still, one never knew what house repairs might hide just below the surface.

Mr. Patterson returned after a brief inspection of the roof. "You've a fair number of broken tiles up there," he informed Aidan. "The back right corner is the worst; if I were you, I'd start there and work my way out." He scanned the house's exterior. "Could I take a peek at the water stains inside, see if they fall where I'm guessing they would?"

"Of course." Aidan led Mr. Patterson inside. As they walked through the house, Mr. Patterson noted accents of marble, mahogany, birch, ceramic tile, and crystal throughout the hallway and expansive rooms.

"This house must have been stunning back in the day. You've quite a job ahead in taking her on."

"I do," Aidan agreed. "Still, she's a grand old lady and worth the investment, don't you think?"

"Aye." Mr. Patterson nodded, catching a bit of the vision Aidan had felt. "I've always hoped someone would see her worth and set her to rights again."

They reached the upstairs where Aidan pointed to the largest of the water stains. "Here, the worst of the stains are in this corner, and down along the wall. There's some in the corner there as well." He pointed across from them. "In the room next door as well there's a bit."

Mr. Patterson surveyed the guest room and hallway ceiling and walls Aidan had shown him, relieved they were the same locations he'd anticipated. "Right. These leaks are where the broken tiles on the roof are situated. Once they're replaced, you should be fine, although I can tell you tile roof repairs are never a hundred percent guaranteed."

"I've heard that. What kind of cost am I looking at?" He held his breath, fearing the worst.

Barry Patterson eyed the young man before him and the grand house surrounding them. He found himself intrigued by Aidan, who seemed to be taking on the enormous restoration challenge alone. If he could help the lad, he would.

"I've a number of old tiles we can use. That will save you some money." Mr. Patterson jotted numbers down on a pad he withdrew from his coat pocket. After he finished his calculations, he considered the young man again and rounded his numbers downward.

"A thousand quid should do her."

Aidan released his breath in a slow, silent exhale, thankful the figure was lower than he'd feared. "Alright, fair enough. When could you start?"

"I've two wee jobs to finish up before I could take yours on. Let's say Wednesday?"

They shook hands, then Barry Patterson drove away.

After Barry left, Aidan walked through his house, surveying each room. He felt again the rush of excitement as he imagined the past grandeur of the house and envisioned anew what it could look like restored. This time, though, he saw with fresh eyes the cracks in the marble, the missing wood trim, the broken window panes that would need replacing. He noted the missing crystals in wall light fixtures and ceiling chandeliers. In his mind's eye, he saw gleaming wood banisters and panelling, fireplaces aglow, and fresh paint giving new life to tired, damaged walls. For all the years it had been neglected, the house could be in worse shape; still, the list of tasks was long, and the price tag would be sizable.

He reached the guestroom next to his own, now filled with his father's bedroom furniture, and sank down into the chair. "I wish you were here with me Da. I might have taken on too much this time. I don't know if I can pull this all off."

Silence echoed back. Aidan hadn't expected any answers, although he would have given his entire house up to hear his father's voice again. Still, as he sat in his father's chair an air of encouragement swept through him, as though his father was reaching across the divide between physical and spirit worlds to give his son the support he needed. Aidan sat for a few minutes longer and allowed the feeling to fill him head to toe. Then he rose, returned downstairs, heated fresh tea water and cut a piece of Mrs. Donoghue's soda bread, and then headed back to the carriage house to continue cleaning.

Niall watched from the barn where he'd been repairing doors and bars to some of the sheep pens as his father unloaded sacks of pellet feed from his truck, or rather tried to, struggling to lift the sacks, dropping one, leaning against his truck and wiping his brow with his sleeve.

"Da!" Niall dropped his hammer and ran to his father's side. "Why did ye not call me for help? You shouldn't be doing this yourself."

Mr. Donoghue brushed Niall off. "I've always handled the sacks myself." Still, a groan escaped his lips when he lifted the next one and Niall stepped in.

"Let me take that." Together, they unloaded the truck and carried the sacks of feed into the storage shed. When the job was finished, Niall saw how flushed his father's face was and the pain in his eyes his father could not hide. "I could use a break now," he suggested. "How about you?"

Mr. Donoghue wiped his brow with his coat sleeve. "Aye. Your mam should have lunch ready just about now."

Mrs. Donoghue had set the table and was pulling a hot casserole dish out of the oven when they entered the kitchen. "You both finished just in time." She set the steaming hot dish in the center of the table. "Go get cleaned up before this grows cold."

As her husband went upstairs to wash, Mrs. Donoghue drew Niall aside. "What was going on out by the truck?"

"The sacks were heavy," Niall explained, downplaying how much his father had struggled. "I was just lending a hand."

"He's never needed a hand before." Mrs. Donoghue's eyes were clouded with concern. "He's not well. I caught him in the middle of the night clutching his stomach like he were in terrible pain. When I asked him about it he brushed me off, told me it was nothing. I didn't believe him, though."

Niall shook his head. "Don't believe him. He was in pain this afternoon as well."

"Thanks for telling me. You best hurry and get cleaned up now before he finds us talking behind his back."

At lunch, Niall and his mother watched the elder Donoghue eat a third of his ham and potato casserole then push his plate away.

"Is there something wrong with your food?" Mrs. Donoghue asked, worry etched on her face.

"No. I'm full is all."

"You left half your breakfast this morning. You couldn't be all that full."

Niall listened as his father and mother traded words back and forth, both of them raising their voices a degree louder with each round, until he spoke up. "Mam's right, you're not yourself today."

"Not you too!" His father exploded. "The pair of you need to just leave me alone." With that he bolted from the table and stormed outside, letting the door slam closed behind him.

Niall rose to follow his father and apologize, but his mother stopped him. "Give him time. He's got something on his mind. He'll tell us when he's ready."

Niall returned to mending the sheep pens, listening for his father's approach or call as he worked. Hearing neither, he stole over to the barn door for frequent breaks to see if his father was okay. He watched as his father worked on his truck, checking hoses and topping off fluids. He kept an eye out as his father raked gardens clean, wanting to lend a hand but reluctant to set his father off again. Twice his mother stepped outside, once to take shirts and overalls down from the clothesline, once to add some refuse to the compost pile. Each time, Niall saw her glance over at her husband yet stay clear of him and return to the house without a word between them.

The day grew late, the sun slipped closer to the hills west of the Donoghue's farm. Niall and Farley gathered their sheep home, then headed in for dinner. The mixed aroma of chicken and bacon greeted him as he entered the kitchen; Niall knew his mother had made her chicken pie with bacon crumble topping, his father's favorite meal.

Niall and his mother took their seats at the table. His father stood by his chair, hesitating. He cleared his throat and announced, "I'm sorry for being so angry earlier."

"You know we're only concerned for you." Mrs. Donoghue motioned for him to sit down. "Still, I know if you were truly ill you'd tell me."

"That I would." Mr. Donoghue took his seat. "I see you've made my favorite dish. You're too good to me."

"Go on with ye." Mrs. Donoghue brushed her husband's compliment off. "Say the prayer, and let's eat before your favorite meal has gone cold."

Niall watched but didn't say a word as his father managed a half serving of the chicken pie, then shook his head and pushed his plate back.

"Anna, this is delicious as always, but I can't eat any more. All that work today has worn me out. Think I'll go in and lie down a wee while."

Niall and his mother exchanged furtive glances and held their tongues, not wanting a repeat of the earlier argument. As his mother cleared the table and started washing dishes, she whispered to Niall, "Go keep an eye on him while I finish here."

"You don't mind if I turn the telly on do you?" Niall asked as he entered their living room. Without waiting for an answer, Niall turned the set on. "I want to catch the news." As he watched the program, he kept one corner of his eye on his father, now reclined on the sofa. He was so intent on watching his father he jumped, startled, when his mobile phone rang.

"Are we still on for the pub tonight?"

Niall hesitated. In all the worries of the day, he'd forgotten about the plans he and Aidan had discussed the night before. "I don't know. My father had a bit of a rough day. I think I should stay home."

"Don't do that." Mr. Donoghue, who had not been asleep but resting with his eyes closed, interrupted. "Don't change your plans on my account."

"Hush, Da," Niall started, but his mother broke in.

"Your father's right. He'll just go easy tonight and be fine in the morning, no doubt. You should keep your plans."

Niall watched his father resting on the sofa, and his mother knitting as she watched the old movie that had come on after the news. They were right, he admitted to himself. They would spend a quiet, uneventful evening. His staying home would serve no purpose; and he and Aidan were long overdue for a night out. "Okay," he agreed. "Why don't you pick me up in a bit."

The Harp, the nearest pub after Rafferty's, was smaller than Niall's former local, with three tables lining the wall opposite the bar. Whitewashed walls offset with dark wood beams and paneling evidenced The Harp's age, while the karaoke machine in the corner indicated its owner's attempt to draw in a new, younger crowd. With all three tables occupied, Niall and Aidan sat at barstools along the stone and wood bar.

"I'll be right with you," the girl behind the bar called out, then returned to the patrons she was serving at the other end of the bar.

While they waited, Niall returned to the topic they'd started discussing in the car. "What if my father's very ill? What if it's something like cancer? You hear so much of that these days."

"And why would ye be thinking it's cancer?" Aidan would have laughed if Niall hadn't looked so flat out serious. "I swear, you do know how to borrow trouble. Your father's not got cancer. He's just got some kind of virus."

"He doesn't get viruses." Niall corrected. "I don't remember ever seeing him sick a day in my life."

"I still say it's a virus, and by tomorrow he'll be right as ever." Aidan saw the seriousness spread across Niall's face, no hint of the spark of humor that always hid just below the surface in his friend's eyes, and realized Niall needed support rather than teasing. "If he's not better, you'll call tomorrow and get him in to a clinic. Whatever's going on, you'll look after him and your mam as well as you ever do. It will all be okay."

Niall hoped Aidan was right. Still, his father's intense pain and lack of appetite were so out of character, Niall had a nagging suspicion something more than a virus was underway. He let the subject drop, though. The evening was meant to be fun.

By now, the barmaid had returned to where Niall and Aidan were seated.

"Two pints," Aidan requested, "and one for yourself."

As she drew their pints, Niall found himself captivated by her. Her long, raven black hair held to one side by a large ceramic green clip shone like the black of the roads in town in the rain. Her emerald green eyes sparkled as brilliant as their namesake gem.

She set their pints before them and asked, "New here, aren't you? I don't recall seeing you before."

Niall froze, unable to connect his tongue and voice with his brain. Aidan stepped in, "First time here for us both, but sure we'll be back, I'm Aidan, my friend here is Niall."

"Nice to meet you both. I'm Pauline." She shook each of their hands. Aidan caught how she held Niall's hand a bit longer before turning away to serve other guests.

Changing subjects, Niall asked Aidan, "Was that the roofer I saw going over your house earlier today? What did he have to say?"

"Aye, that was Barry Patterson. He's located the places where roof tiles are broken and causing some leaks. He'll be back Wednesday to start his repair work."

"Will the roof need much?"

"I don't think so." Aidan shrugged. "We'll see. If I've taken on too much of a job with the house repairs I might be moving back into your guest room!"

Niall countered, "Or you could sleep in your carriage house, and rent the main house out. I'm sure my mam wouldn't mind dropping a hot meal off for you once in a while."

"I doubt I could rent my place if repairs aren't done. Hey, we'll rent your farmhouse, and you and your folks can move in with me!"

They kidded over various scenarios, interspersed with more serious discussions of work at Aidan's house and chores at the farm. To Niall it felt wonderful to laugh, even for the smallest amount of time after a day filled with so much stress. As he and Aidan downed their second and third pints, he found himself stealing occasional glances at Pauline; three or four times he caught her looking his way as well. Each time, he felt his face burn hot and was thankful for The Harp's dim lighting.

After their third pint, Niall checked his watch. "I don't know about you, Aidan, but I better get home. I'll be on early morning duty if my father's not feeling any better."

As they left Niall promised Pauline, "We'll be back."

"Wonder if Gary and Mary will miss you now that you've discovered The Harp?" Aidan teased as they drove home.

"Who? Oh no, I won't miss them."

"That's what I thought! Too bad the barmaid tonight wasn't a little easier on the eye. I wonder what the rest of the staff at The Harp looks like."

"Pauline was fine." Niall defended. He glanced at Aidan, saw the smirk spread across his friend's face, and understood Aidan's game. "Go ahead, laugh. Someday you'll be sorry she didn't catch your eye first."

Aidan was still laughing when he returned home. Not yet ready for bed, he heated water for tea and flipped through papers he had gathered on the kitchen table, looked again at Mr. Patterson's roof repair estimate and prayed he was making the right decision even as he knew it was the only decision he could make. When the kettle boiled, he poured hot water into a clean mug and watched out the window as his tea brewed.

Even in the dark some shapes in the landscape were visible, the line of trees that ran across his and the Donoghues' properties, the shrubs and hedges on his own land, and the carriage house. He remembered he had not locked the carriage house door before he'd left for the pub, and retrieved the key to take care of this now.

As he reached the carriage house door, a sudden shiver ran down his spine. He remembered the apparition he'd seen the night before. Part of him wanted to enter the carriage house now and see if the ghost would reappear; part of him wanted to leave well enough alone and never see the ghost again.

"Glad to see you're back, young Aidan."

The voice behind him made Aidan jump. He wheeled around to see the same translucent figure he'd met the night before. "Who are you?" He demanded. "How do you know my name?"

The strange man tipped his cap. "Timothy McCabe at your service. I know everything about this place. 'Tis glad you've bought the house I am; I was getting a wee bit lonely here."

Still trying to make sense of the vision before him, Aidan asked, "What do you want with me?"

"There's a task you must do." A faraway, sombre look crossed Timothy McCabe's face. "Find the writings. Find the stones."

Puzzled more than ever now, Aidan sought clarification. "What writings? What stones?"

"You'll know when you find them." Timothy McCabe tipped his hat again. "You mustn't fail." With that, he faded from sight.

Aidan stared several long minutes into the darkness around him. Nothing moved, no sound could be heard save for the occasional lapping of waves from the lough between his house and Niall's as it came up against land. The odd Mr. McCabe had disappeared with the same unpredictable action with which he'd arrived.

Find the writings, he had said. Find the stones. Aidan looked out over the landscape before him. Even in full darkness, his mind's eye saw a thousand stones strewn across the fields and hills. Hell, in his house alone hundreds of thousands of stones had been stacked one upon another. And he was to know which of them were the ones meant to be found? Aidan laughed out loud. "Oh great! I've inherited a ghost, and a crazy one at that!"

Niall glanced through the open door into his parents' bedroom, careful not to make any noise that would wake them. Satisfied they were both asleep, he tiptoed over to his room and closed the door, leaving it open a crack in case any problems arose in the middle of the night. After a full day of work, he was tired and expected sleep to overtake him the minute he fell into bed; but when he closed his eyes all he saw repeated over and over on the darkened screen of his mind was his father bent over in pain. He fought against the vision as long as he could, then sat up and turned his bedroom light on.

This is ridiculous, he thought. I'll be of no use tomorrow without sleep, and I can't sleep worrying about my father. I've got to turn my mind to something else.

Pauline from The Harp came to his mind. He saw her smile, lips tinged with a hint of peach gloss, smile bright and natural as if she always wore it. He saw again the light in her eyes, as if all the stars in the heavens resided in them. He recalled her laughter, easy, airy, and the velvet smooth tone of her voice. He turned his light out again, slid back down under his blankets, and closed his eyes, falling asleep to visions of Pauline.

3

Wind and rain beat hard against the stone walls and thatched roof of the whitewashed cottage the Leahy family resided in; but inside, with a fire in the hearth and steaming hot shepherd's pie served up for dinner, they were as cozy as ever.

After Patrick said a blessing over their meal, as Conor and Caitlyn raised forks and dug into their plates, Moira addressed them. "You know your father and I went to see the doctor today don't you?"

Conor nodded, "Yes Mum," while Caitlyn stopped eating, her fork held mid-air. Wide eyed, she asked, "Are you very ill Mum?"

Moira's heart melted at Caitlyn's concern. "I'm fine, pet. In fact, your father and I have good news."

"We do indeed." Patrick gave Moira's hand a light squeeze. "Your mum's going to have a baby."

"Really?" Conor asked.

"Oh Mum!" Caitlyn exclaimed.

Moira winked at Patrick, then told their kids, "There's more. I'm going to have twins."

Her announcement was almost more than Conor and Caitlyn could take in. Even Caitlyn's enthusiasm waned as she tried to digest how two new babies would impact their lives.

Patrick laughed, "Don't look like it's the end of the world, will ye? We're going to have two new babies for you to play with and help us look after. Won't that be grand?"

A smile spread across Caitlyn's face, small at first, then growing brighter as the hills shine brighter when clouds recede. "Can I really help with them Mum?"

"You both can." Moira turned to Conor seated next to her. "With two new babies in the house your father and I will both need all sorts of help."

Caitlyn, now almost bursting with excitement, tossed out question after question. "Can I help bathe them? Will they be boys or girls? Can they sleep in my room?"

"They're not sleeping in my room are they?" Conor blurted out.

Patrick flashed him a stern look. "And what if they were? In fact, what if I chose to make Caitlyn's room a music room and move her and the babies in with you?"

Conor's round eyes in his solemn face grew enormous, afraid his father would carry out his threat. Moira shook her head and gave Conor a hug. "Your da will not be doing that. We'll sort everything out. I will need one thing from you, though."

"What's that?" Conor asked, suspicious of what curve they'd throw at him next.

"Our new babies will need a big brother to teach them things and protect them as they're growing up. Do you think you would help us that way?"

Conor's eyes lit up. "Yeah, I can do that!"

After dinner Patrick pulled out his fiddle, and he and the twins played music while Moira cleared the kitchen and washed their dinner dishes. "I'll need your help soon enough," she'd responded when Patrick had offered to help. "Let me do this while I'm still up to the task." As she worked, she relished the sounds of music and laughter that filled their house.

Two more kiddies, she thought, two more voices of laughter to hear, two more sets of hands to try out new instruments. She stopped her work long enough to watch Patrick teach Conor and Caitlyn the first few lines of a new song. What a patient teacher he was. Moira felt a rush of gratitude spread through her as she thought of how blessed their new twins would be to have such a loving, caring father watching over them.

After both kids had bathed and were tucked into bed, Moira stretched out on the sofa while Patrick settled into the armchair across from her. He admitted to her, "I could have knocked our Conor's head earlier. All he cares about is losing his room?"

"You've never knocked our kids a day in your life, and you never will. Conor doesn't like change is all. You know that. He just needs some time to adjust to our news."

"You're right. He did have a good point though. We do need to figure out where the babies will sleep."

They both scanned the cottage surrounding them from their vantage point in front of the fire. With the open kitchen behind them, the living room they sat in had always seemed large enough to meet their needs. The narrow alcove by the doorway held their coats and boots or shoes; Moira doubted they could convert that to any kind of bedroom. The three bedrooms off the hallway that ran from the living room to the end of their house were each so small Patrick could think of no way to break them into any other floor plan. Even their master bedroom had just enough space for their bed and dresser, with little to spare.

"We might have to add onto the house." Patrick suggested at last.

"We don't have the money for that." Moira ran a hand over the place where two tiny infants grew. Don't you worry, she thought, sure her thoughts transcended to them. Your mummy and daddy will work this all out.

To Patrick, she said, "They can sleep in our room when they're first born. We'll manage."

Michael watched Susannah straighten the area rug in front of the sofa, fluff the pillows for the fifth time, switch the end table lights brighter, then softer, then brighter again. She shifted the dining room candles closer, then farther apart, adjusted the fold in one of the white linen napkins, and changed the hour old water in the centerpiece vase of red roses for fresh water.

"We should have eaten out." She complained to Michael. "I knew eating in would be a mistake."

"This whole evening could be a mistake." Michael muttered so low Susannah only caught the words "evening" and "mistake".

"What?"

"I said, how could it be a mistake?" Michael lied, not wanting her to explode. "The evening's not even started yet."

Susannah double-checked her panko-crusted salmon recipe's directions one more time. "Are you sure your father will like the salmon?"

"He'll love it." Michael assured her, not sure at all the panko crust would go over, wishing she'd stuck to the chicken he'd suggested, sure his father would prefer that.

"I should have chosen rice instead of quinoa for the side."

Michael could see tears rise in Susannah's eyes, and knew she was close to full blown panic. He drew her close and wrapped his arms around her. "Suze, it will be fine. The dinner will be delicious, and he will love you." He pushed a stray hair away from her face. "I'm more at risk, you know. My parents will no doubt fall in love with you; but I'll be that much harder to sell to your folks. They dreamed a doctor or barrister would give you a life of wealth and security, and here you go getting yourself engaged to a musician with less than five hundred Euros to his name."

"They've always liked you." Susannah insisted, but Michael cut her off.

"They liked me well enough as a friend, even a boyfriend. Sure they didn't expect you to marry me, though." Michael had to laugh. "Listen to us! Arguing over whose parents won't like whom. The truth of it is, they'll all band together and tell us we're both in the wrong! What do we care what they say? We're engaged, we'll have a lovely wedding, and in fifty years or so they'll see we were right all along."

Susannah wanted to believe Michael, wanted to think that both families would like each other, or at least accept each other, that the evening would be peaceful, that any discord would be minor. She knew her parents well enough, though, to believe nothing about the evening would be that easy. She checked her artichoke-spinach and flatbread appetizer for the third time, laid her small dessert blowtorch on the counter where it would be ready for use when she presented her crème brûlée dessert, and checked her wine glasses for any smudges or water spots.

Fionna Fallon surveyed the crowd of tourists strolling the grounds of Dublin Castle. Her art class assignment was simple: capture a scene from an iconic Dublin location. After considering several sites, she had chosen Dublin Castle, intrigued by its medieval history and later elegance. Touring the castle and grounds with camera in hand, she sought that one powerful image that would grab people's emotions over anything her classmates would submit. She had recorded two little girls dancing under the entrance arch, a young woman deep in thought as she stood in the long arched walkway leading away from the main door, and was studying a forty-ish couple as they pointed out the medieval round tower connected to the newer part of the castle, when a flash of gold hair caught the corner of her eye.

Aidan! She took two steps towards him, almost called out his name, then realized when he turned his face it wasn't Aidan at all. Instead, a stranger looked past her to the tour guide leading the group he was with. He moved on, but Fionna's heart was stuck, fixed on the image of the beach walker she'd fallen in love with this past summer.

While she'd always gone to Gweebarra alone with her parents, she had never felt the pangs of loneliness as sharp as she had this year. Her parents had discarded her dream of attending art school like so much rubbish, and instead steered her towards a career in library sciences. Oh, she loved books almost as much as she loved painting; but she'd had no desire to make books her life. She wanted instead to capture on canvas the many stunning scenes that fixed themselves on her mind and set her heart on fire. She'd had a bitter fight with her parents before they'd set off on their trip to Gweebarra. She had been overwhelmed by a sense of being trapped that summer, until Aidan had come along. Something about him had hooked her on sight. Even though their conversations had been few, their time with each other limited, he had gotten under her skin. She remembered most the night she had spent at his camper, his compassion, and the feel of his touch as they'd made love. She had been devastated the next morning to learn he'd checked out. She'd listened to the conversations of other guests and the caravan park owners for any clues that would lead her to Aidan, had even gone so far as to spy on the park register for Aidan's last name and address, all to no avail.

Aidan had ignited something inside Fionna, though, that his leaving could not dim. She felt a new strength and determination she had never felt before rise up in her, a courage to stand up for herself and take charge of her destiny. As she finished her stay in Gweebarra with her parents she said nothing of her ideas to them. Instead, she formulated plans in her mind as she continued to draw and walk along the beach. When she returned home, she spent hours on the computer researching options, made phone calls while her parents were out, and even travelled by bus to Dublin for a long weekend, telling her parents she was visiting a friend. She had never lied to them until that summer and didn't like the feel of it, but knew there was no other choice. Only when she'd had all the details of enrollment, housing, and the larger part of the finances sorted did she reveal her plan to her parents.

"I'll not have you wasting your time and money there!" Her father had exploded after he'd heard her out. "You'll not find a job in arts, you'll have nothing to show four years down the line. You'll not be fit for any real jobs. I won't be having this for you."

"It's already set." She'd replied, glancing to her mother for help.

Mrs. Fallon hesitated, agreeing with her husband yet not wanting to hurt her only child. She understood Fionna's dream; she, herself, had once had hopes and plans. "Jerry," she said at last, "would a year hurt? At the end of a year we might know better if this is the right path for Fionna."

Disapproval spread clear across Mr. Fallon's face. Fionna had been afraid he'd scream at her mother and lock Fionna herself away in her room. He had turned scarlet, glared at his wife, then turned a warning look at Fionna. "One year. I'll give you that. At the end of a year, if you aren't top of your class you'll change over to library science."

Now Fionna stood at the courtyard outside Dublin Castle watching the blond stranger walk through the exit at the far end, wishing it had been Aidan, then shaking both images from her mind. She turned her camera back to the storm clouds gathering over the clock tower and clicked away, hoping one photo would capture just the right feel, just the right light, that would translate into the one drawing that would keep her at the top of her class.

Susannah listened to her father and mother chat with Michael's parents while they ate the dinner she'd prepared. They had praised her salmon, admired her quinoa, thought her asparagus tips were cooked to perfection and Michael's wine selection an ideal complement to her dinner. They had talked of the weather, the places they'd traveled, golf and theater. So far the evening had been perfect. Too perfect, Susannah thought. As she cleared their dinner plates to make room for dessert, she nodded to Michael. "Could you give me a hand?"

"Sure." Michael gathered his parents' plates, followed her into the kitchen, and set the stack of plates next to the sink. "What's up?"

"Oh Michael, it's all wrong tonight."

"What is?" Michael asked, confused. "Your dinner was perfect."

"Too perfect! Listen to how polite they're all being. They're so artificial with each other. And no one's even mentioned our wedding."

"They're just getting to know each other." Michael assured her.

"No. Your father and mine are both too direct with people. They don't play the polite game."

Michael shrugged. "You wanted them to get along."

"Get along, sure; but everyone's avoiding the main topic."

She was right, Michael knew; their parents had been too agreeable, too eager to discuss everything except the one subject that had brought them all together. He'd have to be the one to open that round of discussion. "Leave it to me."

They returned to the table, Susannah carrying her crème brûlée and Michael bearing a tray with brandy and six glasses. As he passed the drinks around he suggested, "Now that we've all gotten to know each other, let's talk about our wedding."

Susannah pulled out her wedding folder. "We've booked Markree Castle for the weekend. Next we should work out our dinner menu, the cake and music. Mom, I thought you, Mrs. Sullivan and I could go dress shopping together . . ."

"I'll not be paying for your dress." Mr. Tierney cut in. "I'll not be paying for any part of your wedding."

Michael almost dropped the brandy bottle in his hands, while Susannah turned stunned eyes upon her father.

"James, not here, not now." Mrs. Tierney cautioned. "We can work this out later."

Mr. Tierney shook his head and looked to the surprised faces around him. "No, now. We're here to talk about this God-forsaken wedding aren't we? Let's get it all out in the open." He turned to Michael. "Nothing personal, but you're not the ideal husband for my daughter."

"Stop it, Dad!" Susannah cried out.

"It's about time someone spoke the truth." Mr. Sullivan stood and tossed his napkin on the table. Looking straight at Michael and Susannah he announced, "I'll not be paying for any part of this fiasco either. Susannah, you're a lovely girl. Sure you can do better than my son here. Michael, if you're ready to give up this folly of music, come see me. I'll find you a job that will support you and your lovely wee bride. Until then, you'll get no money off me."

"We're not asking for your money!" Michael stood so he was eye to eye with his father. "Nor yours." He told Mr. Tierney. "We invited you over so you could get to know each other, and Susannah could share some details about what should be the happiest day in our lives, not to ask for handouts we don't need."

"I'm still opposed to this wedding," Mr. Tierney stated, rising to join Mr. Sullivan. "From the sound of it, so is your father. I can't stop you from making your plans, but I don't have to support them." He turned to his wife. "Lillian, it's time we left."

"James, we can't leave like this." Mrs. Tierney protested.

Mr. Tierney glared at her. "Let's go."

Mr. Sullivan had already reached the door. "Marie, are you coming?"

"Please, let's all calm down." Susannah begged. "Come back to the table. We can work this out." She turned to Michael, tear-filled eyes pleading for help.

Michael burned with rage for his father and Susannah's and the way they had both ruined the evening she had so set her heart on. "Let them go; we don't need them. The evening's over."

"How could you!" Susannah exploded once her parents and Michael's had left. "How could you kill the evening like that?"

"How could I? Are you kidding? Our parents killed the night, not me."

"They wouldn't have done if you'd convinced them to sit back down and work with us."

"Work with us?" Michael slammed the tray of dessert dishes on the counter. "The last thing in the world they want is to work with us. They don't want us to go through with the wedding at all. Or did you miss that part?"

Susannah threw the leftover salmon and quinoa into the trash. "The only thing I missed was you helping me calm them down and sort things out. You just let them go! I can't believe you caved like that."

"Suze," Michael took her arm, thinking to draw her away from the dishes out to the living room, to quiet music and wine and a chance to diffuse the anger the evening had stirred.

Susannah jerked her arm away. "Leave me alone. Just let me get the kitchen cleared." When Michael picked up a dish towel to help, she pulled the towel out of his hands. "Alone. Just leave me alone for now."

Michael retreated to the living room and pretended to browse through the newspaper while listening to the clink of glasses, plates and silverware as Susannah washed their dinner dishes. When she finished in the kitchen, she pulled her laptop out and worked on he wasn't sure what, her polished nails clicking hard against the keys. He pretended to work as well, scanning e-mails on his phone, although five minutes later he couldn't remember what they contained. When Susannah stood at last and announced she was going to bed, he rose as well.

"Where are you going?"

"To bed."

"Not with me, you're not." Susannah stood in the doorway of their bedroom blocking Michael's entrance.

"You're joking!" Michael couldn't believe what he heard. "I know the evening didn't go your way, but you don't think I'm sleeping on the sofa for it."

"Then I will." Susannah yanked her pillow and blanket off their bed and threw them on the sofa.

"No." Michael grabbed her bedding and pushed it back to her. "I will."

Susannah let her bedding fall to the floor. "Fine. Have it your way." She slammed the door closed between them. Michael heard her settle into bed and saw the ray of light under the closed door go dark. He picked her pillow and blanket up from the floor and arranged them and himself on the sofa. After an hour of tossing and turning, punching the pillow into various uncomfortable shapes, and covering and uncovering himself half a dozen times, he drifted to sleep. In his dreams he chased after an elusive bride who always slipped out of his reach at the last minute.

Patrick re-read Mack's e-mail while Moira retrieved wash from the line outside. Mack's e-mail confirmed next week's rehearsals they had all agreed to, the recording schedule for the new album, and the first several gigs Mack had scheduled for the band in the coming months. All the arrangements looked fine and Patrick was excited to return to work, except for one thing.

Moira.

As he watched her unpin the shirts and socks she had hung on the line that morning while he'd driven Conor and Caitlyn to school, bending and stretching now with caution, he knew he could not leave her on her own. Conor and Caitlyn would help, of course, but Moira would insist on doing most of the household tasks herself. If she were sick, and they were at school, what then? What if something went wrong with her, the babies or the house?

No, there was nothing for it but to call Mack and beg off rehearsals, at least.

What then, he wondered. If he missed rehearsals, how could he be prepared for recording? How would the band be in shape for upcoming gigs? Was it even fair to the rest of the group for him to miss the hard work of rehearsals then expect to reap the rewards of their new album release?

Sad realization swept over Patrick. He would have to leave Macready's Bridge. He would call Mack that evening. In the morning he would call the concrete foundry and see if he could get his old job back.

No other way made sense.

He waited until Moira had settled on the sofa with the laundry basket next to her, folding the wash she had just brought in. Sitting in the chair across from her, Patrick drew a deep breath, held his breath a long moment, then released a long, slow exhale.

"I'm going back to the foundry."

Moira cast a doubtful look Patrick's way while she continued to sort and fold laundry. "You are, are you? And what brought this decision on?"

"I need to be here to look after you and our family."

"You don't think I can manage things the few times you're gone?"

"There will be more and more times. Mack's just sent a schedule for the next several weeks. There's a lot of away time on it."

"How will your working at the foundry change that? You'd still be away every day." Moira studied the resolve on Patrick's face and realized he was dead serious about his decision. Part of her was grateful all over again for the man she'd married who would put his family's needs over any of his personal desires. She loved him for his choice. She also knew she could not let him carry it through. "No, Pat. You'll not be leaving the band."

"It's for the best."

"For whose best? Yours? Or ours? Because I can tell you right now what's best for you is the band, and what's best for us is your happiness."

Patrick gave her shoulders a light squeeze. "Moira, love, how could I be happy traveling with the boys when all the time I'd be worried about you?"

Moira placed one of her hands on Patrick's arm. "Pat, my mother can come out and stay with us when you're away. Even if she couldn't, you'd not be so far away you couldn't get home in a hurry. I could call one of the ladies from church in the meantime. I promise, we'd be fine. Chances are we wouldn't even have need of help. If you left the band, though, you'd end up regretting it; and I'll not have you resenting me or our kiddies for a choice you didn't want to make."

Patrick considered her words. She was right; between her mother and the church ladies she would have any help she needed. If he walked away from his music there would, indeed, be a corner of his heart that would grow resentful no matter how hard he fought against it. He'd have to go along with Moira, at least for now, and trust that no harm would come to her or their babies.

"Alright," he relented at last. "I won't call just yet. We have rehearsals at Aidan's next week; we'll see how that goes."

"Fair enough." Moira handed the folded laundry to him. "Now how about you put these away while I put my feet up before Conor and Caitlyn come flying through the door."

4

"Find the writings. Find the stones."

The whispered words, so close in Aidan's ears he swore he could feel someone's breath as they were spoken, woke him from a deep sleep. He glanced around his room but saw no one. He listened hard to the house around him but heard no creaks, footsteps or voices. Sure he'd dreamed the voice, Aidan closed his eyes and drifted back to sleep.

"Find the writings! Find the stones!"

The voice was louder, more insistent now, followed by a loud thud that shook the room. Aidan bolted upright. This time he recognized the voice as Timothy McCabe's. He remembered the man's words the night before in the carriage house. Far into the night he'd puzzled over what writings and stones Timothy had meant and where to begin his search. He'd had no answers before he fell asleep, and by no means had any now. Even if he knew what writings Timothy had meant, they could be anywhere if, indeed, they still existed. And stones? He pictured again all the stones visible to him in his house, in the carriage house, in the farmhouse behind him and in the fences and fields as far as his eyes could see. Unless a stone jumped out and attacked him, there was no way he'd ever be able to pick out one particular, special one.

"Could you give me a clue?" Aidan called out, thinking if Timothy had been the voice that woke him he might answer back. "What am I looking for? Where do I start?"

An empty, silent house echoed back. Feeling how futile Timothy McCabe's request was, Aidan rose, showered, dressed, and went downstairs to start his day. In less than a week, his Macready's Bridge mates would arrive for rehearsals. He had a good deal of work to do to finish cleaning and setting up the carriage house for them to practice in, make sure his guest bedrooms were in order for Mack, Michael and Patrick to sleep in, and stock food for at least the first couple of days.

By mid-morning he'd cleared the rest of the refuse out of the carriage house, swept cobwebs from corners and swept the cement floor twice. He then stood back, admired the expanse of room before him, and felt excitement rush from his heart through his veins to every part of him as the first stage of realizing his dream was underway.

"This is it, Da." He spoke in half whispers to the air around him, sure his father's spirit was present. "Roisin Studios is starting at last."

As he surveyed the space around him, memories of every plan he and his father had discussed for a music studio named after his mother came alive, racing through his mind in such rapid succession he could not keep track of them all. No matter, he thought. The plans had become so ingrained in him, were such an integral part of him, that he knew each idea would return at its proper time.

Visions of his father and mother, sister and grandmother swarmed through the carriage house, each one seeming so real he wondered for a moment if Timothy McCabe had conjured up their ghosts to witness his work. If Mr. McCabe knew his name, perhaps he knew Aidan's history as well, and had tracked down his family in the spirit world and led them here. Unsure how the spirit world worked, Aidan entertained the thought a few moments, wishing it were true. How good it would feel to see their forms and hear their voices again, even if they were just apparitions.

Then he shook his head hard to clear the visions and memories away. "You've got too much work to do," he ordered himself, "to be strolling down memory lane. You best get at it or you'll have no place for the group to rehearse in next week."

Aidan moved four old chairs from the carriage house into a semi-circle in the center of the room, set another chair off to the side for Mack, and carried a table from the back of the room to the bank of windows along the right wall. Then he stepped back and surveyed his work. It was a good start, he thought, but it needed something more, some kind of color, something to give the cement and stone building a little pizazz. He remembered seeing an old rug rolled up in the house's attic and hoped that might provide the accent he wanted.

He climbed up to the storage space on the top floor of his new house and ran a cursory scan around the room before heading to the far left corner. Picture frames leaned against walls on the other side, an old floor lamp he thought he would someday repair stood behind him. Trunks and boxes shared a corner off to his right; someday he would take his time in sorting through their contents. For now, all he cared about was the rug he'd seen rolled up and cast aside.

The rug was heavier than he anticipated; it took Aidan an hour of dragging, lifting, carrying, resting, and dragging again before he was able to roll the rug out on the carriage house floor. As he stepped back, he was elated to see a red, blue and gold patterned oriental rug unfold before him. Threadbare though it was, with colors worn and faded, even worn through to the backing in one corner, the antique rug lent an air of sophistication to the hard cement floor and cold interior. He set the chairs back in place around the rug, then returned to the attic. If his memory was right, one of the trunks he'd seen up in the attic had a flat top. He was sure it would complete the scene if he set it in front of the chairs in the center of the studio.

The trunk stood to the right of the storage room, partially hidden by old picture frames. Aidan moved the frames aside and ran his hands over the dark wood of the trunk, thrilled to see it was in fair shape, did indeed have a flat top, and would make a perfect table. If the trunk was sturdy inside, he thought it might serve for storage as well. He slid his hands along the worn, scarred wood and faded brass fittings, then lifted the lid, hoping the interior would be as sturdy as the exterior.

A musty smell from too many years closed rose to his nostrils when Aidan opened the trunk. In order to inspect the interior, he lifted out the contents of the trunk: a lace shawl, yellowed with age; an infant's white satin dress, a christening gown he supposed; a mid-sized brown wool suit; a packet of letters tied with string so fragile it almost fell apart at Aidan's touch; a woman's black hat with a scrap of netting across the front; and a pair of black ladies' gloves.

Aidan set the trunk's contents aside, then ran his hands along the sides and bottom of the trunk, checking its sturdiness. To his surprise, the bottom slid the slightest bit under his touch. He moved his hands slower along the sides near the bottom, discovered two small latches, pressed them in, and lifted the false bottom out.

The secret compartment he'd discovered held several papers that, at first glance, looked quite official and important. As he set the false bottom aside, turning it over in the process, he found a separate piece of paper, thin and yellowed, taped to the wood. The tape had deteriorated to the point where it all but disintegrated as he pulled the paper away. Written in old Irish, this paper appeared to be some sort of legal document.

Brimming with curiosity over what he had stumbled upon, Aidan set the false bottom and the rest of the contents back in the trunk, closed it, and carried the papers downstairs to examine them in better light.

The top paper, written in English, was a deed to the house sold to William Gallagher by one Charles Brainerd in 1878. Under that were three papers written in Irish and a handwritten map. Aidan studied the map, noting lines he guessed might be roads, a shaded area in the center, and rudimentary lines that seemed to represent buildings. Four circles had been marked on the outer boundaries of the map, each one equidistant to the others.

Find the writing. Find the stones. Timothy McCabe's words echoed in Aidan's mind as a course of excitement ran through his body. Could what he'd found in the trunk be the writings Timothy had meant? He studied the papers again. He wished he'd taken more time to learn the native Irish Gaelic the papers were written in. If Jeannie were here, she'd be able to translate. On his own, very few words were recognizable. He set the papers aside and studied the map again, turning it to different angles, and wondered if it could be an old drawing of his land. That would make sense, as it was tied together with the deed. From where he guessed the house was situated on the map, though, the property outlined was far too large. The shading behind the house could be the lough, he thought. That would fit in proportion to the building, but would still not explain the rest of the outline. Aidan focused on the four circles. If the shaded area was the lough, and the other drawings were buildings, one of them perhaps his house, then one circle was situated across from the house, near what the drawing indicated might be a road.

Aidan carried the map outside, hoping he could decipher what the circles represented. Across the road from his house was a large, old oak tree. He walked over to it, studied its broad trunk and multiple branches, but found nothing unusual about the tree. If the circle represented the oak, he concluded, the map was no more than a random drawing.

Yet it had been secured away in the secret bottom of the antique trunk. Intuition told Aidan the map held some significance that tied it with the papers he was unable to translate.

Niall gathered his pipes and the song list Mack had e-mailed the band. With rehearsals due to start at Aidan's next week, he had a lot of practicing ahead so he would be ready. After spending the morning helping his father store the fountain and patio set away in their storage shed for the upcoming winter, he felt sure he could take time out now for his music.

"I'll just be up the hill to the field beyond," he told his parents as they finished their lunch. "I'll have my phone with me. If you need anything call me."

"We will, lad. Sure our sheep will enjoy your entertainment."

Niall nodded to his father and flashed a concerned look to his mother. She understood as soon as he sent it; their shared worry over the elder Donoghue the past few days had honed their communication skills to quick looks and immediate knowledge of what one another intended. If she had a need while Niall was out practicing his pipes, she would summon him straight away.

The pasture where Niall chose to practice stood at the top of a hill behind his family's barn and afforded him a grand panoramic view of the farm, Aidan's home, and the countryside surrounding them. In the fields nearby, his family's sheep dotted the grass like cotton balls spilled across a green towel. Beyond that hills rose and fell away in varying heights, some rock strewn, some tree capped. Above them, a pale blue sky had started to give way to grey clouds.

We'll have rain by evening, Niall thought. He pulled out his uilleann pipes first; they would take the longest to put away if rain swept in faster than he expected.

As Niall looked out over the landscape spread below him, and in particular the home he'd grown up in, a sense of pride and love for this corner of the world swelled inside his heart. He was filled with gratitude for the blessings God had showered on him with the land he called home and the parents who had raised him. With his best friend now living on the other side of the lough behind his farm, he felt even more blessed. His ability to make a living, no matter how modest, at the music he loved was the greatest blessing of all. As he practiced now, all of the feelings that filled his heart poured out through his fingers to the tunes he played on his pipes. Each note rose and fell like the hills around him, like the music the birds sang overhead as they circled and arced against the expanse of sky.

In the space of an hour Niall had run through the first four songs multiple times until he felt comfortable enough with each one that he could move on to the next. He was halfway through the fifth when he heard shouts coming from the direction of his farm. He looked across the fields to his house and barn, saw his father lying on the ground and his mother bent over him, calling for Niall to help. He dropped his pipes and ran to them as fast as he could.

"Da! Get up!" Niall shook his father's shoulders, easy at first, then harder. Alarmed when his father didn't respond, he ordered, "Mam, call for an ambulance!"

Mrs. Donoghue remained frozen with fear, feet glued to the ground. "Now!" Niall ordered. "Call now!"

Fear had complete hold of Niall himself as his father remained unresponsive on their gravel driveway. With one eye fixed on his father, Niall ran to the hose by the side of their barn, filled a bucket with water and hurried back to his father. Not sure at all whether he was doing the right thing, but knowing he had to try something, he threw the water as hard as he could straight into his father's face.

Mr. Donoghue came to, confused and gasping for air. "What the hell?" He wiped his face with his hand as he struggled to stand.

Niall held his father's shoulders down. "You're going nowhere. Just lie still."

"I will not. There's work to be done." Catching sight of the bucket on the ground next to Niall, he demanded, "And what the hell do ye think you're playing at, trying to drown me?"

"I wasn't trying to drown you at all. You were out cold."

"The ambulance will be here soon." Mrs. Donoghue called to Niall as she dashed out from the house, then rushed to her husband's side. "Will! Thank God you've come around. You had us that scared."

"I don't need an ambulance, woman." Mr. Donoghue insisted, not at all happy with the fuss his wife and son were making. "I was dizzy. I blacked out. There's an end to it. Let's all just get back to our day now." He tried again to rise, but Niall stopped him.

"You were out several minutes. You're going nowhere until you've been seen by a doctor."

"That'll take hours. I have inventory and records to tend to; and who'll look after our sheep if we're not back by evening?"

"They'll be fine." Niall insisted. "They've been out late before. If it will make you feel better though, I'll ask Aidan."

Ignoring his father's protests, Niall ran across their yards to where Aidan was heading into his house.

"Aidan! Wait!" Niall yelled.

Aidan turned to see Niall running towards him and an ambulance speeding into the Donoghues' driveway. He hurried to catch up with Niall by the lough where their two yards met.

"Niall, what's wrong? What's with the ambulance?"

"It's my dad. He collapsed. We're taking him to the hospital."

Aidan read the fear etched all across Niall's face and embedded deep within his eyes, and tried to reassure him. "I'm sure everything will be okay."

"I hope so." Shaken by the way the afternoon had turned and anxious to get back to his parents, Niall rushed through his request. "Could you go with Farley to bring our sheep home if we're not back by dark? And pick up my pipes along the way if you could. I left them on the ground up on the hill."

"Of course. You go on. I'll look after things here."

Niall glanced out the curtain that separated the emergency room cubicle his father had been placed in from others around them. Nurses and aides hustled here and there. No one panicked but each moved with purpose and efficiency. He wished one of those purposes was his father, that a nurse or doctor would enter their curtained world and explain what the x-rays they'd taken over an hour ago revealed.

As if reading his son's mind, Will Donoghue ordered Niall, "See if you can't get a nurse in here to tell us what's going on."

"They're all busy, Da." To convince his skeptical father, Niall peered again out the space between curtains. "I don't see anyone free to ask."

Mr. Donoghue sat up, swung his feet over the side of the hospital bed and ordered his wife, "Anna, fetch my clothes. We're going home. We've been here long enough."

Mrs. Donoghue refused to move. "By God, you do make the worst patient ever. We're going nowhere until we hear the doctor out."

"I see I got here just in time."

All three jumped at the voice and figure that had just entered their space.

"I'm Dr. O'Hara. Let's see what's brought you in here today. I've reviewed your records and test results. Aside from dizziness, did you feel anything else before you passed out?"

Mr. Donoghue nodded, "Aye, my gut were hurting something fierce."

"How long have you been having stomach pains?"

Mr. Donoghue glanced at Anna and Niall before confessing, "Three or four weeks." Mrs. Donoghue and Niall exchanged perturbed looks, but kept silent.

"Have you noticed any change in appetite during that time?"

"Aye, my eating's not been up to par."

Mrs. Donoghue added, "He's lost a fair amount of weight these last several days."

"Right." Dr. O'Hara noted their answers on the papers he carried, then set his clipboard and pen aside. "Alright, I'm going to ask you to lie back down on the bed there so I can check things out for myself."

Mr. Donoghue complied and allowed the doctor to examine his abdomen, wincing a couple of times when the doctor's poking and prodding hit a tender area, gritting his teeth and inhaling sharply in an involuntary reaction when the doctor pressed on the spot where his pain had been the worst.

Dr. O'Hara noted his examination finds and Mr. Donoghue's reactions on his chart. He glanced at each of the Donoghues, then fixed his eyes on Will.

"Your x-rays show something in your abdomen, in your small intestine, the same region where your pain is sharpest. We won't know what it is until we run a few more tests. You'll have to stay here overnight at least."

Niall spoke up, knowing neither of his parents would ask any questions of a doctor. "I know you can't say for sure, but what do you think is wrong with my father? You must have an educated guess."

Dr. O'Hara held them all in his sight as he weighed his words. "If you're asking whether I think it's cancer, I can't say. We'll know more after tomorrow's tests. If we still can't determine what's going on, we may have to operate. Even if it's a blockage of some sort, and I will say the x-rays point in that direction, it might not be cancer. It could still be a number of other things."

"Fair enough." Niall spoke for them all. "If surgery is required, when would you do that?"

"I'd schedule it in the next few days."

"That fast?" Mr. Donoghue was stunned.

"Yes. You've been in pain long enough. Let's do whatever we can to get you well as soon as possible."

After Niall and his family left, Aidan tried to focus on work. He set the papers he'd found aside and returned to his carriage house/studio to put the finishing touches on the room where he and Macready's Bridge would rehearse next week. If rehearsals were held. If Niall's father was okay. Aidan fought back his fears that whirled around the word if. The image of Mr. Donoghue flat on the ground had shaken him more than he would admit to Niall. His own family tragedy had been hard enough to get through; he didn't think he'd be able to cope with anything happening to Mr. Donoghue, to say nothing of how devastated Niall would be. No. It wouldn't turn out that way. It couldn't. Niall's father would be fine. Niall would be hard at work with them next week. No other option would do.

Aidan returned to his kitchen and finished applying fresh white paint to faded walls. As he worked, he kept an eye on the Donoghue's farm, hoping the truck Niall had driven behind the ambulance would return with its family intact and all would be right once again.

With no truck in sight, when Aidan finished painting he set out with Farley to collect the Donoghues' sheep. At first the dog was reluctant to break with routine and follow someone else down the lane that led to the far pasture. Aidan tried coaxing Farley by rubbing behind the dog's ears and reassuring him. When that didn't work, he reverted to the more forceful command he'd heard the elder Donoghue use at times: "Farley! Sheep!"

That set Farley off at a fast pace, with Aidan close behind. Aidan paused to retrieve the pipes and carrying case Niall had left on the ground, then caught up with Farley in time to open the pasture gate. Needing no direction, Farley herded the sheep by running four circles around the field, each one tighter and smaller, until all the sheep moved as one fluffy, creamy white body through the gate. Aidan and Farley then guided the sheep back to their home.

After securing the sheep in their pens back in the Donoghues' barn, Aidan filled Farley's food and water dishes, then sat on the steps to the Donoghues' back door while the dog ate.

As he sat, he wondered how Niall and his family were getting on. The day's light had faded to a point where Aidan found it hard to discern where the hilltops surrounding his and Niall's home ended and the sky began. The Donoghues were away longer than he or they thought they would be. He hoped their delay didn't mean problems. He knew something serious was going on inside Mr. Donoghue for him to have collapsed. With nothing else to focus his thoughts on, Aidan's mind rushed to worst case scenarios. Could Niall's father have had a sudden heart attack? No, he'd had too much stomach pain the past few days; whatever the problem was now, it had to be centralized there. With nothing to hold it back, his mind leapt to the thought of cancer. What if Niall's father had that? What if it was widespread, and nothing to be done for it now? His thoughts raced ahead like a runaway train. He tried to imagine how Niall and his mother would manage if Mr. Donoghue was gone. He would step in and help, of course, but the farm would be hard work; and he knew first-hand the agony Niall would go through without his father.

"No!" He spoke out loud, scaring Farley. "They're fine. Hospitals just take forever is all."

He had to keep busy, keep his mind from imagining any more horrible scenarios. He secured Farley in the barn where he'd protect his sheep charges until Niall came home, then walked across to his house. As he entered his house, his mind returned to the papers he'd found earlier. Increasing darkness made the challenge of unlocking the circles on the drawing futile that evening. He studied the papers he'd found with the drawing. Written in old Irish, faded with time, he could pick out few words. After twenty minutes trying, he knew he needed help translating them. He remembered a man Jack had once brought to their house who was fluent in the language and had an archaeological background. Sure this man could help, Aidan called Jack.

"I was wondering," he explained after he and Jack exchanged greetings, "are you still in touch with the history buff you once introduced my dad to?"

"You mean Allan? It's been a while, but yes, we do stay in touch. Why?"

"I've come across a couple of things I'd like his input on. Do you think he'd help out?"

"I'm sure of it. When would you like to meet with him?"

"No hurry, whenever he's available. The band is rehearsing here next week; after that I'm free for a bit."

"Fine. Let me call him and get back to you."

Jack called back twenty minutes later. "Allan's available the week after next. Why don't you come for dinner? Rita and I would both love that."

Aidan agreed. "I'm looking forward to seeing you both, and I'll be glad to have Allan's input as well."

Aidan pulled his camera out from its storage bag in his study, took photos of the writings, printed and slipped them in an envelope for Allan, set the envelope and original papers in his father's desk, now central to his own study, then peered out the window to the Donoghue's farm. Relieved to see a light on in their kitchen and someone moving back and forth between the stove and table, he grabbed his jacket and dashed across both yards to their house.

Niall answered Aidan's first knock on the door. "Come on in; I was going to call you after we ate."

Aidan noticed two plates and cups on the table. Niall set bread and butter out while Mrs. Donoghue stirred a pot on the stove. "Where's your dad?"

Niall's face clouded. "They're keeping him overnight. They've scheduled a few more tests for morning." He hesitated. Should he admit the rest, the fears he and his mother carried with them on their drive home? Aidan was family now. He might as well know it all. "They found something in his stomach, some kind of blockage they think."

Aidan read the same fear on both Niall and Mrs. Donoghue's faces, and guessed what they were thinking. "Cancer?" The world came out in almost a whisper.

Niall looked to his mother first, then to Aidan. "I don't want to think so, but it does sound like that doesn't it?"

"Maybe not," Aidan lied, hoping to reassure Niall and his mother. "Even if it is cancer, it might not be a worst case scenario. Sure he'll be home and all of this behind him before you know."

"I hope so." Niall picked up the boiling tea kettle and poured fresh tea for his mother and himself. "Would you like some?" He offered the hot kettle to Aidan.

Aidan declined. "You're both tired; you've had a long day. Relax and enjoy your meal. If you need anything, just call. I'll check in with you both in the morning."

5

Niall woke up at four, far ahead of the break of dawn over the hills outside his window. Myriad thoughts flew into his brain the minute he opened his eyes, as if they'd watched all night for his waking moment. Now that moment was here, and him with a mind full of nagging pulls and pushes, he found he could not return to that peaceful place where sleep held worries at bay. He rose, taking great care to make no noise and so rouse his mother out of her own slumber. He slipped on jeans and a flannel shirt and tiptoed downstairs.

"You needn't be so quiet moving about the house. I'm already up."

Niall jumped at his mother's voice calling out from the kitchen.

Dressed as if she was ready to go to hospital the moment Niall appeared, Mrs. Donoghue poured a fresh cup of tea for her son and pushed a plate of scones his way.

"Mam, these are still warm. When did you bake them?"

"Oh, an hour or so ago."

"Did you get any sleep at all?"

She shook her head. "I tried, but the bed were too empty. I gave in a couple hours ago, baked these, and baked some oat cakes. He were always fond of my oat cakes, your father. Loves them with his tea, he does. We can take him some as soon as you're finished there."

"They might not let him eat them, with all their tests to be run." At his mother's crestfallen look, Niall softened. "We'll take them with us though, just in case."

"Fine. Finish your tea so we can be off. Sure he'll be watching the door to his room for us to appear."

"Mam, the day's not even born yet, and when it is I'll have the sheep to tend to and all. You best go back upstairs and try to get a bit more kip."

"It's no use." Mrs. Donoghue shook her head. "I'll get some laundry done while I'm waiting."

Niall watched his mother head off in search of dirty laundry, sure she'd find none; she'd finished as much laundry as she could when they'd returned from the hospital the night before. When she returned empty handed, she dragged out the vacuum and devoted the next hour to removing every trace of dust in their house, as if banishing dust would set their lives back in proper order.

Funny, he thought to himself, how we always fall back on routine when our lives are thrown into disarray. The house could be spotless, yet she'll clean it all over again tomorrow morning if my da's not home.

He laughed a short while later when he caught himself doing the same thing, falling into blind routine, finding comfort in familiar actions. At first light he and Farley led their sheep to new pastures, rotating fields according to the schedule his father always followed. He returned to the barn, cleaned sheep pens and hosed them down with the same sweeping motion he'd watched his father use. He coiled the hose in his father's same way when he'd finished. Then he glanced at the clock that hung on the barn wall, noted the time in the spiral bound diary his father kept on a makeshift desk in a corner of the barn, along with a comment as to the field rotation. The diary served no real purpose, he knew, as his father kept a more detailed journal in his desk in the house. It was blind tradition, as was the way he coiled hoses, as was his mother's cleaning. Habits formed over a lifetime became comforting lynchpins, anchoring their lives when storms rattled their windows and beat down on their roof.

By the time he finished it was just past six and his mother was pacing the floors. "Let's go. Your father will be expecting us."

Niall knew they'd arrive too early. He knew they'd have to wait hours before they could see his father. Still, his mother would feel better at least being in the same building as his father. "Alright," he agreed. "Don't forget your box of oat cakes."

The hospital they entered was early morning quiet. A uniformed woman swept the shiny waxed floor and emptied refuse containers into a larger wheeled bin. A young man spoke in low tones into his mobile phone in the lounge area. Two women, one young, one older, sipped tea and watched for someone to appear through the bank of elevators to their right.

Niall directed his mother to the reception desk, where a middle aged woman with blonde, almost white hair sorted through papers and answered phones.

"We're here for Will Donoghue," he informed the receptionist when she'd finished her current call.

Mrs. Donoghue added, "We know we're early, but I couldn't bear to be away any longer."

The receptionist typed information into a computer, studied the screen before her, then directed them to a chair in the nearby lounge area.

"If you'll have a seat, I'll have someone out for you in just a moment."

Niall thought he caught a shadow behind the receptionist's eyes, a quick warning flash that indicated she knew something she would let the medical staff reveal. His pulse quickened with fear; he forced himself to hide his worries from his mother.

"Who do you think she's calling?" Mrs. Donoghue asked as the receptionist picked up her phone, her back to them to block the conversation from their ears.

"I don't know, Mam. We should find out soon, though."

The receptionist finished her call, informed Niall and his mother someone would be down soon to speak to them, then turned her attention to her next call.

Mrs. Donoghue turned worried eyes to Niall. "Why would they be sending someone to talk with us? We know it's not visiting hours yet; we don't mind waiting."

Sure now something was wrong, Niall thought to forewarn his mother while at the same time keeping her calm. "I don't think it's about our early call. Maybe my da's had a restless night, or he may be scheduled for early tests today. We'll know soon enough; here's someone off the elevator now coming to speak with us."

"Mrs. Donoghue? I'm Dr. Carson. Let's have a seat." He nodded to Niall, and sat down across from them both.

"Your husband's had a very hard night. He's in a great deal of pain, and we suspect there may be some internal bleeding going on. We need to take him to surgery straight away."

"Dear Mother of God." Mrs. Donoghue's face drained of all color, her eyes flew open wide as the windows behind the receptionist's desk. Niall placed a hand on her arm to settle her.

"Do you have any idea what you think is going on with my father?"

Dr. Carson held them both in a level gaze. "You know we've detected a suspicious spot on his x-rays. We'll be looking at that first, then go from there. I need you to sign this release, then we'll get started."

Before handing the form to Mrs. Donoghue Dr. Carson added, "You should know there are some risks to the surgery. We don't know what we'll find. We'll do our best to deal with whatever we come across, but I can't say how long surgery will take, and there may be complications."

"I understand." Mrs. Donoghue took the release form, skimmed over it, then handed it over to Niall, her mind too full of Will to comprehend all the form stated.

Niall scanned through the form, knew it contained standard language, that the doctors and hospital would not be held liable in the event of . . . he didn't want to think beyond the words in front of him.

"It's okay, Mam." He handed the form back to her. "Here, sign here."

He watched her sign it, caught how her hand trembled a bit, and placed an arm around her shoulder as Dr. Carson, signed form in hand, disappeared in the next elevator up.

"We may have a long wait ahead of us, Mam. How about some tea and some of those oak cakes you brought?"

Gale force winds blew hard against the brick exterior and rattled the windows of their apartment as Michael and Susannah sat at breakfast.

"Sounds like a good day to work at home." Michael poured fresh coffee for them both. "I can practice my songs in the bedroom if you want to work out here."

"Fine." Susannah reached for her coffee while keeping her eyes on her phone's calendar.

"You don't have to go out in this wind for anything do you?"

"No."

"If you did, I'd take a break and go with you."

"I'm fine." Susannah repeated while scrolling through her e-mails.

Impatient with the same short answers she'd given him for days, Michael snapped. "How long are you going to do this to me?"

"Do what?" Susannah acted innocent, even though in her heart she knew what made him angry.

"You've been short with me ever since our dinner fiasco last week."

Susannah glared at him. "Yes, and you know why."

Michael gave an exasperated sigh. "You're taking it out on me because our fathers don't want to see us married."

Susannah shot back, "No! See, you don't listen. You've got it wrong."

"Then what is it?"

"Have you called your father yet to persuade him to change his mind about our wedding?"

Michael shook his head. "Suze, you have to understand. I know my father. Calling him won't make him change his mind."

"Right, then you best know I'll start calling tonight to cancel our wedding plans."

Michael couldn't believe what he'd heard. He set his coffee mug down hard and sat back, staring at her. "Are you serious?"

"Very much so."

"Why? Because our fathers are two stubborn old men too set in their opinions to see sense?"

Susannah shot him a look of cold steel. He'd seen that look before, recognized it as a warning shot fired across his bow, and knew if he didn't tread with great care a full battle would erupt. Most times, that look would cause him to retreat.

Today, though, there was too much at stake. If he had to wage a battle for their future together, Michael loved Susannah enough to take that conflict head on.

"Suze, it's each other we're marrying, not our fathers. If they choose to not be a part of our wedding, it's their loss, not ours."

Susannah frowned and spoke in slow, even tones, as if she was explaining something to a child. "All my life I've dreamed of a large wedding with all the trimmings, and my father walking me down the aisle. I've made concessions as it is. I've scaled down the size and cost of our wedding as much as I can. It's already not the wedding I'd dreamed. I can't let go of this one final piece, having my father there. It's too much to ask."

Through all her words, Michael focused on only one phrase, not the wedding I'd dreamed. He felt a knife slice through his heart at those words, as if choosing him at all was a let-down, a compromise.

"Not the wedding you dreamed," he repeated, his tone even, flat, measured while he forced himself to remain calm. "I'm sorry this is such a let-down for you."

Exasperated that he'd missed her point, Susannah shot back, "Oh Michael, give over! That's not what I meant at all. This is not about you or what I've let go of. It's about having my father at my wedding. I can't give in on that, it's too vital to me."

Michael considered her words, sure there was a deeper truth she didn't want to admit, well aware the deeper truth would cut him to his core. Unwilling to push her to expose that level of truth, afraid of where it might lead, Michael conceded, "I get that your heart is set on your father's presence."

"Your father's as well." Susannah insisted.

"Okay, our fathers' presence. I'll call my father, but I won't make any promises he'll change his mind."

"Fair enough. If you can convince him to give in, I'm sure I'll be able to persuade mine as well."

"Your techniques are very strong."

Fionna steeled herself, sure Mrs. Cross's praise would be followed by criticism.

"You excel in painting, your drawing skills are quite good and showing improvement." Mrs. Cross reviewed several more pages in Fionna's portfolio. "Sculpture isn't your strongest medium, but we can't be good in all things, can we?"

"No," Fionna agreed and waited for her advisor's next criticism.

Mrs. Cross closed the portfolio, sat back, and passed her eyes over the nervous student before her. They were always so scared in the beginning, she thought, afraid she would rip their works apart and tear their tiny, tender hearts out of their fragile bodies. This one was no exception, sitting on the edge of her chair, hands clasping and unclasping in her lap, straight, hard line of a mouth where a smile should be. Mrs. Cross knew she held the power to either crush the girl's hopes and dreams now and give the poor girl a chance to build her life around another, more attainable goal, or encourage her dream and let her find out her own way, in time, as she herself had, how competitive and hard making a living on dreams could be.

Yet the girl had talent. Mrs. Cross had to give her that. Her work had an inner light, a hidden spark that drew viewers in. Not all of Mrs. Cross's charges had that. Perhaps in time and with proper guidance Fionna could be one of those rare artists who rose above the crowd and made a proper name for herself. Mrs. Cross chose to encourage the girl and see how much farther her talent would develop.

"Your themes are all similar," Mrs. Cross said at last. "No matter what your class assignment is, you always fall back on the same subject in the end: a solitary young man facing whatever world you set him in."

Fionna nodded, but found her explanation stuck in her throat.

Mrs. Cross smiled, hoping to soften the atmosphere, make Fionna less afraid. "Is this young man a relative? A brother or something?" Perhaps he was a family member who had passed on, and Fionna paid homage to him in her artwork. Mrs. Cross would never want to crush that.

Fionna shook her head. "No, no one in particular."

Young love, Mrs. Cross realized. She recalled her own turn at the wheel of romance. In her day she, too, obsessed; all of her artistic creations bore strong John Lennon resemblances. The memory warmed a corner of her heart she'd long thought had died.

"Fine. I understand. Sometimes an image stays with us a long time, until it plays itself out."

"I'll try to choose different themes from now on." Fionna promised, not sure she could keep her word but certain it was what Mrs. Cross wanted to hear.

"You do have talent." Mrs. Cross told her. "Exploring new images will only make your work stronger. I'll see you again in a month."

Fionna exhaled all the breath she'd been holding back as she stepped out of the administrative building. She hadn't been told her work was rubbish and that she'd have to leave the art school, as she'd been sure would happen. Change her themes; that's all she'd been advised. She crossed the grounds of the art school, one eye on the lead grey clouds racing across the sky, hoping she could catch the bus back to her apartment before the storm the clouds promised let loose.

She was three blocks from the bus stop when the skies opened and great torrents of rain poured down, falling so thick and hard she could just make out the sidewalk and buildings in front of her. When a coffee house appeared on her left she ducked in, shook some of the wet from her coat and hair, then scanned the crowded shop for an empty table.

"Over here! Fi, come join us!"

Fionna turned to the corner booth where the voice had come from. She recognized Gwen from her textile design class, but not the two lads who shared the booth with Gwen.

"Come join us," Gwen repeated. "We have room."

The boy across from Gwen slid over, freeing a spot for Fionna. With the driving rain forcing other pedestrians to seek the shop's shelter, the spot Gwen offered was the only empty one in sight. Fionna grabbed it.

"Thanks so much. It's raging out there!"

"Lucky we got here before the storm started." Gwen nodded to the boy beside her. "This is Paul, and the guy next to you is Hugh." To the boys Gwen explained, "Fi's in my textile class. She's best in the class." When Fionna shook her head Gwen insisted, "Well you are!"

"Nice to meet you," Fionna told Paul and Hugh. "Gwen's too kind in her praise of me, though. I'm just passing the class."

"You're loads ahead of me." Gwen confessed. "Paul's in metal arts and Hugh's studying architectural design."

"Architecture, that sounds fascinating."

"I've always been drawn to it." Hugh told her. "Would you like some coffee? Cappuccino? Latte?"

"Just tea," Fionna reached for her wallet, but Hugh stopped her with a hand on her arm.

"My treat. You've already suffered enough with that downpour."

Paul rose and joined Hugh. "Another for you?" he asked Gwen.

"Sure, thanks." When both boys were out of earshot, Gwen leaned in close to Fionna. "Isn't Paul dreamy? I met him at The White Rose a month ago."

"He is. He reminds me of a young Liam Neeson." Fionna smiled. "Thanks again for letting me join you."

Gwen waived Fionna's thanks off. "Fate sent you here, and at just the right time. Paul and I are going out tonight. We were looking for someone to go out with Hugh. Why don't you join us?"

Fionna stiffened inside, the same reaction she had when she thought of dating anyone since she'd met Aidan. "I don't know. I have two major projects to work on."

"It's Friday night! You can't stay in. You can work on them tomorrow. Come on, please? You'll have fun; and Hugh's a sweet guy, you'd enjoy him."

Fionna heard Mrs. Cross's words again: explore new images. At the thought of going out with Hugh, a vision of Aidan flew across Fionna's mind. Each time that happened Fionna tried to grab the image, hold it a while before it faded; this time she forced herself to let the image go. Inside she still felt locked tight, unsure she wanted to let anyone in her private world. Still, she had to start somewhere, and this was as good a chance as any.

"Okay." She agreed. "I'll come along."

Michael practiced the songs Mack had suggested, warming his voice up with scales first then going through song after song, relishing how rich each note was, how smooth the tones of the various songs sounded. His pulse quickened with each song he sang, thrilled to be back to the work that made every fiber of his body come alive. If only he could get his father to understand, to feel what he felt when he sang, to know how every cell in a body could feel so electrified, so fulfilled.

His father. As daylight dimmed and shadows danced across his bedroom walls, Michael remembered the phone call he'd promised Susannah he would make. Now was as good a time as any, he supposed. He doubted he could sway his father; still, singing always raised his spirits and brought to him a sense of optimism for life. Praying that optimism would send positive vibes over the phone waves, he took three deep breaths and rang his parents' house.

"What do you want?" His father answered with bear-like gruffness.

Undaunted, Michael asked, "Can we talk?"

"I have work to do."

"I'll just take a minute. Dad, I'd like to ask you again to come to my wedding. I'm not asking for money, just for you to be there. It would mean so much to Susannah and me."

"Your mother may go. I won't."

"Dad, please. I'm begging you."

"Don't beg. It makes you weak. You know how I feel about your wedding. Get a proper job and build a responsible life for you and your bride. Then I'll come around."

With that, his father hung up.

Michael stared at his phone a long time, angry with himself for begging, for appearing weak in his father's eyes, and angry with his father who'd turned out to be more hard-hearted than even he had imagined possible. Truth be told, he was mad at Susannah as well for setting her bar so high she could not bend when what she demanded could not be obtained.

Michael entered the living room and sat down across from Susannah. "I've called my father. Tried my best. He won't budge."

Susannah paused from the proposal she was typing out for a new client, held still a moment, then returned to her work. "Then I know what I have to do."

"I tried everything I could. I even begged."

"I'm sorry."

"I can't believe you're being so stubborn on this."

"I can't believe you can't understand how important this is."

"Suze, when my father digs his heels in he can't be moved. I could take him to dinner at the most exclusive club in all of Ireland, ply him with Dom Perignon champagne and the finest caviar on earth, and he wouldn't give in. I know what you want and what it means to you, but you have to understand. My father doesn't love me enough to want to be at my wedding. Do you love me enough to be able to move past what I can't give to you?"

He held his breath as Susannah stared at him, studying him inside and out, measuring him against a scale he could not perceive. When she shifted her gaze to the window behind him he exhaled and, for the second time that night, prayed.

"I won't cancel yet. I'll give it a few more days and try again with my father. If I can't win him over, though, I'll cancel our plans."

Michael had hoped for more, for Susannah to declare more love for him than anyone had ever provided, for her at least to offer a word of understanding that he'd tried his best. Her words fell far short of what he'd hoped. She'd promised more time though; true, only a few more days, but it was a start, a glimmer of hope, something to hang onto. In that window of time he was sure he could make her see sense.

"He doesn't look well, does he?"

Niall watched his father, still asleep after his long surgery, then turned to his mother. "He's bound to look poorly after his ordeal today."

"He will be okay though, won't he?"

Niall directed his mother to sit on the lone chair near his father's bed. "You heard the doctor, Mam. They removed the whole tumor and found no signs the cancer has spread any further. It doesn't appear to be an aggressive form of malignancy."

Mrs. Donoghue nodded. "Aye, I heard the same as you. Still, it's cancer your father has, and removing it can't be as simple as surgery."

"No, he may still need chemo, or radiation, or both. We'll know more soon enough."

"What if it never goes away? What if he gets worse? What if . . ."

Niall cut her off, "Stop it, Mam. Don't do this to yourself. The doctor said he'd be fine. Let's have faith in that."

They both fell silent then, each focused on the man who was the center and anchor of their lives, now lying still, monitors tracking his heart beat and pulse with rhythmic beeps while he slept.

Mrs. Donoghue, for the twentieth time that day, prayed her rosary, smooth Connemara marble beads slipping through her fingers with familiar, comforting ease, lips reciting silent words. As she prayed, Niall noticed how the lines of her face softened as her faith turned her fears to peace.

Niall, though, despite his own prayers, found his fears increased. Sure his father would soon come round. Even so, he would be weeks or more in recovery. Niall thought of all the work involved in keeping their farm going. While his father could manage some of the light chores while he continued to get well, and was no doubt stubborn enough to push beyond his physical condition, some work would be too demanding and would require Niall's help. Niall could not imagine how he'd be able to handle his parents' needs, including transportation to and from doctor's appointments as his mother had never learned to drive, plus all the heavy chores their farm would need, plus his Macready's Bridge work which was becoming more demanding with rehearsals, recording and increased performing ahead of them. In the end, he could think of only one solution. He'd have to give up his music, at least for now.

6

Aidan rose before his alarm pierced the morning quiet. Today Mack, Patrick and Michael would arrive. He wasn't sure which he was more excited about: a chance to show off the progress he'd made in repairs on his new house and the carriage house-turned studio, or the chance to once again be about the business of making music. He raced through his shower and shave, double checked that all the painting and cleaning supplies he'd left lying around the house the last few weeks were put away, and dashed out to the carriage house. In a few short hours, songs and laughter would ring out from the once empty building, and his dream of a home studio would be well on its way.

"Roisin Studios," he whispered, the name almost sacred to him as he thought back over the years he and his father had shared their home studio dream. "Da, I wish you were here to see it come to life."

As he surveyed the chairs and trunk table positioned on the rich oriental rug, he envisioned how the studio would someday look. On one side, by the windows, there would be a massive mixing console, all shiny and new, large enough to manage a symphony's recordings. Microphones on their sleek, solid bases would stand before musicians' chairs. Along one wall gold records and awards received by Macready's Bridge and other artists Roisin Studios had produced would be hung. On an opposite wall, a picture of his mother, the studio's namesake, would oversee all the studio's comings and goings.

In that instant he imagined them all, his grandmother and sister setting up tea, water and pastries at the table on one side of the studio for incoming guests, his mother greeting musicians as they arrived to spend a day of recording, his father seated behind the great control panel, joking with some of the musicians already gathered before their serious work began.

It would have been the family business they'd all dreamed of. Now he would carry it on alone. Tears rose in his eyes, and for a moment the rush of memories threatened to derail his exhilaration for the day ahead. Then he felt it, a touch on his shoulder so real he spun around to see who had snuck up behind him. No one was there. The feel of the touch remained though, followed by a warmth in his heart that spread throughout his body.

"You're doing fine, lad. Keep moving forward."

His father's voice filled his mind, then evaporated as did the inner warmth and the touch on his shoulder. Perhaps he'd just imagined the voice and the feeling. Even if he had, he thought, the feel and the message pleased him, and he held on to them as he returned to the house and waited for his friends to arrive.

Mack arrived first, bearing a tray of meat and cheese slices and rolls. "I thought we could eat here and not lose any rehearsal time by going out for lunch."

Aidan laughed and pointed to a shelf in the refrigerator where he'd already stacked sandwich meats, cheeses and side dishes of potato and pasta salads. "I had the same idea."

Mack scanned the living and dining rooms, where Aidan had patched plaster, washed windows and polished the marble fireplace mantles in both rooms. "Look how much you've accomplished already," he noted, impressed. "You should be proud of yourself."

"Thanks. There's still tons to do, though. I may switch our instruments out for paint brushes before you're all gone this week."

"If you pay us enough," Mack countered, "we might all stay on another week and help you out."

"Help you out with what?" Patrick's voice behind them made Mack and Aidan jump. "I'm sorry; the back door was open. I just came ahead in."

Aidan accepted the box Patrick handed him. "You can just walk in anytime. What's this?"

Patrick smiled. "You know Moira wouldn't let me show up with nothing in hand. She sent an apple pie along with me."

"Thank God for Moira! I forgot about dessert." As Aidan took the box from Patrick, he thought the band's fiddler looked tired or worried, or both. He asked no questions, guessing over the course of the week if anything was on Patrick's mind it would soon come out.

Patrick scanned the large living room where they stood, noting its tall windows, high ceiling, and marble fireplace. "I still can't believe you own this house."

"I can't either," Aidan admitted. "Once the others are here I'll give you all the grand tour of the work I've done so far. I can show you the outside now while we're waiting."

They stepped out and Aidan pointed to the upper corner where the first section of roof repairs had been completed, the various windows and trim that would be next in line for work, and the places where he had cleared away overgrown or dead vegetation. They were discussing options for repairing several worn and cracked steps on the front stairway when Michael pulled up.

"Hey! No fair starting the tour without me!" He hurried to where they stood, carrying a large bag of crisps and a bottle of wine which he handed to Aidan. "I thought we might want to stay in tonight. You don't want to risk inflicting us all on your local too soon, now do you?"

Aidan laughed. "I'm not sure I want to inflict you all on them ever! Come on in, though. I've held up the inside tour until you arrived."

Michael glanced around. "Niall's not here yet. Shouldn't we wait for him?"

"No, he's seen the interior so many times he's no doubt bored with it. He should join us later." Aidan led the others inside, saying nothing of Niall's father and the concerns his family now faced. He knew Niall's news would come out soon enough.

Starting in the kitchen, Aidan showed them the cleaning and repairs he'd done as well as the color palettes he'd chosen for each room. "You've seen the blue and white I've painted the kitchen, which was always my grandmother's dream combination. In the dining room, here, I'm going for sand and salmon tones. They remind me of the beach and of the fish my dad and I used to catch." They moved to the living room, where Aidan showed them chips of green, brown and gold paints. "The colors of the oak leaves and acorns that are the symbols of Derry," he explained and added, "I might also use some terra cotta accents, the color of the Guildhall, my sister's favorite building."

As they followed Aidan to the library at the back of the house Patrick commented, "I love how you're paying tribute to your heritage with the colors you're choosing."

"Thanks. I like the connections they'll represent." They reached the library, now Aidan's study, where he showed them a palate of soft greys and blues, explaining, "the colors of the Derry sky and Lough Swilly waters."

"It looks like you spend most of your time here." Michael pointed to the mementos Aidan had set on the bookshelves, and one of Jeannie's paintings Aidan had stood on an easel in a corner of the room.

"I do. The front room still seems a bit too big and empty."

"I'd stay here too." Mack admired the view out the large window at the far end of the room which looked out over the great expanse of lawn that once boasted a vibrant garden and the lough and farm behind them. "It's very peaceful back here."

They stood for a moment admiring the view, taking in the figurines, painting, photos and tokens of his family Aidan had displayed, reflecting on the colors Aidan had selected and what those choices meant to him. When the moment grew too long and thoughts of Aidan's loss threatened to weigh them down, Mack suggested, "We best get about the business of music. Why don't you take us out to that carriage house studio I know you're so anxious to show us?"

"Let me call Niall first." Aidan pulled his phone out. "Even he hasn't seen the studio yet; I've kept that a secret until it was finished."

"Niall, the boys and Mack are here." Aidan explained when Niall answered. "I'm just checking to see how you are and if you're able to come by today."

"I'm sorry, I meant to call you earlier." Niall paused and drew a deep breath. "I'm at hospital with my mam. My father had surgery yesterday."

"Already?" The surprise in Aidan's voice caused the others to turn his way. "Is he okay?"

"He will be. I'm not sure when I'll be over though. It might not be until this evening."

"If you can't be here until tomorrow, or later this week, that's okay. Can we do anything to help?"

"No, thanks."

Aidan turned to the worried faces around him. "Niall's father had surgery yesterday. Niall's at the hospital now." To all the questions directed to him Aidan could only answer, "I'm not sure what the surgery was for. All I know is he hasn't been feeling well and they had to rush him to hospital the other day."

Mack gave them all a moment to digest Niall's news, then suggested, "Why don't we have lunch now, then we can start rehearsing here in the house. We can see the studio later, when Niall can join us."

Aidan's spacious living room served well as a rehearsal spot that afternoon. Michael, Patrick and Aidan practiced all the songs they could without Niall, while Mack listened and wrote comments in his small wire-bound notebook. They broke at seven for the chicken casserole Aidan had prepared that morning, and were just getting back to work when Niall walked in.

"I'm sorry I couldn't be here earlier. Aidan told you about my father, didn't he?"

"Yes," Mack answered. "How is he?"

"A little better thanks. He has stomach cancer. The surgeon said they were able to remove it all, they don't think it spread anywhere else."

There. The words were out. He almost choked on them, hated pushing them through his mouth, hated the feel of them on his tongue, the sound of them slicing through the air. The first time speaking them was the hardest. At least that was over now.

"It's good the cancer hasn't spread." Michael hoped his words would help, although they felt and sounded hollow to him.

"Will he need chemo or radiation?" Patrick wanted to know.

"I think so, just as a precaution. I'll know more in a few days." Niall looked straight at Mack. "Can I talk to you alone?"

"Sure."

"You can use the study if you want," Aidan offered.

Mack followed Niall to the back room and closed the door behind them.

Niall stood in front of the window where his family's farm was visible in the distance. He watched the farm a moment, saw the light in his parents' upstairs bedroom go on and hoped his mother was settling in for an early sleep. Then he turned to Mack.

"I think I'm going to have to leave the group. My dad won't be able to work around the farm for a while, until he's healed from his surgery, and maybe during whatever chemo or radiation treatments he needs. I'll have to be there to help out."

Mack studied the young piper as he spoke. He knew how devoted Niall was to his parents and the sheep farm he'd grown up on. Of course Niall would place that as a top priority. He also knew first hand

Niall's passion for the pipes he devoted so much time to. Maybe he could help the lad find a way to work around both the farm and the band.

"Niall, I know your parents and the farm come first. You might not have to step away from the band, though."

"I don't see how I can do both."

"For one thing, you know Aidan will help. I'll do anything I can as well, although I admit my farming abilities are a bit of a joke."

Niall laughed in spite of his dilemma. "I'll give you something easy, like cleaning the pens out."

"Thanks!" Mack wrinkled his nose. "Niall, I'll do whatever I can. Perhaps you have neighbors you could call on as well."

Niall considered the idea. "My parents do have some friends around town and at church. I doubt they'd call on anyone though. They're proud. They wouldn't accept help."

"You should discuss that option with them. Other than that, we'll work our schedule around you as best we can."

"Mack, there's tons to be done between rehearsals, recording, and the gigs you're setting up for us. I don't want to hold you and the boys back."

Mack saw the weight of stress and fear bearing down on the young musician before him. How would he feel, he wondered, if he were in Niall's place? If he were young and responsible to help his family out, would he set aside the thing that meant most to him? Or would he pursue his dream and let his family sort things out for themselves? He hoped he would make the right choice, just as Niall was trying to do now.

"I appreciate your concerns for the band, Niall. This week, do whatever you need to with your family, and join us when you can. After that, we'll see what we can sort out. Will that work for you?"

Niall weighed Mack's suggestions. He didn't believe they would work, that things would fall into place so easy. It wouldn't hurt to try, though. By the end of the week he should know if staying with Macready's Bridge would be possible after all. "Okay," he agreed. "I'll try it your way and see what happens."

"Fine. Now why don't you go relax with the boys for the evening. Aidan can warm some dinner for you unless you've already eaten, and we can all use a good catch up."

"Everything okay?" Aidan asked as Niall and Mack returned.

"I think so." Niall spotted the leftover casserole on Aidan's kitchen counter and realized he hadn't eaten since the full breakfast his mother had prepared early that morning. "Any chance you'd heat some dinner up for me after you show me that carriage house you've been keeping so secret?"

"Sure!" Aidan grabbed his keys off the coffee table. "We've been waiting for you so I could show you all at the same time."

He unlocked the door to the long, low stone building, switched the lights on and stepped back, allowing his friends to enter first. As he watched their reactions, he admired again how the carriage house, once filled with clutter and debris, had been transformed.

"Aidan, this is amazing."

"I had no idea this building was so spacious."

"I love how you've set everything up."

"Your father would love what you've done here."

This last comment, from Mack, pleased Aidan the most. "My dad would have loved this, wouldn't he?"

Mack nodded. "He would be very proud of you. You've handled the decision to move, which home to buy, and the repairs and restoration very well. It can't be easy, though. How are you really doing?"

Aidan sat on the wooden chair nearest him. "I'm okay. All the work is a good diversion."

"It must be hard living in this big house alone." Patrick thought of his own small, crowded home, soon to become even more cramped. "The silence must be overwhelming at times."

Aidan shrugged. "Most of the time it's fine. There's so much work to do the days fly by, and by the time I hit bed I'm well tired and sleep straight through the night. Mornings are hard. Every morning I lie in bed and listen for voices and movement. When no sounds arise, I have to remind myself they're gone, there won't be any noise. I have to force myself to get out of bed and start the day off. Once I've done that, I'm okay."

"I know that feeling." Mack admitted. "In the years while Kate and I were apart, every day started out empty, a huge hurdle to overcome."

"How are you and Kate doing now?" Michael asked.

Mack smiled, thinking of Kate, her bright blue eyes, her spicy fragrance that lingered in his mind wherever he went. "We're fine. In fact, I haven't hinted to her on this, and you're all sworn to secrecy, but I'm thinking I'll ask her to marry me again. I think we're both at a place in our lives where this time it would work."

"Mack, that's great!"

"Ask her as soon as you get home!"

Aidan handed over his mobile phone. "The hell with later! Call her now. Make up an excuse to get her out here, tell her you forgot something you need. And when she gets here, propose!"

They all laughed, imagining Mack on bended knee before Kate. When the laughter faded Mack asked Michael, "How are your own wedding plans coming along?"

Michael shook his head. "They're stalled. Susannah's threatening to cancel the whole affair."

"Are you joking?"

"She wouldn't do that."

"Why? What's gone wrong?"

Michael, still puzzled over the turn their plans had taken explained, "Both our fathers refuse to attend. They think we're wrong for each other. No, the truth is they think I'm wrong for her, that she could do better. Neither of them want anything to do with our wedding. She won't get married if our parents aren't there. If I can't convince them to change their minds, she's going to cancel it all."

"Sure Susannah wouldn't do that, Michael." Niall assured him. "She loves you that much, she'd choose you over her parents any time."

"Niall, she has a dream of what she wants her wedding to be." Michael held back her words about how much of her dream she'd already compromised and how those words had cut through his heart. "She's dead set on our parents being there."

"Your parents and hers will see that," Patrick suggested. "Sure they'll come around."

"I hope so." Michael glanced over to Patrick. Their fiddler always seemed to have the perfect life, he thought. Finances may be tight at times, but Patrick and Moira always managed to come through;

and their twins, well, they were pure charmers. More than any musical or financial success, Michael wished he could have Patrick's life. "Someday I want Susannah and me to have all the blessings you've found."

Patrick laughed, "Aye, we've blessings alright. In fact, we're about to have more. Moira's pregnant. Twins again, can you credit that?"

Aidan teased, "I don't know what's in that Sligo water you're drinking, but you better move away from it as soon as those new twins are born!"

"I know we're crazy," Patrick admitted, "but we want these new twins as much as we ever wanted Conor and Caitlyn. Sure things will be tight, but there's nothing like looking into the face of a child of his that sets a father's heart on fire. I'd not only take the next two, but a dozen more like them if I could. Although," Patrick looked out one of the carriage house's windows to the farmhouse across the lawn, "our wee cottage is already stretched to its seams. We'd be better served moving to a larger place, maybe a farm like yours, Niall."

At the mention of the farm, Niall grew serious. "The farm's grand, sure, but there's a lot of work that goes with it. In fact, that's what I was discussing with Mack. My father should be coming through his cancer okay, but with all my parents and the farm will need for the next while I'll not have much time for music."

Aidan sensed where Niall's thoughts were heading. "Don't think too far ahead," he cautioned. "One step at a time."

Niall knew Aidan was right, as Mack had been. His father wouldn't be side-lined forever. He was worried and tired, and felt like he carried the world on his back. A few days on, he might not feel so overwhelmed. He'd take Mack's and Aidan's advice and see how the week played out.

As they rehearsed, Michael thought of Susannah, never far from mind but lying on it much heavier now. In order to gain their fathers' approval, he knew what they wanted. He'd have to change careers, use his Trinity College business degree for what it was intended, to work his way through a company to the point where he ran it. Susannah's father would expect him to become president of a large corporation someday. His own father would be satisfied with nothing less than him owning two or three companies. As for Susannah, no matter how she supported him, in her heart he knew she wanted the same lifestyle she'd been raised on, and that would not happen while music was his career.

While he rehearsed though, while the music they played struck the deepest parts of his heart, he knew this would be his choice. If his father and Susannah's couldn't accept that, so be it. And if Susannah chose to cancel their wedding, well, that was her loss. He had to follow his dream.

Patrick played his fiddle hard that week, on slow airs, fast jigs, sometimes solo, most often with the rest of Macready's Bridge. As the fiddle's vibrations ran through his fingers and hands, through his veins and along his whole body, he thought back to Moira and their expanding family. He recalled his resolve to leave the band and return to the cement quarry. The money would be better, no doubt. The hours would fit better too. Moira could never handle four wee ones on her own, although she'd protest that she could. No, leaving would be the only reasonable option he could see, although with Niall's news he'd have to choose his timing with great care.

He would not leave Macready's Bridge down two members at once.

Still, as he played he knew that to leave the band would be to leave the best part of him behind. He would hate it, truth be told. He'd just have to settle for teaching music to Conor and Caitlyn, and the new wee dotes when they were of age, and the odd gig in town when he could get it. That would have to suffice until they were in a position for him to take music on full time again.

Aidan, as he rehearsed, thought how close he'd come to giving music up. He was right, playing music without his father was painful. Standing here in Roisin Studios, bare bones as she was, without his father or family cut deep as well. There was no choice for it though. They were gone, he was here; and joining his bandmates now in music, he knew, had been the right choice. Music and laughter filled the studio, giving life to once abandoned space. As he rehearsed he recalled again how music had connected his father with so many people, how it had stirred so many of their hearts. The past few months had brought numerous changes, and Aidan knew more lie ahead; yet this week, as he rehearsed with his bandmates in the studio space he'd set up, he felt the thrill of purpose seep back into his life through the music they shared and the friendships they'd formed.

Niall ran his hands over each of his pipes as he packed them away, rehearsals over for another night. He'd been able to participate more than he'd expected, and it felt good. No, wonderful. Playing his pipes always filled a place in his heart nothing else could; playing with Macready's Bridge always provided a connection with friends he'd sometimes missed growing up on a remote farm with no brothers or sisters and no neighbors close by. Macready's Bridge gave him a taste of a dream he'd carried inside him since he was nine, watching other pipers at the small fairs and festivals around town in summers gone by. The dream had come alive the past couple of years, every moment of it exhilarating and satisfying.

Now, as he packed his pipes away, he felt he was packing his dream away as well, at least for a while. His father was due home from the hospital the next day. He'd had fun rehearsing with the boys this week; but now reality would take over, his parents and the farm would come first. They had to. Each day he'd driven his mother to visit his father in the hospital, then returned home to manage work on the farm. He'd spent a couple hours mid-morning rehearsing with the boys, then finished with the farm before returning to the hospital to pick his mother up. He'd caught a couple more hours rehearsing before bed, then repeated the cycle the next day. It had worked, but he was exhausted. Once he'd hinted to his parents that calling on friends might be wise, but his father had shut the idea down straight away. Rather than argue, Niall had dropped the idea. Now, though, the band had recording sessions and gigs coming up. They needed a piper who would be on hand in a moment's notice, which he doubted he could do.

Aidan, Patrick and Michael had already gone into the house, Aidan to start dinner, Michael and Patrick to make phone calls. Mack alone remained in the studio sorting and packing papers away, and no doubt waiting on Niall to finish.

"Mack, this week has been fun. I've enjoyed being with the band again."

"It has been," Mack agreed. "I'm glad you could join us."

"I am too." Niall stepped away from the table his pipes sat on. "This is the end, though."

Mack had been expecting this. "It shouldn't be, Niall. We can work around you. We've already discussed it."

Niall shook his head. "You need someone who can give you one hundred percent. I can't do that right now."

"I wish you'd give it more time."

"You're recording in two weeks. My dad will still be recovering from surgery. I'll need to be here."

Mack considered Macready's Bridge's options. They could find another piper; every town had one or more waiting for a lucky break and a band to join. Talent and technique were just half the requirement, though. Chemistry with the rest of the band was another vital factor. Niall and the others had formed such a tight, cohesive unit, Mack was unsure he could match that with another player.

Still, he understood Niall's dilemma. "I know timing's hard. We could record around you the first few days, but you would be needed after that. You must be able to find someone who could help you and your parents out for a little bit, at least. I know your parents are proud, but I'm also convinced they would not want you to give up your dreams, would they now?"

"My father's not keen on calling in help," Niall confessed.

"Mack countered, "Would he be keen on you giving up the music you love?"

"No. He'd feel a great deal of guilt."

"I doubt that would help his recovery."

Niall considered his choices. Give up the band, deal with his father's guilt, and hope someday another band would come along, or step on their pride and force his father to bring some help in for the farm. He picked up the canvas carrying bag his pipes had been packed away in, felt their familiar weight and how even just holding them lifted his heart. Who was he kidding? He could no more give up Macready's Bridge than he could breathing, or eating, or sleeping.

"Alright, Mack. I'll see what I can do."

That night, their last in Aidan's house, Mack lie awake long after the others had fallen asleep, considering again each of the boys, their places in the band and the challenges each one faced.

Aidan, for all he'd come through, had reached the other side of his dark days. What he'd done with his new house was remarkable, and would continue to keep him busy for months on end. Even though hard days were still sure to come, he'd shown he had the strength to get through them. He would be fine.

Michael would be fine as well, although whether he'd end up with Susannah remained to be seen. Mack thought he'd like to knock Michael's and Susannah's fathers' heads together, knock some sense into them. What was wrong with them anyway? Michael was a fine lad, better than most. Susannah could do a lot worse. Still, Michael was strong. If Susannah chose to turn her back on him, Michael would be hurt but he'd survive.

Then there was Patrick. New twins on the way? Mack almost laughed out loud. Well, Patrick and Moira were wonderful parents, they'd look after four kiddies in fine fashion, even if on a wire thin budget.

Of all four Macready's Bridge members, Patrick was the one Mack worried about least.

Last, Mack considered Niall. He hoped he'd been right in advising the boy to stay on. He admitted to himself now his reason for wanting Niall to stay, some of it professional, some very much selfish on his part. All the boys had become a family to him. To lose any of them would be like losing one of his sons.

He wished he could talk to Kate. She would tell him whether his advice had been right. His clock showed half two in the morning. Kate would be deep in sleep, as he himself should be. He forced himself to close his eyes and set his worries aside. To keep them at bay, he focused on Kate, her soft hair, her elegant pearls, her tender voice. Tomorrow he'd be back home with her. He fell asleep thinking, again, how wonderful life would be if, no when, they remarried.

7

Mack, Michael and Patrick left after Saturday breakfast, schedules and set list in hand, excited for the recording sessions to come. After they left, Aidan turned back to the writings and drawing he'd found in the attic trunk. He would be meeting with Jack and Rita and their history buff friend on Sunday, and would love to have deciphered what the circles on the drawing represented by then.

The first circle, as he'd guessed before, appeared to be across from the front of his house, although he'd not been able to see what it connected with on his first cursory search. Now he carried the drawing outside. Not sure what he was looking for, he walked the length of his driveway, scrutinizing every stone and blade of grass but seeing nothing out of the ordinary. He crossed the paving to the gorse shrubs that lined the roadside. Gnarled, tangled and hard to search through, Aidan nevertheless poked around their roots, finding nothing unusual and scratching his hands in the process.

Straightening up, Aidan checked the drawing to confirm he was where the circle indicated, then surveyed the scenery before him. The road, he thought, might not have been here when the drawing was created. What if the object the circle referenced was under the pavement? In that case, he'd never find it.

He should move to the second circle, he figured. If he could find something there, he might stand a better chance of unlocking the circles' code.

He turned, took three steps toward his house, and froze.

Was that a whisper he heard?

He turned back and stared at the gorse hedge, at the road, at the field beyond. Seeing nothing, he continued to walk away.

This time, the sound of rustling called him back. When he turned, he saw a section of the hedge shaking though no wind blew and the shrubbery on either side of the quaking section remained still. He strode over to the rustling gorse, peered at it, but found nothing noteworthy. He stood, shook his head in bewilderment, and spoke to the air around him, "If you've got something to show me, let's be having it."

Words came to him, a whisper so close to his shoulder he jumped. The words came in Irish first, then in English. "Look in the roots."

Aidan kneeled in front of the section of gorse that had moved without cause and felt closer around the base of the shrub.

There! Hidden by branches, half buried in dirt, was a stone, its surface cold and smooth and rounded on top. As his hand ran over the stone, his fingers felt lines on one side, a long solid one running straight down, and several smaller ones running side to side.

A rush of excitement ran through him as he hurried back to the house for his camera and his grandmother's gardening tools. He returned to where the stone was and, working with great care, trimmed a few lower branches away then dug around the base of the stone, careful not to scratch its surface. When he had removed enough branches and dirt to allow his camera access, he took a few photos then examined them.

Ogham, he thought. The lines on the stone looked for all the world like ogham markings, the ancient form of writing used by the early Irish.

Aidan sat back on the ground. He knew ogham stones were rare. To find one was remarkable. If the other three circles held the same type of stones, their findings would be a treasure indeed.

He gathered his tools and the branches he'd cut away. Best to leave the site undisturbed so no one else would stumble upon his find, he thought, as if anyone even frequented that spot of ground. Back at the house, he packed his camera and tools in a knapsack then carried that out to what he perceived to be the location of the next circle on the map.

Aidan walked eastward to a spot halfway between his land and Niall's. So many rocks lie strewn across the ground here, he wasn't sure he could find one that stood out from among the rest. Still, he'd give it a try, his excitement fueled by the gorse hedge stone discovery. He studied stones as he walked past them, seeing nothing unusual. Several times he bent down and examined a stone closer, then moved on. After forty minutes of looking, he was about to give up and move to the third circle, when he saw it. There, near the trees, to the right of where he'd been looking, standing at a tipped angle as if the ground were trying to eject it, rose an oblong stone. Worn smooth by wind and rain, the series of lines along the east-facing side of the stone were faint but still visible. Aidan took several photos of the second ogham stone and its position near the tree line, then moved on.

The third circle appeared on the drawing to be opposite the second, as if the paper had been folded in half and a mirror image had been left by wet ink when unfolded. Aidan walked west in as straight a line as he could, given the lough he had to walk around. Before long, he was near the road at the far edge of his and Niall's lands. A small stream bubbled up here and fed into the lough. Stones galore lie scattered among the stream and the banks on either side. To pick one special, different one would be madness, he thought. He sat on a small boulder and studied the stones the water flowed over. Each one was brown, small or mid-sized, and rounded by the water's constant flow over them through so many decades of time.

By now the weak autumn sun was slipping towards the horizon, taking daylight with it. Aidan rose to leave, thinking the third and fourth stones would have to wait for another day.

As he bent to pick up his knapsack, something from the boulder he'd sat on caught his eye. Could it be? He almost burst out laughing at the absurdity of it, but there, carved into the boulder, facing away from the stream, were worn but unmistakable lines so similar to the stone near the tree line they could be twins. Aidan took photos, ran his hands over the lines, caressing them as if to bless or thank them, then strolled home satisfied he now had enough of value to show Jack's friend tomorrow.

Aidan parked his car in front of the house he once lived in. Outside it hadn't changed much. He thought his grandmother would not like the bright blue curtains that hung in the front upstairs windows, and the way they clashed with the lime green curtains in the living room, nor would she like how the lavender she'd planted in front of the house several years earlier had now died out. She would, though, smile at the sound of children playing that emanated from the back garden, as would his father. New life in the house would make them happy. For a few minutes he sat in his car and watched the house, envisioning his sister Jeannie bounding from room to room, full of laughter, energy and life, seeing his granny cook and clean and keep general order, picturing his father, tired from work but always ready with a joke, a story, a song. Moving away from the house had been the right thing to do, especially knowing Jack and Rita's daughter now lived there; still, seeing it now brought back such an overwhelming flood of feelings and memories he feared he would drown in them if he sat there too long. He hurried out of his car, past the house to Jack and Rita's next door.

Rita swung the door open before he could knock, and wrapped him in a fierce hug before he could hand her the chocolate mousse tarts he'd picked up on his way. "Aidan, love, it's so good to see you!" She stepped back and held him at arm's length. "You're looking well, dear. Your new home must agree with you."

"It does," he admitted as they stepped inside. "I can't wait for you to see it again."

They entered the dining room, where Jack sat with a stranger Aidan guessed to be Allan. Jack rose, extended a hand to give Aidan a warm, hearty handshake, and pulled out the chair next to him. "Here boy, sit here. Allan, this is Aidan, the wee lad I've told you about. Aidan, my friend, Allan McStrainer." As they exchanged handshakes Jack continued, "Aidan's just bought a grand old house out Minterburn way."

"Lovely country, that." Allan smiled, his eyes far away recalling his own travels through the Minterburn region.

"It's beautiful indeed. My friend's family has a farm behind me, there's a wee lough between us and the views all around are remarkable."

Rita brought in fresh tea, and a tray of cheese, crackers and fruit which she placed in the center of the table before settling into a chair opposite Jack.

Jack, never one to beat around the bush, opened their discussion. "Aidan, tell us what you've found."

Aidan chose to start with photos of the stones he guessed might be easier for Allan to explain. He pulled up the photos he had taken on his phone and passed the phone to Allan. "I found these on the grounds around my place. They all look the same. There are three; I think there might be a fourth." He excluded any mention of Timothy McCabe's instructions to him, not sure how to explain that apparition.

Allan studied the photos, turned them to several different angles, enlarged them, with each new angle his smile growing broader. After several minutes of intense scrutiny, he handed the phone over for Jack to view.

"They look to be ogham stones," he confirmed. "How did you find them on your property?" To Aidan's puzzled look he clarified, "I mean, how were they spaced apart? At regular intervals? Or set in a more random fashion?"

"They're at three different locations, not close to each other, but I think there's a regular pattern to their spacing." Aidan received his phone back and turned it over to Rita so she could see the photos as well.

"Why do you think there's a fourth?" Allan noted the slight flicker in the young man's eyes. The boy's keeping something from us, he thought. That was fine, let the lad have his secrets for now. They'd come out soon enough.

Aidan pulled out the drawing with four marked circles, three of them now checked off. "I found this up in the attic of my house. The first three stones were found in the circles I've marked off. I haven't checked for the fourth yet."

Allan studied the map. "Can you tell me what features are in the land around where you found the stones?"

Aidan indicated to Allan where on the map his house was, where Niall's family's farm sat, the road's path, and the pastures where the Donoghues' sheep grazed. Allan nodded his head as Aidan pointed each item out. When Aidan was done, Allan spoke.

"My first guess is these are property markers. The lines on each of the stones look to be the same, possibly a name; the same name on each stone around the vicinity of your property could be boundary markers." Excitement rose in Allan's voice as he continued. "It's quite rare to come across three or four stones in the same general area such as this. I know a number of people who would love to come out and inspect what you have here."

Aidan hesitated. He hadn't even shared news of what he'd found with Niall and his family yet, let alone having them find strangers traipsing all over their land. "Would you mind if I asked you to keep this just between us for now?"

"Of course not. It's your land, your discovery. With your permission, though, I would like to research this a bit further."

"I was hoping you would. I'd like to know what they mean." Aidan considered the additional pieces of paper he carried with him. "Can you read Irish?"

"I can," Allan responded, even more curious as to what Aidan would produce next. When the young man laid three pieces of paper on the table Allan tried to act casual, while inside his excitement built like a sea at high tide. The papers were old, yellowed, marred along the right edge by a tea or water stain, the writing faded, yet the numbers 1579 stood out on one of them as did the Irish words "land title". Allan spent several minutes studying the writings, some of them almost indecipherable but all of them, together, pointing to the same answer.

"Aidan, what you have here appears to be an accounting of who has owned certain pieces of land in the past, I'm guessing to the land your home sits on. One paper tells the history of who has owned the land up to and including 1579, when it was issued. The title and the ogham stones, on their own, are each remarkable finds. Together with the additional papers, they are a very important historical and archaeological record."

Allan then launched into a discourse of the history of land ownership and records throughout Irish and Northern Irish history, some of which Aidan found fascinating, some dry and difficult to follow. As he listened he thought of Timothy McCabe. He doubted the spirit, or whatever he was, cared for the archaeological value of the writings and stones he had driven Aidan to find. What other purpose could there be? What secrets did the papers and stones hold? Aidan hoped Allan's research and translation would make the reason clear.

After his speech was done, Allan turned back to Aidan. "Could you mail me copies of the photos and papers you brought so I may research them further? You have my word I won't show them to anyone else."

Aidan opened the envelope he'd brought with him. "I brought copies with me just in case. Here's a set you can have. Thank you for agreeing to keep them private."

Allan left with the copies and a promise to get back to Aidan soon with his results.

After Allan left Jack cautioned Aidan, "You best store your photos and original papers in a safe spot until you know for sure what they all represent and what you want to do with what you're learning."

"Jack's right," Rita agreed. "You want to be careful with your find. Now, you'll stay to dinner won't you? We could even stop next door a bit; our Lizzie can show you what she's done with your old house since moving in."

Aidan considered what stepping into the house he grew up in would feel like now, with his family gone and another family living there. He wondered what changes he would find. Jack and Rita had already informed him of the fresh paint and new colors the walls had received and he'd seen the curtains when he first drove up. The thought of seeing those changes, though he knew change was inevitable, was more than Aidan could deal with. "I don't think I'm ready to go next door yet, if that's okay. I will stay for dinner though; in fact, I'd like to take you both out for a meal."

Jack shook his head. "Save your money there, lad. No doubt you're needing it for repairs around your own place."

"You're right there," Aidan admitted. "I've just had some roof work done and more to come."

"Well there you go, then. You mind your expenses, and have dinner here. Our Rita's already planned for that as it is." Jack offered Aidan a bottle of stout and opened one for himself. "Are you managing the place okay? Do you need a hand with anything?"

"Thank you, no, it's all under control. I've cleaned out the carriage house; I guess I can start to call it my studio now. It's not a proper studio, mind; I need a lot of equipment for that. I've moved some chairs and things into place in it though, and the band was able to rehearse in it last week."

Rita was pleased to see the smile that spread across Aidan's face as he spoke of the studio. "You sound happy enough love, and for that I'm so thankful. We've been worried for you."

"We did worry the big house was a bit much to take on," Jack confirmed. "Sounds like you're coping fine though."

"I am, I think. The house is starting to take shape. I enjoyed having the boys there. I'm seeing more and more potential in the house; I can even see myself raising a family there someday, although that's a long way off!"

"You've a grand place there to build your future on." Rita told Aidan. "You made the right choice."

Driving home that night, Aidan thought the same thing. He did have a future to build, and his home was the best place for it. Someday Roisin Studios would be properly fitted out and become a recording hub, a mecca for musicians dedicated to their craft, with him at the helm. Someday his house would be restored to its former glory, no, to a new glory decorated with his personal tastes and touches, bright lights shining from its vast windows, a showplace people from all over would drive by to admire. He would host parties in the house's massive rooms again such as Mrs. Donoghue dreamed of, and this time she'd be attending and even have the thrill of helping him plan it all out. He'd raise a family here too, with children running over the lawn, playing in the lough between his house and Niall's, maybe Niall's children playing with his own, while he and Niall and their wives sat back with wine and food, enjoying the world they'd fashioned for themselves.

A spark of inspiration ignited Aidan's heart and mind. He parked his car in his driveway and hurried inside to grab his guitar, paper and pen. Playing with notes and chords, experimenting with sounds and words, three cups of tea and a midnight sandwich later he'd set down a song he hoped Mack would like well enough to include on their new album. As he headed up to bed, the tune he'd written still ran though his mind. He could imagine Niall's pipes intertwining with his guitar throughout the melody of the song that celebrated the sweet spot his life had found and the friendship that had helped him find his way through the dark period he was emerging from. As he slid under blankets and turned his light out, his favorite line of the chorus still rang in his mind, "and the lough between connects the fields that carry our hearts and dreams."

Will Donoghue watched through the kitchen window as Niall stored sacks of protein pellets in their supply barn to feed their sheep through the winter ahead. Their son was a hard worker, he thought, never breaking stride once even though the feed sacks were heavy and Niall's frame slight. He'd give anything to be out there helping the lad, or doing the work himself as he'd always done. Soon, he reminded himself; you'll be out there soon enough once you've recovered from surgery and the chemo to come. He hoped he was right.

"That's some boy we've got there," Will told Anna as she stepped up to the sink to wash their breakfast dishes.

"Aye," she agreed. "He's a hard worker, never complains."

"I swear he loves this farm as much as I do, maybe more. He'd be hard pressed to choose between the farm and his music if the choice were ever necessary."

Anna watched as Niall, finished with the job of storing sacks of feed, secured the door to the supply barn and bent down to pet Farley, the dog sitting down and wagging his tail, watching for the treat he knew Niall would soon produce.

Turning away from the window Anna ordered her husband, "You have to tell him."

Will sat down at their kitchen table. "I know. I don't know how, though. How do you put an end to your own son's dreams?"

"It doesn't have to be the end. He needs to know, though. He deserves as much."

"He does that."

"Tell him tonight. I'll make his favorite dinner, happen that will soften the blow."

"Lamb chops?" Niall asked as he sat down to dinner a few hours later. "What's the occasion? I know I haven't missed any birthdays."

"No occasion." Mrs. Donoghue passed him the dish of cheesy potatoes. "We're celebrating your father being home."

Niall looked suspicious. "He's been home four days now. And you've made all my favorites, not his. What's up?"

"Can't a body prepare a wee dinner without someone questioning what they're up to?" Mrs. Donoghue shook her head as she passed the applesauce around. "I do declare you're as bad as your father there. Eat up, and you best enjoy my food without another question coming out of your mouth."

After that they filled their dinner conversation with small talk, how Will was feeling, the price of apples and fresh fruit at market, news that the church's choir director was resigning and discussion of who would take her place. Niall, as he often did, listened more than he talked, enjoying the easy flow of conversation between his parents, the chemistry between them years of marriage had refined. Pauline from The Harp flashed across his mind, and he played with the thought that someday he'd have with her what his parents had. Perhaps he and Aidan could take a run up to the pub before Aidan left for recording next week.

After dinner, Mrs. Donoghue set a fresh custard pie before Niall. Suspicion returned; Niall raised his eyebrows and asked, "Alright Mam, now I know something's up. What gives?"

"It's my fault," Will confessed. "I told your mam to make all your favorites tonight."

"No, it were my idea." Anna countered. "I wanted to make something special for you."

"But why?" Niall demanded. "I don't care whose idea it was, I just want to know what's behind it."

Anna sat across from Will as he drew a deep breath and started in. "It's about the farm, son. This wee health scare has made your mam and me realize it's time to set the record straight on something."

Niall glanced from his father to his mother, then back to his father, his heart skipping a few beats in the process. "What is it Da?"

Anna nodded encouragement as Will spoke, "We've always led you to believe we own this farm. We don't, though. We did once, mind. Back in the day, generations ago, one of your ancestors saved the life of the English landlord's son and was granted this land in return. I grew up believing it were still ours. When my own Da passed on, though, the paperwork didn't fit."

"What do you mean didn't fit?" Panic rose in Niall. If the farm wasn't theirs, why were they still on it? How long could they continue to claim ownership?

"Paperwork wasn't always kept up over the years," Will explained. "Oral history meant almost as much as paperwork did. Records were lost, arrangements and understandings worked out. When my father passed he left the farm to me as my inheritance, only then we discovered it wasn't his to give. The bank couldn't trace proper ownership and had let us stay on, glad to have the land worked. We've only paid rent all these years, not a mortgage. The house, the farm, the land, none of it's ours."

"My God, Da! Why did you never tell me this before? Why did you keep the lie up?"

"Pride, I guess. I didn't want you to think I were a failure."

"I'd never have thought that of you."

Anna stepped in. "Niall, today your father and I watched you carrying on your work here. We both know how much you love this place. This farm is as much your dream as your music is. We can't let you go on dreaming of something that might not be yours in the end."

Niall looked at his parents, their faces lined with the same fear he knew spread across his own. "Do you think we could lose the farm?"

Will nodded. "Aye son, if the bank ever decides to sell the land outright."

"Then we'll have to start saving the money to buy it. Or find the paperwork that proves it's always been ours. We'll have to do some digging around, but the records have to be somewhere."

"I've got a box of old papers," Will told him. "I don't think there's anything there; the solicitors sifted through it years ago, when your grandda died. Still, it might be a good place to start."

Niall studied his parents. They must have been so afraid to tell me this, he realized. He thought back over the years to all they'd done for him, providing a loving home, protecting him from every danger, every worry. He owed them love, not anger in return. "It's good you told me all this," he said at last. "Good you're not carrying it all yourselves. In the morning we'll start sorting through your papers, see where we stand with them, and then plan our course of action from there. Now, let's be having some of this custard pie before it spoils. Then you're off to bed. You've both had a long, hard time of it the past few weeks."

Aidan called Mack in the morning and played "The Lough Between" for him.

"That's a wonderful piece," Mack acknowledged when Aidan was through. "Do you think Niall would be able to learn his part by the time he joins us?"

"I know he has a lot on his plate, but I'll run it by him and see what he thinks."

"Fine. It's a very good song. If you and he can pull it off, we'll record it."

Aidan waited until evening, when he guessed Niall would be through his work for the day. "Do you have a few minutes? I have a song I'd like to share with you."

In his heart, Niall didn't care about the song. He was tired, not in his body, he could work well into evening if required, but in his mind and heart. All the fear of his father's illness, all the stress of overseeing the farm and juggling his parent's appointments and needs had worn him out, if he were honest. On top of that, now he wasn't even sure they could keep their farm - if it were even theirs. It was almost too much to handle.

Still, Aidan would be heading off for recording in the morning. If he had something he thought important enough to share now, Niall would meet him. "I'll be over soon."

"Bring your pipes with you."

Niall obeyed. Pipes in hand, a few minutes later he entered Aidan's house through the back door.

Aidan held out a tea mug and a can of stout. "What's your preference?"

"Stout." Niall pointed to the can in Aidan's right hand. After his father's revelation tonight, a stout at the very least was in order.

"Good choice!" Aidan grabbed a second can and motioned for Niall to follow him to the living room. "I wrote this song last night. If you like it, and if we can get it down this week, Mack will let us record it."

Niall admired the even paced, melodic tune as Aidan's fingers drew gentle notes from his guitar, imagining which pipes and notes he would add to the mix as Aidan played.

The words spoke of dreams and hopes for the future, of friendship and the strength and support it brought to a person's life. When Aidan sang the chorus, his words vibrated in Niall's heart as Niall realized the song might be about himself and Aidan and their adjoining homes.

"Do you like it?" Aidan asked when he was through.

"Very much." Niall forced himself to not think of future dreams that might come crashing down. Instead, he spoke of how his uilleann pipes, Aidan's favorite, could complement the tune.

As they tested various harmonies between instruments and voices, fine tuning what Aidan had written and broadening the song out, an unseen visitor looked on. Timothy McCabe, perched on the fireplace mantle, witnessed the camaraderie between the two friends, how well they worked together, how deep the bond between them was, and smiled an invisible smile.

After an hour and a half of work, Niall returned home and Aidan set about packing his guitar and music, clothes and shaving gear, and preparing for the recording sessions ahead. When his packing was done he washed dishes he'd allowed to pile up in the sink, sure he could hear his gran lecturing him from above. He then turned to clean the kitchen table where, as usual, a stack of papers had accumulated. He sorted through bills, threw trash in the bin, and placed the others in his desk in the library.

Opening his desk drawer, he spotted again the papers he'd found in the attic. He pulled them out and studied the drawing. Judging from the map and his knowledge of the land around him, the fourth stone, the one he hadn't found yet, must be somewhere in the Donoghues' fields. He gazed out the window. As he studied the land opposite his home, a memory came to him. He'd seen a stone near one of the Donoghues' pasture gates that looked odd, oblong, a marker of sorts. Could this be the fourth ogham stone?

Aidan grabbed his keys and hurried out to his car, thankful Niall and his parents had gone to bed. He wasn't sure how he'd explain the stones, nor the map and writing he'd found, at least not until Allan reported back with his findings. Aidan reached the pasture gate, used light from his mobile phone to guide his way, and searched through the tall grass near the gatepost until he found the stone. Similar to the others, it was oblong, weathered, and decorated with lichens that had multiplied over the years and now formed a pattern of intricate white and light brown circles over the stone's surface. On the stone's northern side, Aidan found the same carved lines he'd seen on the other three stones. Satisfied he'd solved the puzzle that had nagged at him, Aidan took several quick pictures of the stone, then returned home and printed the photos. Adding them to his collection, he closed and locked the desk drawer, hoping Allan would report back to him soon.

8

Fionna sat on a bench along the lake at the north end of St. Stephen's Green. She had grown to love this quiet corner of the city. While buses, cars and people rushed about their business behind her, she found peace in the steady flow of the water before her, in the birds that chattered in the trees overhead, and in the trees themselves, now fading to autumn brown. Ducks and swans still floated by despite the season's change, comrades in her solitude. She set her pencil to paper and drew them, the lake, the rocks near her corner of the park, and the trees which had started shedding their leaves. She knew her assignment was to create an abstract of a local scene, but first she would follow her heart and paint a realistic watercolor.

"I love to watch you work."

The voice behind her made Fionna jump, causing her pencil to draw a sharp line through the heart of her work.

"Damn!" She cried out, then turned to the voice behind her. "Hugh, don't ever sneak up on me like that."

Full of remorse, Hugh held fresh cappuccino and a chocolate biscuit out to her. "I'm sorry. I didn't mean to startle you. I just like watching you work. You're so focused, so intent on trying to capture what you want, and you always create such vivid, memorable pictures."

How could she stay mad at that? "Thanks," she told him and accepted his offerings. "And thanks for this. How did you know I was here?"

"I was over at the mall across the way and spotted you." He eyed the empty space next to her on the park bench.

She gathered her coat and bag closer to her to clear room for him. "I'm sorry. Here, sit down."

"Thanks."

"What were you doing at the mall?" She noted he carried no shopping bags. "You didn't buy anything?"

"No, I'm working on a project for class. Architecture and Ecology. I chose the mall because I love its unique lines."

Fionna gazed across the street to St. Stephen's Mall with its curved white exterior and multiple windows. "It is a pretty building. Maybe I should do an abstract of that for my class."

Hugh shook his head. "I like what you're doing now. Your heart is here, isn't it?"

"Aye. It's my solace spot in the city. Still, I'm meant to be creating an abstract. I'm afraid I'm wasting my time on this."

Hugh shook his head. "No you're not. You've got good lines here. I can't wait to see the colors you use to fill it in."

"I'll still need to turn in an abstract." She turned to a fresh piece of paper and opened her watercolor paints. In a few quick movements, she painted a swath of green on both sides for the trees, a slash of blue lake in the middle, angular grey marks to represent rocks, brown and white ovals for waterfowl atop the blue, and two black lines to represent public benches such as the one she shared with Hugh now.

"There!" She laughed as she presented the painting to Hugh. "Best I can do, and if I receive a failing grade so be it."

Hugh laughed as well. "It's no Picasso, mind, but I like it."

"Fine. After it's graded, it's yours!" Fionna set her paints aside and warmed her hands on the sides of her cappuccino cup.

Hugh watched as she sipped her drink, her eyes still fixed on the waterfowl dipping into the water searching for food. He loved the fire in her emerald eyes as she studied them and the fire in her copper hair as sunlight played off each individual shaft. Did she know how beautiful she was? He doubted it. She always seemed a bit on the insecure side.

Fionna focused on the swans in front of her, three of them, one, no doubt, this year's cygnet. Hugh's presence next to her felt unnerving as she wondered what his next move would be. He'd seemed trustworthy enough the two other times they'd met up, at a party with Gwen and Paul, and then at a pub where they'd listened to a band Paul knew. Still, it was early days. He hadn't yet revealed his true self. If she focused on the river and its inhabitants she could keep her senses about her if he tried anything.

"There's a new art exhibit opening next weekend, glass and industrial fusion, kind of an abstract display." Hugh told her. "Would you like to go with me? I think Paul and Gwen are going as well, we could make it a foursome."

Fionna felt her bones and muscles relax. Hugh wasn't here to make any moves on her. She was safe. The art exhibit would be interesting, she thought, and she could get to know Hugh better in a safe setting. "Sure," she agreed. "Thanks. I'd like that."

Mack dropped his suitcase at the foot of the stairs and stepped into the breakfast nook off the kitchen where Kate sat waiting, their small square table set with her best silver and fine bone china, white on white rose pattern, one of their wedding gifts decades ago. Aromas of bacon and coffee stirred his hunger as he kissed her cheek and sat down across from her.

"Waffles or eggs?" Kate rose to prepare whatever he fancied.

"Waffles please." From where Mack sat he watched Kate stir the waffle batter she'd prepared in advance and pour a portion of it into the waffle iron she'd preheated, knowing waffles were his favorite and sure they would be his choice. He loved to watch her work. She had smooth, economical moves, no motion wasted. She carried an air of assurance about her. He loved the soft tune she hummed as she worked.

Within minutes Kate returned with a plate of waffles for him and toast for herself. "Are you looking forward to recording?" She asked as they started to eat.

"I am." Mack felt a surge of excitement at the thought of working in the studio with the Macready's Bridge boys. He couldn't wait to be about the business of making music, overseeing the boys as they poured all their energy, emotions and heart into the one thing they loved best. Rehearsals at Aidan's the week before had fueled his drive to make this, their second album, their best work ever.

This time though he felt conflicted as well. He hated the thought of time away from Kate.

"You don't look too excited."

Mack paused his eating. Should he confess his feelings? Or lie about what dampened his joy? For the dozenth time since the week of rehearsals Mack found himself tongue-tied, unable to force out the words he most wanted to say. With all his heart, he wanted to propose to Kate and settle their future together. If she weren't ready though, if she felt he were pushing, she might bolt, move back to an apartment in town, and refuse to see him again.

Mack chose a middle path. "I hate leaving you," he confessed. "Every day we're apart seems endless, now we've restarted our lives."

Kate set her coffee cup down, click of china on china muffled, soft like all of her moves. She looked across the table to her former husband, the man she'd tried to leave but found she'd never stopped loving. "I hate it too. Still, you'll only be gone a week. That will give me time to sort through your closet and toss away all those old flannel shirts you refuse to let go of."

"Don't you touch those shirts!" Mack warned, and both of them laughed, her laughter sounding to Mack like the tinkling of a hundred bells in a gentle breeze high on Himalayan mountains. Their conversation turned to teasing and how they would pass the week ahead, yet Mack left an hour later knowing he'd wasted another opportunity.

Malahide Recording Studios, north of Dublin, looked from the outside like an old two-story warehouse wearing a grey brick exterior with black wrought iron bars across its windows and doors. No signs indicated what the building's business was; only the frequent movement of cars in and out of its

129

parking lot gave any indication that business was conducted there at all.

Inside, oak paneling lined hallway walls and the main reception room while sea green carpeting muffled footsteps. Two soundproof recording rooms, with their adjoining control rooms, stood one on each end of the building while in the center, across from the reception room, a lounge with two brown leather sofas, two matching easy chairs and an iron-grated fireplace provided a place to relax between recordings. A kitchen to the side of that offered space to prepare and eat meals if one chose that option instead of dining out.

Into this world Mack entered, followed a short time later by Patrick, then Michael and last of all Aidan. Most times their meetings would start out with teasing, horseplay and similar exhibits of the close camaraderie that had developed between them all. Recording sessions were different. They knew reserving studio time was expensive; they wasted no time in digging into the work they were there for.

While Michael recorded vocal tracks for the first song, Aidan and Patrick practiced their parts in a separate room. When Michael was through, Patrick entered the recording room and laid down his background fiddle tracks, then Aidan took his turn with guitar. They repeated the process for each of the songs on Mack's list. Mack oversaw each recording, observing from the control room while Owen Connelly, Malahide's mixing engineer, mastered the multi-buttoned console. Some tracks had to be recorded several times, whenever Owen detected the slightest odd noise or waver of tone or note in a song.

Tuesday night, rather than stay at the nearby hotel Mack had arranged, Michael chose to return to his apartment. He entered to find Susannah packing her suitcases. Puzzled, he asked, "Going on a trip are you?"

"No." Susannah fixed her eyes on the clothes she was packing. "I'm moving out."

Michael froze, shocked. "What?"

"Diane has a spare room. I'll be taking that until I sort out a proper place for myself."

"Why are you doing this?"

"Have you called your father yet and convinced him to come to our wedding?"

Michael sighed in exasperation and shook his head. "No. I've been busy rehearsing and now recording. I told you it would have to wait until next week when our recording is through."

"And I told you it can't wait that long. We have to get this sorted, Michael."

"Good God, woman! You sound a broken record on this!"

Susannah brushed past Michael. "I have to get my laptop."

As she passed him Michael grabbed her arm. "Stop it. This is madness."

Susannah yanked her arm free, anger setting her emerald green eyes on fire. "No! Madness is falling in love with someone who won't do the one thing that's most important to me."

Michael matched her anger for anger. "No, it's falling in love with someone so self-centered they only care about what they want, no matter how outlandish!"

"Outlandish?" Susannah exploded. "You call wanting my father at my wedding outlandish? I sure had you figured wrong!"

"As I did you! I thought you loved me more than anything else in the world. Your father refused to be a part of the most important day in your life and you're ready to pack it all in? Well go ahead! If you're so much a daddy's little girl that you can't stand up to him now, when it counts the most, we don't stand a chance."

"You don't get it!" Susannah's anger was still crystal clear although now she lowered her tone a degree. "This isn't about my father. It's about how little you care about what I've dreamed of most."

"Yeah, I know your dream. Walking down the aisle on daddy's arm. What about my dream? What about our future? Marriage is compromise, Suze. It's hard work and it's both of us bending at times, placing the other person above what we ourselves want. Only right now I don't see you bending. I see you throwing a fit when you can't get your way, drawing an impossible line, and not understanding when I say you have to wait until next week for me to see if I can sort our parents out. You didn't even tell me you were leaving. You just hoped to disappear before I found out. Sorry I came home early and spoiled your plan."

Michael withdrew to the kitchen, poured himself a glass of wine and hoped Susannah would calm down and change her mind, although he knew he had a better chance that Bono himself would walk through their door. Before he'd finished his wine, their door slammed and Susannah was gone.

From her back room office where she ate the turkey sandwich and tomato risotto soup she'd brought with her for lunch, Kate heard the laughter of children mixed in with the voices of Deirdre, her assistant, and a customer. A child giggled, another child, she guessed a little girl, called out "Look, Mammy! It's pink!" That was followed by a laugh that sounded for all the world like liquid sunshine. Kate found herself drawn to the voices, and peeked around the curtain that separated her back room from the dress shop. While Deirdre helped the customer, a woman Kate didn't recognize, select a sweater and slack ensemble, a wee blonde-haired baby cooed and giggled from her stroller and a ginger-haired toddler pirouetted, fingered dresses on the racks in front of her and called out colors to her mother. "Mammy, red! Ooh Mammy, pretty blue!"

Kate slipped back behind her curtain as a wave of old feelings rushed over her. She'd thought she had moved beyond them long ago. Stunned to find they'd returned, Kate sat in her chair and squeezed her eyes shut hoping to force the feelings back in the corner of her heart where she'd locked them away.

After all these years they still called to her, the children she'd never had, the children she'd given up hope for.

Why now, she wondered. Why had their memories returned? What had drawn them back from the desert she'd banished them to?

The answer, she knew, was easy. Mack. In returning to him she'd opened the door to the past.

Long after the woman and her two children had left the shop, Kate still juggled her emotions. She was beyond the age when she could bear children even if she'd been able to become pregnant, which had always been denied her. She'd rejected the thought of adopting years ago and was perhaps no longer eligible. Or was she? Could there still be a way? As she finished the day, locked her shop up and drove back to the house she again shared with Mack, the questions remained on her mind.

"And what do ye think our man would say?" She asked Seamus and Kellan as she took the dogs for their evening walk. "If I told him I wanted to adopt, or at least be a foster care giver, do ye think he would laugh outright?"

The two setters stared up at her and waved their copper plumed tales, more at the sound of her voice than the words she spoke. Yes, I know, she thought. You're both children enough for me now.

Still, her longing remained through the night as she ate her salad and pan-seared chicken, as she thumbed through a magazine waiting for Mack's evening call, as she settled herself afterward into their king-sized bed. Funny, she thought as she ran her hand over his empty side of the bed, how easy it's been to slip back into our old lives. Three days you're gone and I can't wait for your return.

The sound of little girl laughter rang in her ears again and filled the dark room.

"What would you think, Mack?" She whispered into his pillow. "Would you say yes? What if they only agree to let us foster or adopt if we're married? Would you marry me Mack?"

Kate laughed into the dark around her. You're a daft fool, she thought. Some things are best left as they are now and not stirred up again. You've got a good life with the man you love. Don't look for anything more than that.

She pulled the blankets closer around her and forced her mind to retire for the night.

Thursday morning Niall joined them, grateful he'd been able to line up assistance from two of his parents' friends at church. "I'm sorry I had to miss so much this week." He told Mack. "I'm ready to run through it all now, though."

"You were missed." Mack admitted, handing Niall an updated song list. "Here's the rundown; we can start as soon as you're ready."

Niall spent the day laying down tracks for two thirds of the songs for which the other Macready's Bridge members had already recorded their parts. They broke for a late dinner before Niall and Aidan would take their turns on the tracks for Aidan's new song.

They were just finishing dinner when Aidan's phone rang. The name on the phone screen showed Allan McStrainer; it took Aidan a moment to recognize the caller as Jack's friend. Excusing himself from the table, Aidan stepped out to the lounge area to talk.

"I hope I'm not catching you at a bad time," Allan started. "I've been able to confirm some of what you've found and I wanted to share that with you now rather than waiting. I also hoped I could set a time to see the stones myself, if you didn't mind."

"This week my band and I are busy recording an album. I can show you sometime after that. Jack and Rita could bring you out, maybe next week? What were you able to confirm?"

Allan glanced at his notes. "The writing is what I thought, title to your property. It covers the land your house sits on and surrounding property. Didn't you tell me your friend's family owns the farm behind you?"

"Aye, I did. I'm not sure which of us owns the lough though."

"You do." Allan paused. "In fact, you own the farm itself and surrounding fields unless I'm missing something with land records."

Aidan tried to recall the images of the drawings and writings stored safe in his desk at home. "That can't be right. I don't own the farm."

Allan spread the map out on the table before him and consulted his notes. "Aidan I believe you do. I'll check some more though. If you have the title from when you bought the house I can check that, if you'd like. What I found at public records, though, indicates that you do indeed own the farm."

"I'll have to take a look at my papers when I get home." Aidan told him. "If you want, you can call Jack and Rita and see if they're available to come out with you early next week."

"Will do." Allan tried to curb his excitement. To see Aidan's grand house would almost be enough in itself; to view and touch ogham stones no one else knew of would almost put him over the moon. "I'll leave a message for you if you're back to recording when I call. Good luck with the album."

Aidan remained in the lounge area several minutes after his call was through. What Allan had said was preposterous! The Donoghues owned their farm. Niall would have told him if it were otherwise. On the other hand, Allan was a skilled researcher. As a historian and archaeological expert he would know how to confirm what Aidan had found. He seemed to have a solid basis for thinking Aidan owned the farm behind him. He wondered how he would face Niall as he returned to the kitchen where Mack and the boys were clearing dinner dishes away.

"Everything okay?" Niall asked.

Aidan nodded, unable to look Niall in the face. I own your farm, he thought. Except I don't. That can't be right. Allan must have missed something.

As Niall and Aidan set down their tracks for "The Lough Between", Aidan couldn't help wondering if the friendship the song celebrated would hold up if Allan's information proved to be true.

They returned to the studio one last time on Friday to record each of the tracks as a group, a system of recording Mack liked to use feeling, no matter how well Owen mixed the tracks they'd each recorded alone during the week, there was a difference between that and having the boys play a song in one live track. By the time they finished recording and listening to playbacks, evening had set in.

"How about a meal at one of the pubs in town?" Michael asked. "Marble Arch might be a good place."

"You mean the fair Susannah's not going to make us one of her gourmet meals?" Aidan teased.

His teasing stopped short at the sight of Michael's face turned so sad. "No. She's moved out."

Patrick asked, "When did this happen? You never said a word."

"Tuesday. After we finished here I went home to find her packing her things."

"Why would she do that?" Aidan wondered.

"She's still angry that I haven't convinced my father to be at our wedding. Not that I've had time to call him; I've been a wee bit busy but she doesn't see that."

"Oh Michael, I'm so sorry." Niall spoke. "Maybe she just needs a break. She'll be back once she clears her mind and thinks about what she'd be losing if she let you go."

Michael thought, if she loved me she wouldn't need a break. To his friends, though, he forced a half smile. "I don't know, maybe she will. Tonight I think a meal and a few pints with friends is what I need. What do you say?"

The Marble Arch, at the foot of Dublin's Ha'Penny Bridge, was crowded by the time they arrived, as were all of the Temple Bar District's pubs. The bartender recognized Michael from him singing there on occasion and waved them in. "Tight quarters," he informed them, "but I can give you a table upstairs if a couple of you don't mind standing."

Aidan and Niall stood along the upstairs level rail while the others sat at table. Downstairs music blared from a sound system, while upstairs wall-mounted television screens broadcast football and other sports. In the spirit of the good-natured fun they always enjoyed when their hard work was over, Niall and Aidan each took turns pinching food off the others' plates and drinks off various pints when one of the others' heads was turned. True they had their own plates and full glasses, but their antics made Michael laugh and that was as good a reason as any to ramp up the fun. Lip synching the next song the sound system played, exaggerating arm and body movements to match the saccharine love song, Aidan turned and for a moment, from the corner of his eye, caught sight of a girl he thought he knew. He stopped his playing around and took a closer look.

Fionna! He couldn't have mistaken her long, cascading copper hair or her face. She sat at a table on the lower level along with three others, one girl and two guys. One of them, the boy seated closest to her, slipped an arm around her shoulder and whispered something to her.

Fionna hadn't seen him, Aidan guessed. He stepped away from the railing to make sure she didn't now. Sure she would have looked back his way if she'd known he were here. Or would she? So many months had passed since their brief encounter along the Gweebarra shore, perhaps she had moved on. And why wouldn't she? He'd given her no reason to think she would ever see him again. If she'd found someone else, he was glad for her. Still his heart fell a wee bit, and he felt like he'd lost something he'd very much wanted.

Fionna returned to her apartment still smiling over her evening with Hugh, Gwen and Paul. The art exhibit had been inspiring, a display of glass and metal sculptures that opened her mind to the world of abstract art in a new way. Tomorrow she would try to paint abstracts of gleaming blue and green glass intertwined with silver and copper, although her canvas would not shine the same as the sculptures had.

Tonight though, as she soaked in a hot tub of lavender bubbles, she thought beyond the art exhibit to the meal the four of them had shared at the Marble Arch after the show. Hugh and Paul had debated the uses of color and shape in the designs they'd seen that night, while she and Gwen discussed abstract versus realism overall. She'd found the conversation exhilarating, as she had so many times in classes or afterwards. As scary as it had been, she'd been right to go against her parents and enter art school. The friendship developing between herself and Hugh was an unexpected bonus. Now after her bath, as she turned lights out in her apartment she found her mind full of thoughts of Hugh, his laughter, his kind voice and his bright smile. Only when her eyes fell on one of her paintings did she realize she hadn't thought of Aidan in days.

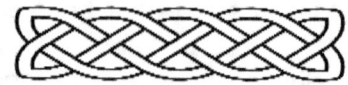

9

Aidan woke with a start, noticed the shadows on his bedroom walls and realized half the morning had already slid by. His phone rang; guessing that must have been what woke him up he grabbed his phone from its customary overnight spot on the small table next to his bed and answered, "Hello?"

"Aidan? It's Jack. How are you?"

"Fine." Through the fog of sleep interrupted, he had a vague recollection of Jack and Rita coming to see him today. "Are you still coming out with Allan?"

"We are if that's still okay."

"Sure, two o'clock wasn't it?"

"Yes," Jack confirmed. "We'll see you then."

Aidan recalled Allan's phone call a few days earlier and wondered if he'd learned any more in his research since then. A hard rain had fallen overnight; as he looked out his bedroom windows now he wished he'd thought to remind Jack they should bring proper footwear for traipsing through wet, muddy fields. Ah well, he told himself, Jack is wise enough to have thought of that on his own. At least the rain had ended and a weak sun was pressing to break through the thin grey clouds stretched across the mid-morning sky.

"What a grand place this is." Allan remarked two hours later as Aidan guided them through his house. "Have you given any thought to opening this up to tours once you've restored it?"

"No I haven't. I don't think I could do that. I mean, it's where I live and all. I wouldn't want strangers invading."

"No, of course not. It was just a thought."

After they viewed his new studio, Aidan led them across the road to what he knew Allan most wanted to see. "The first stone is here." He bent down and revealed the stone among the gorse shrubs.

Jack and Rita, having never before seen an ogham stone, eyed Aidan's find with deep interest. Allan ran a careful hand over the surface of the stone, fingered the lines carved into its side then measured it with a piece of string he pulled out of his coat pocket.

He repeated the same ritual with the second and third stones Aidan led them to, the twin stones on either side where his land and the Donoghues' blended together.

"Were you able to locate the fourth stone?" Allan asked after he'd inspected and measured the third.

"Aye." Aidan pointed towards one of the Donoghues' northern pastures. "It's up that way a short piece. I haven't told Niall about any of this yet; I'm not sure I should take you up on their land without telling them first. I can show you pictures though."

Disappointment clouded Allan's face. "I would very much like to see the stone itself."

Jack pointed out, "We'd not hurt anything, just take a look. Five minutes and we'd be gone from there; sure they couldn't mind that. You do what you think is best though."

Aidan surveyed the farm in front of him and found no sign of Niall or his parents. Perhaps they'd be safe if they hurried, he thought.

"Alright. I'll drive you up in my car; it's faster than walking."

He drove them to the top of the hill and the gate where he'd uncovered the fourth stone. While Allan gave the stone a quick inspection and measurement, Aidan kept an eye out for Niall. Full of guilt at the thought he was trespassing, all he wanted was to return to his car and the house unnoticed. As it was, as they drove back down the hill he thought he saw Niall watching them from a corner of the barn.

Back at Aidan's house, Allan spread several papers on the dining room table, copies of the original Gaelic writings Aidan had given him along with the drawing showing four circles and several papers written in English, which they all gathered around to examine. Starting with the crude map, Allan explained each piece in turn.

"The four stones are in fact ogham stones, ancient stones that bear ogham markings, our earliest written language. In this case each of the four stones is connected one to another, each bearing the same name, each one a marker to confirm property boundaries. The locations of the stones you showed us today coincide with the circles on the drawing.

"As we thought, the first writing is an ancient deed setting down a record of land ownership. It dates back centuries, quite rare for this area as so much of the land here fell under British control. Some property owners did retain their land. Yours is one of those properties."

Allan drank some of the tea Rita had set before them all, then focused his eyes on Aidan as he explained the next set of papers. "Based on what I found in the original papers I did some searching through public records regarding your land and the land around yours."

More curious than ever, Aidan pressed, "What did you learn?"

"As I told you last week you own a larger piece of land than you realized." Allan pulled the crude map closer. "This is a drawing of the property you own."

"I wondered about that when I first looked at the drawing. It seemed too large to have fit only my land."

Allan slid two more pieces of paper towards them. "Back in the late 1800's there was an arrangement to let some of the land here out, including the farmland at the back of your property. There's a clause here that spells out if new title papers weren't filed by a certain date ownership would revert back to the original owners. The papers for the farm were never filed. And here, the way your title reads it includes property as bounded and described in the Griffiths Land Valuation dating back to the 1800's. What you bought is the whole of the property, not just the piece that ends with the lough behind you."

Jack repeated, stunned, "You own Niall's farm."

Aidan studied Allan and the papers spread out on the table. He thought of the lough between the two pieces of land, of Niall and his family and the farm that had been theirs for decades. Two families had existed side by side, neither aware where one boundary ended and the other began. Own Niall's farm? Impossible. He weighed Allan's words. "That's a lot to take in. I'm not sure whether I should bring this up to Niall and his parents or just leave things as they are." He turned to Allan. "What about the ogham stones? I know you're fascinated by them. Will you tell anyone else what I've found?"

Allan thought of the photos Aidan had given him and looked at the map and ancient Gaelic writings. "You must know this is a very rare find, the stones in particular. Ogham stones themselves are rare. To find four in one setting, each in fair condition, coupled with the drawing and the writings, from an archaeological and historical sense these are priceless. People from all over would come to see those stones, and your house if you ever reconsidered opening it to the public."

"Tourists." Aidan shook his head. "I can just see summer tourists flocking all over the Donoghues' farm. They would hate that."

Allan gathered his papers and handed them to Aidan. "You should have your solicitor go over this and double check your title. I may have missed something, although I'm quite sure what I've told you stands. As for the stones, tempting as it is I'll not say a word. If you change your mind though, please let me know. I can help you work out the best way to share this with others if you ever decide you're interested."

They turned the conversation then to Jack and Rita's family, to the house Aidan had sold them and the joys and challenges of their daughter living next door, to Allan and his family, wife and two grown sons, both living in Australia now. They talked of the rising cost of food and petrol and the colder than normal winter the weathermen had forecast.

After his visitors left Aidan stood by the kitchen sink, gazing out over the land behind him. He owned Niall's farm? No. There was no way. Still, as he surveyed the land that filled his window's view he entertained the thought of how owning the farm and fields behind him would feel. His status in town would be elevated; he'd be a person to be reckoned with, with a grand estate house and significant tract of land to his name. He allowed himself to visualize what local headlines would read: Son of Auto Repairman Elected to Local Council; Local Estate Restored to Former Glory by New Land Owner. He even projected into the future what the revelation of the ogham stone discovery would bring about: the archaeological treasure trove could yield thousands of pounds as tourists and historians would flock to ogham fields. He imagined the influx of money that would come his way and how that money would elevate his plans for his music studio and house to turn them into the magnificent masterpieces he dreamed of. He could even sort out a new farm for Niall and his family so everyone would benefit. He found his visions tempting and wondered, even though he thought he already knew, what course of action was the best one to take in the end.

Niall scanned the last of the papers he had gathered from his search through the attic. With his parents he'd already gone through all the papers they'd stored in the metal lock box under their bed and in the kitchen drawer where all sorts of bits and pieces of paper had been stuffed over the years. He'd searched through his father's makeshift work table in the barn where his father had saved various receipts and news clippings in an old wooden crate. He'd pulled out and examined every paper in his father's desk, had even flipped through his father's year-by-year journals for any papers that may have been slipped into them for safekeeping. None of those searches had unearthed anything that shed light on the farm title problem. Now the last of the attic papers proved futile as well. He groaned to himself. This would be harder than he thought, though he would not let his parents see his concern.

"Da, Mam, I've got nothing here that will prove we own the land. I think we should talk with a solicitor. Let's write down what you remember of how we came to possess the farm. Who owned it before it was ours?"

"Let's see." Will Donoghue cast his mind back through all the bits of knowledge he'd gathered throughout his life and related, "My dad took over the land from his dad so you're talking back into the mid- to late 1800's at least. Before the partition. Before the rebellion. I remember me Da saying something about filing a paper with the bank, but I were a young lad then, in my school days, and didn't pay proper attention to what he was saying. Over the years the ownership trail was muddied. Not even the bank could make heads or tails of it all. Best leave it be with the rent we're paying."

Niall was astonished. "Da, how can we leave it at that? We could lose the land at the bank's whim. Or the government's. Or whoever else finds they own the land. One wee change in any of this and we could be out by the side of the road, no sheep, no home, nothing but the clothes on our backs."

"They'd not do that!" Anna Donoghue exclaimed. "Not after all these years. Would they Will?" She turned to her husband, terrified.

Mr. Donoghue patted his wife's hand. "No dear, they'd not. As long as we pay our rent we'll be fine."

"I need something more." Niall insisted. "We've got no assurances for our future here. I can't leave it at that."

"You've looked at everything we have." Mrs. Donoghue pointed out. "What else can you do?"

Niall thought a moment. "I'll have to search the public records in town."

"I doubt you'll find anything," Mr. Donoghue cautioned, "but try if you want."

Mrs. Donoghue asked, "Before you do could you be after cleaning the table here so I can set dinner out? And run over to see if our Aidan wants to join us."

Niall did as he was told. He gathered the papers he'd spread across the table and stacked them with others in a cardboard box by his father's desk in their living room, thinking he'd sort them in better order some rainy evening while his parents sipped tea in front of their fireplace. Then he slipped his jacket and boots on and walked across the field to Aidan's house.

Reaching Aidan's house, Niall opened the back door without knocking. Aidan did the same thing at times when he arrived at Niall's house. They were both close enough in their friendship they felt more like the family they had become, sharing so many meals, problems, chores and feelings there were few boundaries between them by now. He stepped inside Aidan's back hall to remove his shoes, now damp from crossing moisture laden grass.

"If you could look into this I'd appreciate it."

Niall heard Aidan on the phone and stopped, not wanting to interrupt the conversation.

"Aye, some old papers with writing on them and a drawing, a map of sorts. The map indicates the location of the ogham stones I mentioned."

Niall's ears pricked like radar focusing on a new sound as he heard Aidan describe the items.

"Right. You remember my friends Jack and Rita, my father's friends, my former neighbors. Yes, it was their daughter who bought our old house. Jack's friend Allan has researched what I've found. He believes it's a title or deed or some indication of property ownership. Based on the papers, he thinks I own more than my house and land; he thinks I own the farm behind me as well. If you could look into it for me I'd be grateful."

Niall froze, sure he should not be listening in now but unable to pull himself away.

"Yes, the ogham stones would be an incredible revelation but please don't say anything to anyone just yet. I need to sort out how I'll handle all this."

Niall had heard enough. He slipped his shoes on and stepped back outside, moving and closing the door behind him without making a noise to betray he'd been there at all.

Could he have heard right? He was sure he hadn't. He replayed in his mind the words Aidan had spoken. He had found papers and stones, ogham stones. Niall knew they were ancient stones whose locations generated a great deal of interest. He could care less about them. The papers, though, gripped his heart. A land title, Aidan had said. He owned Niall's farm, he had said. He had to sort out how he'd handle things. Handle what? Based on the one sided conversation he'd heard Niall made the best guess, the only guess he could.

Aidan owned his farm. The ogham stones were a huge draw. Aidan would claim his family's land and convert it all to a tourist attraction. He'd rake in tons of money while Niall and his family would be forced to give up the livelihood they depended on, the only thing his parents knew how to do. They'd be devastated. They'd be in financial ruins. All at the hands of his best friend.

It couldn't be true, Niall thought as he reached his own home once more. There had to be a mistake. Aidan wouldn't do that. He'd heard the conversation with his own ears though; there was no denying the words.

"Where's Aidan?" Mrs. Donoghue asked as Niall stepped back into his own kitchen. "Didn't he come with you?"

"He's busy Mam." Niall lied. "He won't be over tonight."

Aidan thought Niall had mentioned the night before the idea of him joining their family for dinner; yet dinner had come and gone and he'd not heard a word from Niall. He'd glanced out the window over his kitchen sink once and could see the Donoghues seated at their kitchen table, eating. He had been half tempted to join them but stopped himself. Perhaps Niall's father had had a rough day and they'd decided against company that night. Aidan made a chicken and vegetable stir fry for himself instead and ate his small dinner in front of the television in his study.

After washing his dinner dishes Aidan texted Niall, "How about a night out? Darts and a pint at The Harp? I'll pick you up in a bit."

"Not tonight," Niall had texted back without further explanation, not responding to Aidan's text, "Why?"

Chalking Niall's refusal up to his friend being worn out from weeks of stress and added work, Aidan went to bed early, although he tossed and turned for an hour before the wind lulled him to sleep.

The next morning, before settling in to practice guitar, Aidan strolled across the field to the Donoghues' farm where Niall was helping his father change a tire on their truck.

"Anything I can help with?" Aidan offered.

"No, we've got it." Niall kept his eyes focused on the tire before him.

"Our Anna's got fresh bread and jam," Mr. Donoghue offered. "Get yerself in the kitchen there. She'll be that glad to share some with you and a hot cuppa along with it."

"I think Mam was going to lie down a bit," Niall lied. "She told me her back was bothering her."

Aidan caught the surprised look in Mr. Donoghue's eyes, and heard a tone in Niall's voice he couldn't quite place. Anger? Aidan could think of nothing Niall would be angry with him for. He reasoned maybe Niall was just tired.

"It's okay." He told Mr. Donoghue. "I have to get home anyway. I just thought I'd check to see if you needed help with anything. I'll stop back another time."

"Why did you do that?" Mr. Donoghue demanded of Niall as Aidan walked away. "Your mother's putting up peaches for winter. Why did you tell Aidan she was resting?"

Niall ignored his father's question. "Let me tighten that tire. You shouldn't be straining yourself like that." By the time he finished the job, his father had forgotten about his unanswered question.

Aidan passed the afternoon playing guitar, fine tuning songs for the upcoming gigs Mack was scheduling and playing other songs he'd grown up with. In between songs, he tried to think why Niall had been so cold that morning. He was sure now he was meant to have dinner with Niall and his family the night before. Could Niall be upset because he hadn't shown up? That would make no sense but he could think of no other reason. Hoping he could make amends, Aidan called Niall.

"Is your mother feeling any better? I was hoping I could come by for dinner tonight if that's okay. I'm sorry I missed last night."

Niall waited until he was upstairs, in the privacy of his own room, before responding. "We've got a special dinner tonight in honor of my father starting to feel better. I don't think tonight would be good."

Aidan felt stung. Ever since his family's accident, he'd been taken in by the Donoghues. They considered him part of their family now. They would have invited him to any special dinner they'd planned. This time there was no mistaking the undercurrent in Niall's voice. Aidan knew from all their time working together any problem would best be resolved by facing it head on and chose to do so now. "Hey, is something wrong between us?"

Niall's voice over the phone was flat and cold. "No."

Sure now some problem was under foot, Aidan pressed harder. "You're not yourself. Are you upset with me because I haven't been over to help you out much while your father's been ill?"

"You've helped out every time we've asked."

"I know, but I might have done more."

"It's nothing like that." Niall told him. "I have to go now. Mam's calling me to dinner."

Before he could respond, Niall had hung up. Aidan stood several minutes staring at the phone in his hand, trying to figure his friend out, unable to come to any conclusion as to what might be wrong.

After their meeting at St. Stephen's Green, Fionna received more surprises from Hugh. As she walked to class one morning he greeted her with hot tea and fresh tea cakes. On her way to the bus after classes another day he handed her a candy bar and a single daisy. He invited her to a chamber music presentation, a blues bar and a poetry reading.

"I'm not all that fond of poetry myself," he admitted to her, "but I think you'll enjoy it."

She did. Even more, she found she enjoyed Hugh's company. His manner was quiet and respectful, considerate, confident but never forceful. Over the course of their meetings she learned he was the second oldest of five children, had two brothers and two sisters, that his father was a welder and he'd been expected to follow in the trade, that he'd had to put up a struggle similar to her own in convincing his parents to allow him to enter architectural school. At first guarded in her interactions with him, the more time she spent in Hugh's company the more Fionna found herself warming to him. When she stepped out of class on Thursday to find him waiting with two bicycles and two bottles of water, her heart danced a few light steps and a smile escaped her lips unchecked.

"What's this you've got?" She asked, stifling a laugh as he dropped a water bottle while trying to hold both bikes upright.

"Taking a wee chance here, I am." Hugh told her. "If you're up to it, I thought you'd like to see the city up close instead of through a bus window."

They set out then, past Trinity College, past St. Stephen's Green, past the National Concert Hall and along the Grand Canal. They cycled past Kilmainham Gaol, through Phoenix Park and back along the River Liffey. As they rode, Hugh slowed his pace to match hers.

Limited in conversation as they rode, as city noise and the need to ride one behind the other through crowded streets strained their ability to hear each other, Fionna was forced to hold her thoughts inside until they returned, hours later, to the art school. "Hugh, what a wonderful surprise that was! The city looks so much different than what I see from the bus. I can't thank you enough."

"I hope you found some inspiration for your artwork."

"I did, so much I'd be hard pressed to select only one or two sites although I did find the Grand Canal fascinating."

"If you'd like, I'll go back there with you sometime so you can make some sketches or take some photos."

"I'd love that."

"Fine." Hugh hesitated, not sure he should make any moves, sensing Fionna could not be rushed on anything. "Well, I best get these bikes back to the rental outlet, and you've a bus to catch."

"Thank you again." Fionna turned toward her bus stop but took no steps forward.

"Would you care to join me for dinner tomorrow at the café where we first met? Nothing fancy, mind, but it would be fun."

Hugh smiled. "I'd like that."

Fionna found the bus ride home quite boring and very impersonal after the more intimate connection she'd had with the city while bike riding. While she ate her light evening meal of soup and a slice of bread she sketched quick strokes on multiple sheets of paper, anxious to capture as much of what she'd seen as she could. She worked past midnight, only laying her charcoal, pencils and paper aside when her brain and eyes grew tired. Tucked into bed then, drifting to sleep, she found her eyes held a new image, not a golden haired solitary figure along a beach but a young man with dark black hair and glowing sapphire eyes.

"Why don't you call Aidan?" Mrs. Donoghue suggested to Niall, watching him move from kitchen to front room, up to his bedroom, then back to the kitchen. "You're at cross purposes with yourself here. Go on out for a pint."

"Aidan's busy with the house." Niall lied.

"Then go help him or go to the pub yourself. You're bored just hanging around here."

Niall watched his father drifting off to sleep on their sofa, and his mother trying to focus on the sweater she was knitting, her own eyes growing heavier and staying closed for longer periods of time. His watch showed just past nine, far too early for him to retire. Giving in at last, he slipped his coat on and told his mother, "You win. I'll be back in a bit. You don't have to wait up for me."

He intended to drive out to where the Glenelly and Owenkillew rivers met, watch the moon light their flowing waters then slip back into his house once he thought his parents would be asleep. His car had other thoughts though, heading in the direction of The Harp, turning into its small parking

154

lot then shutting herself off before Niall could turn her back around.

He hesitated. It had been hard enough walking into a new pub with Aidan, forcing themselves to fit in with the regulars. Now on his own, he had no courage and would have turned around to leave except Pauline, stepping out to toss a plastic bag into the refuse bin, spotted him.

"Look what the wind's blown our way!" She called out, heading over to his car. "I'd just about given you up for dead. Where have you been?"

"Did you miss me then?" He teased, a sudden smile spreading across his face.

"I missed the money you brought in," she teased back, then added when she saw his smile dim, "and alright, I missed the sight of your scruffy mug the other side of the bar a wee bit as well."

"Enough to pour me a free pint?"

"Not that much!" Pauline threw back. "Get yerself in here. I can't leave the bar unattended, the punters will have the stock emptied by now."

Niall followed Pauline into the crowded pub. "A pint for me please," he requested, "and one for yourself."

"Thanks." Pauline drew two pints, set one in front of him and the other off to the side for herself. "Where's your friend tonight?"

"Not coming. I'm on my own."

"All the better." Pauline poured pints for two of the regulars then returned to Niall. "How are things on your farm then?"

"Busy." Niall decided to level with her. "My father's been sick. I've been handling a lot of things myself."

"I'm sorry. Is your father better now?"

"He will be in time."

"And your band? Didn't you say the last time you were here you all had rehearsals or something?"

"Aye, rehearsals were a couple weeks ago. Since then we've been to the studio recording our next album."

"That's grand." Pauline drank from the pint Niall had bought her. "When do I get to see this band of yours play?"

Niall shrugged. "Mack, our manager, has been booking gigs for us but I don't have the dates with me. I could let you know though."

"I'd like that. I wouldn't mind a wee peek at that farm of yours either someday."

"Really?" Niall was surprised. No girl had ever asked to see his family's farm, nor had he ever relished the thought of showing them. To him the farm, its barn and sheds, pastures and brambly borders were heaven, the warm, familiar place he'd spent all his life. Others, he was sure, would see it as drab, even run down and remote. Thanks to Aidan, now he couldn't even call the place his or his family's. For all he knew a year from now, even six months from now, he'd be living someplace else.

Still, Pauline's interest in the farm seemed genuine, and her face all lit like a tree decorated with a hundred fairy lights and the sight of her smile warmed a place in his heart he'd thought had been closed off forever. "Sunday," he found himself offering to her. "How about Sunday after Mass, if you attend."

"I do, and family dinner after. We're through by half two though. Could I come to your farm after that?"

"We'll hold dessert for you." Niall drew her a map and gave her his mobile phone number in case she got lost.

By the time he returned home his parents had withdrawn to bed, leaving the kitchen light alone on for him. He turned it off, tiptoed upstairs, cursed the fifth step that creaked as it had every time he'd set foot on it the past several years, and listened for any noises in the dark. Relieved that no sound of stirring escaped from his parents' bedroom, he entered his own room and got ready for bed. Before he turned his light off he looked across the field to the light in Aidan's bedroom. He felt torn. The thought of Aidan owning the farm, and the plans he had to turn it into a tourism hub, angered Niall more than he'd been angered in years. Then again, if he'd still been friends with Aidan and Aidan had accompanied him to The Harp, Pauline might not have been so open. They might not now have plans for Sunday. He turned his light out and fell into bed, anger tempered by thoughts of what Sunday might bring.

Aidan saw the light go on then off in Niall's room. He wished he knew what was bugging Niall, what had caused a rift between them. He thought over the past several days. Niall had seemed fine at the recording studio and their evening at Marble Arch when recording was done. He'd been fine the day after they had returned home, as they waved to each other across their lawns, he caulking open spaces around lower windows in his house, Niall giving Farley a thorough brushing.

The only thing Aidan knew had changed was the confirmation from Allan over the stones and the ownership of land. Niall couldn't know that though. Aidan himself wasn't certain Allan's findings were true; he wouldn't know until he heard back from Mr. Maloney. He was sure that couldn't be Niall's problem.

As Aidan turned to go to bed, a familiar shadow appeared in the room before him.

"Timothy." Aidan half whispered into the dark.

"You've not forgotten me then." The spirit answered.

"As if I could. You're the only spirit I know."

"'Tis a grand thing, that. I like to be unique."

Aidan let Timothy's comment pass. "I found the stones and the writing."

"I know. Your solicitor will call next week to confirm what your friend has told you."

Aidan found himself a bit unnerved by the ghost's statement. "How did you know about my conversations with them?"

"I know everything that goes on here. Your music, by the way, is quite good. Not like in my time mind, when the pipers and fiddlers played until dawn and we danced in the fields after harvest. Now that was fine music. Still, yours will suffice."

"I'm glad you approve. I'm not so happy though knowing you watch every move I make."

"I don't watch with evil intentions." Timothy studied the young man before him. A fine young man he was, Timothy thought, though he carried such a heavy air about him. Ah well, in time that might dissipate. "Now, what will ye be doing with yer findings?"

Aidan stared hard at Timothy McCabe, trying to discern the spirit's intent. "I don't know. What would you have me do?"

"'Tis no decision of mine to make. They're your findings."

With that, Timothy faded into the walls. Aidan remained frozen in the same spot a good twenty minutes listening for any noise Timothy might make, searching the walls, windows, ceiling, even into the hallway for any sign of the gossamer spirit. He gave up at last and crawled into bed but remained awake long into the night, unnerved at the thought Timothy's eyes still watched him.

10

Patrick parked the car in its usual spot by the house and hurried over to open Moira's door for her. "I'll bet you're tired after such a long appointment. You go rest for a bit."

"I am tired, but did you see those babies of ours? Aren't they a sight to behold?"

"Aye, they're a grand sight to be sure!" Patrick helped Moira out of the car. "I'm still blown away at seeing two wee heads, four feet, four tiny hands." Then, sensing an air of disappointment still clung to Moira he asked, "Do you mind that I didn't want to know their sexes yet?"

Moira didn't answer straight off. In truth she had felt let down. After weeks of carrying the babies inside her she had looked forward to knowing if she carried boys or girls. To Patrick it hadn't mattered but she was their mum, their hearts beat within her and she was eager for every new insight into who they were.

"I just wasn't ready to know." Patrick explained now as if he could read her mind. "There are so few surprises in our lives anymore. I want to hang onto this one surprise as long as I can."

Moira smiled at him. "I guessed that was your reason. As anxious as I am to know, I can wait." Her face glowed as their living room did when their hearth fire was at its brightest, as the sea behind their house shone when the sun descended to its bed at night. As she walked toward their house though, a cloud of worry dimmed her shining joy. "Patrick, have you thought any more at all where we'll put two new babies?"

"I have." Patrick opened their front door and held it so Moira could step in before him. "I don't have an answer yet."

"Nor do I." Moira sank to the sofa and shifted until she found a comfortable position.

Patrick sat across from her and scanned the cottage around them. "I don't see any walls we can break down. We may have to squeeze them into our room for now. Come spring perhaps we can build on, make our cottage a wee bit larger."

Moira pointed to a corner of the living room near the door going outside. "Maybe you could build a closet there. We can shift our clothes into that space, and you could turn the closet in our bedroom into some kind of alcove the cribs would tuck into."

Patrick considered her idea. "That might work. Now you get some kip while I fetch the laundry, then I'll run out to pick up Conor and Caitlyn."

Moira started to protest but was too tired to give any real fight. Her eyes were already half closed when Patrick stepped outside. As he unpinned the towels, shirts and slacks she had hung to dry he eyed their small house from several angles. Their dream home it had been when he and Moira had first spotted it, thatched roof in need of repair, windows broken, whitewashed exterior chipped and faded. They had both seen its potential, fallen in love with its charm and made it their own. Now it gleamed with fresh white paint and shining windows, its roof had been re-thatched, and Moira's green thumb had coaxed forth colorful rose bushes on both sides of their blue front door every summer.

For their family of four, the house was ideal. For six though? Patrick feared no matter what he tried he'd not succeed in finding a place for two new wee bundles of joy. He thought of Aidan's grand home. A palace it was, pure and simple. What he wouldn't give right now for a home like that! He wasn't jealous; Lord knows Aidan deserved the house for all he'd been through. The house made Aidan happy and gave him things to look forward to. All that was fine. Still, Patrick wished whatever fairy or angel was passing blessings around would fly over the Leahy home and sprinkle some kind of good fortune over him and his family. The babies were blessings, sure; but a place to bed them would not go amiss, nor would an extra Euro or two.

Ah well. An answer was bound to come, he thought. Until it did he'd not show Moira his worries; she had enough to contend with. Patrick carried the full laundry basket into the house, peeked around the doorway to the sofa to see Moira had indeed fallen asleep, and tiptoed back out to the car to collect Conor and Caitlyn from school.

Michael rang Susannah's number for a third time, and for the third time that day reached her voicemail. His anger reached a new high and he left a second message. "Susannah, call me back. I have to know what's going on. Have you cancelled our wedding yet? If you haven't, we need to work things out." He paused before adding, "If you have, I want my ring back."

There, he thought, that would shock her into returning his call. The truth was he didn't care about the ring. It would always be for him a painful reminder of failure. He'd tried for a girl beyond his reach and he'd lost. He'd be damned if he'd let her keep the ring though. If she'd called their wedding off, if she decided her father was more important than her fiancé he'd retrieve the ring, return it for a refund and take himself off on a trip somewhere. Spain, maybe. Majorca. He'd always liked the sound of that word. That was it, he'd take himself off to Majorca, let the warm sand, hot sun, and all those beautiful sun-tanned, bikini-clad young beauties erase Susannah's memory from his mind.

As if it could be that easy. Michael had no doubt they could wipe away the thoughts of his mind but his heart had a longer, more durable memory. All the bikinis and sun-tanned bodies in the world could never change that.

"Damn you, Susannah! Damn you for putting me through all this." He threw his coffee mug into the kitchen sink with so much force it shattered into myriad pieces against the stainless steel. So like his relationship with Susannah, he thought. The mug could never be put together again. He wondered if he and Susannah would end the same way.

Diane listened as Susannah played Michael's voicemail back. "Can you believe it?" Susannah mocked. "He wants his ring back. That's all he cares about in the end."

Diane shook her head. "No Suze, you're wrong. It's you he cares about, not the ring."

Susannah stared at Diane in disbelief. "You can't be serious. You heard him yourself."

"I've heard him call you almost every day for three weeks now. Today's the first time he's brought up the ring. He wants you back."

"Well he's blown that, hasn't he?"

Diane watched Susannah toss her phone down onto the sofa and step into the kitchen. "Shall I make a salad for our dinner tonight?" She couldn't believe her friend's nonchalance. Was this the same friend who, mere months ago, gushed over every mention of Michael, eyes glowing and face blushing as she convinced Diane that Michael was the man she wanted to marry? How could she have changed her mind so fast?

"Let's skip dinner for now," Diane suggested. "We need to talk."

Susannah set aside the romaine and carrots she had pulled out. "What about?"

Diane steeled herself, sure her friend would not be pleased with what she had to say. "Suze you've been here three weeks now." She raised a hand to stop whatever comment Susannah was about to make. "I don't care if you're here three months; you can stay as long as you want. That's not the point. In three weeks' time you haven't even tried to work things out with Michael. That surprises me."

"There's nothing to work out."

"I don't believe that." Diane poured wine for them both, a gesture of friendship she hoped would take the sting out of whatever words she spoke next. "I think you should call and talk to him. Not fight with him, mind. Have a proper conversation with him."

"We've tried talking." Susannah told her. "We're at an impasse."

"Impasses are meant to be broken. Someone gives in, then you both move forward." Diane let her words sink in. "You told me your fight was over your parents not attending your wedding, right?"

"It's more than that," Susannah defended, although even to her ears her defense sounded weak. "Michael doesn't care about what's most important

164

to me. It means nothing to him, and that's a bad way to start any marriage."

"I think you're wrong."

Susannah looked at Diane as if she'd grown two heads. "Are you serious? You don't even like Michael."

"I didn't at first but you persuaded me. Let me ask, have you cancelled the wedding yet?"

Susannah thought of the phone calls she'd reminded herself every morning needed to be made, and every evening remained on the undone list in her day planner. "No," she admitted. "I don't know why I'm putting it off."

"I do." Diane smiled. "You're still in love with him."

"No," Susannah protested. "I'm not. I'm through with him."

"You're hurt because you're not getting the wedding of your dreams."

Susannah had no answer for this. She knew deep in her heart her best friend was right.

"Suze, dream weddings are lovely things to be sure, but they're all show. So often there's nothing behind them. It's time you grew up and put the fairy tale wedding behind you. Michael's real, not some made up Prince Charming. He may not be perfect, but by God he does love you and he'd move heaven and earth for you if he could."

"He's not moving anything at the moment." Susannah turned back to her salad preparation. Diane dropped the subject, knowing she'd challenged her friend enough for one night.

Mack sat at his laptop and studied the latest music marketing techniques. Marketing in this industry, as in most other businesses these days, was an ever shifting landscape. Technology changed almost overnight, and bands and individual artists found new methods every week to advertise their products and increase their fan bases. Each week Mack uploaded a new Macready's Bridge video to new programs, and posted new links to the band's website. Every week he read blogs about new equipment, fresh recording techniques and innovative musical styles. Now, as Seamus and Kellan reclined on the slate floor between the dining room and kitchen, both pairs of eyes watching, ready to follow wherever he moved, Mack studied trade journals and articles, jotted down notes on his lined pad, and e-mailed to himself copies of articles he wanted to study further during the week. By the time Kate arrived home for dinner his head was spinning.

"Time for a break for you." Kate insisted, pushing his laptop away. "I'll bet you've been at this since I left this morning."

Mack didn't deny it, just rose and gave her a quick hug and kiss. "I'll start dinner if you want to freshen up."

Kate glanced at Seamus and Kellan, now prancing around the floor, tails waving, nails clicking on stone. She guessed they hadn't been out much while Mack had been so focused on work. "Why don't I just throw jeans and a sweater on now, we can take the dogs for a walk and then we can work on dinner together."

A cool breeze stirred the trees that lined Mack's property and grey tinged clouds scudded across the sky, growing darker and more frequent as they walked. "Storms by nightfall," Mack guessed.

"I think our dinner on the patio just shifted inside."

Mack wrapped an arm around Kate's shoulder as another, colder breeze blew in. "Are you disappointed?"

Kate moved in closer to Mack. "No, as long as we eat by the fireplace."

On a good day Mack's eyes would have lit up at Kate's suggestion and the romantic innuendo it carried. He would have hurried Kellan and Seamus along on their outing, taken a shorter path home and served an abbreviated dinner, rushing through the evening to an encounter with Kate that would warm and fulfill them both more than any dinner and fire ever could.

Today, Kate noticed Mack's lack of reaction to her suggestion. Something bothered him. She'd have to be patient and give him space, sure when he was ready he would tell her what troubled his mind.

They walked the full perimeter of their land, Seamus and Kellan at times romping through the grass with reckless abandon, other times motionless, noses pointed high, deciphering the scents that wafted their way on the breeze now growing stronger. Little conversation passed between Mack and Kate as they strolled, Mack consumed with the myriad industry and technology questions that swirled through his mind, Kate concerned that she not push too hard for Mack to tell her his thoughts.

Kate waited until they had settled in front of the fire, plates of spaghetti set on their coffee table and wine glasses in hand, before asking, "Mack, are you going to tell me now what's on your mind or must I try all evening to pry it out of you?"

Mack set his wine glass down and stared into the orange and yellow flames. "I'm not sure I'm doing right by the boys." He confessed at last.

Kate waited a minute for Mack to expand on his statement. When he didn't, she asked, "In what way?"

"There's so much to keep up with. The business is always changing." Mack turned from the fire to Kate. "I'm an old man playing a young man's game. They might be better served with someone else guiding them."

Kate would have laughed if Mack hadn't looked so dead serious. "An old man you're not. Take my word for it. Sure the business is changing; mine is as well. You're wise enough to keep up with it all. If you asked the boys, they'd tell you in no uncertain terms they wouldn't want anyone else at the helm. You just put that nonsense right out of your mind."

Mack watched Kate lean back against the sofa, leather releasing a hushed sigh as she settled herself, resting her feet on the ottoman in front of her. How like her, he thought, always knowing just what to say, always confident and reassuring. For the thousandth time since she'd returned to their house, he wondered what he had ever done without her and whether she was as happy as he was that she'd come back.

"Do you ever regret moving in here again?" He probed, holding his breath as he waited for her answer.

He didn't have to wait long. "Never," she replied almost before the words had escaped his lips.

"Never? Are you that happy here?"

Kate set her plate down on the coffee table and turned to him. "Mack, I'm as happy as I've ever been a day in my life. I wouldn't change a thing now."

"Nothing?"

"Well, okay, maybe one thing. I'd give up my job."

Mack was surprised. "You wouldn't! You love that dress shop."

"I do, and I'm proud of what I've accomplished with it." Kate peered into the fire, weighing the words she spoke next. "There's something I want more than the dress shop. I don't know if I can do it and I'd need your help."

Hoping whatever she requested was something he could oblige, Mack asked, "What's that?"

Kate drew her gaze away from the fire and turned to face Mack. "I want children. Oh I know I can't have my own. We've been through that. I doubt I could adopt at my age now, either. I might be able to enter a foster care program though. Mack I know it's a lot to ask, especially as you're not home for stretches at a time, but I've thought of almost nothing else the past couple of weeks. Would you be against me looking into this?"

Mack saw an opportunity he'd been waiting for and whispered a quick prayer before stepping through the open door he'd been presented. "Kate, I think it's a grand idea. I do have one suggestion with it though."

Kate frowned. "What's that?"

Mack took her hand. "I've no doubt you can pull this off as a single woman. You can do anything you set your mind and heart to. Still, it might be easier if you were married." He watched her eyes grow large with surprise. "Would you do me the honor? Not just for the sake of any plans you might have; but because I love you. I've never stopped loving you."

There. He'd gotten the words out at last. He'd hoped for a more romantic setting, in his mind he had planned out a luxurious dinner with violins and roses, but one had to leap on the moments life sent one's way. He could only hope now she wouldn't laugh, but would give his proposal the same respect he'd given her idea.

Kate ran her free hand along his arm, sending a flood of warmth radiating from where she touched through his entire body. "Mack, are you sure?"

He nodded and levelled his most solemn look her way. "I've never been more sure in my life."

Kate recalled the day at her shop with the mother and two wee children, her intense longing that night and her wonder whether Mack would ever marry her again. Here he was now asking the question she most wanted to hear, yet she hesitated to answer. Was he asking for the right reason? Was he that in love with her, or did he ask now out of her need to realize a dream of children in her life? She couldn't answer until she was sure of his motives.

"Are you asking because a husband might make the powers that be more inclined to accept me as a foster carer?"

"Not at all," Mack insisted. He detected a flicker of doubt in Kate's eyes though, and guessed she needed more convincing. He stood, pushed the coffee table away from in front of the sofa, and knelt down on one knee. "Kate Monaghan, with all my heart I love you. I can't bear the thought of facing a single day in my life without you. Will you marry me?"

Kate gave a light laugh that sounded to Mack like angels at play. "Oh Mack, you can get off your knee. You've convinced me your reasons are genuine. Yes, I'll marry you. I love you."

Mack didn't know whether he wanted to jump up and dance, or race to the phone and call the boys, or dash outside and shout his good news to the entire world. In the end, he settled for leaning back against the sofa with Kate snuggled in his arms, Seamus and Kellan drifting to sleep in front of the fire, and the sense that all his dreams, at last, had landed upon his doorstep.

Susannah sat on the edge of her bed in the spare room of Diane's apartment, scrolling through photos on her laptop. Every wedding dream she had ever had was contained in the photo collection she'd amassed over the past two years. Romantic castles with lavish gardens, cascades of roses, delphiniums and lavender, elegant tables set with lace cloths and gold plated service ware, pearl and crystal studded wedding dresses with long veils, or tiaras, she'd dreamed it all.

Leave the fairy tale wedding behind, Diane had said. Reviewing her photo collection now Susannah wondered how she could do that. She had invested so much of her heart, her style, her fantasies in her wedding plan collection. How could she cut away such a large part of herself and still survive?

Then she thought of Michael. She'd not met many people like him. He had class and style and an aura that captivated her. So far different from the carbon copy social climbers she'd met time and again, she had found herself drawn to his independent drive to pursue his dreams rather than give in to others' expectations of him. Michael was real, as Diane had said, in a way that both excited and scared her.

Susannah studied a photo of Michael, then a photo of the wedding dress she had selected for her dream day. Which did she want more? Did she even know what she wanted at all? Which could she not live without?

She opened her dream wedding photo collection once more and started deleting photos, one at a time, until they were all gone. Then she set her laptop aside and picked up her coat.

An hour later she stood in front of Michael's apartment, knocking on his door. He didn't answer right away; she feared he'd gone out and she would lose her nerve before he came home. She knocked twice more. Just as she turned to leave, the sound of footsteps echoed behind the door and the door opened.

Anger swept over Michael like a wave against the Atlantic coast in a storm when he saw Susannah before him. "What do you want?"

"Can I come in?"

Michael shook his head. "You can say what you want out here."

Knowing she deserved his rebuff, Susannah remained where she stood in the hallway. She noticed all over again how magnetic his dark eyes were, how the combination of his riveting eyes and velvet voice sent shivers through her. She whispered a quick prayer that her words would soften his heart.

"Diane thinks I should come back to you. She thinks I'm wrong to make such a big deal out of our wedding plans."

She thought she saw a hint of the hardness in Michael's eyes soften a degree. "And here's me thinking she'd be lighting the sky with fireworks to celebrate your leaving me."

"Quite the opposite. She told me I needed to grow up." The words still stung Susannah's heart, but not as deep as when Diane had first spoken them.

Michael ran his eyes over the woman before him. Time was the sight of her, so elegant in her classic cream slacks and sweater coat, pearl necklace and earrings and long golden hair would have driven him wild with passion. Today though he found himself cautious, not wanting to take for granted Susannah's thoughts would match Diane's. "What do you think?"

Susannah lifted her eyes to meet his. After a long pause she admitted, "I think she's right."

"Michael allowed himself to let go of a portion of his anger. "I'm surprised it took someone else to make you realize that. Does that mean you're moving back in with me?"

"If you'll still have me."

"Have you cancelled our wedding?"

"No."

Michael pointed out, "We still don't have our parents agreeing to attend."

"I know." Susannah closed her eyes. No matter what decision she'd made in Diane's spare room hideaway, giving voice to that decision was harder than she thought it would be. Hoping she'd made the right choice she inhaled deep, opened her eyes and told Michael, "They're not necessary. I'm marrying you, not them. If they choose to not be a part of our day, so be it."

The roller coaster emotional ride Michael had been on with every twist and turn in their plans Susannah had forced him through had taken its toll. He found he could not trust what she said now. He'd survived three weeks without her; it had been hard, but he'd made it. If she put him through that again though, he was afraid he might not pull through.

"Are you sure?" he asked. "I'll not fight this battle anymore. If you come back now there's an end to it. We go through with our wedding no matter what."

"Agreed." Despite her assurance, tears rose in Susannah's eyes which she tried to hide from Michael.

Michael's heart gave way at the sight of her crying. He drew her to him. "There now, there's no need for this. You move back in with me. We'll have our wedding, it will still be a glorious day, and at the end of it all we'll be together forever."

Susannah rested her head against Michael's chest. "I know; and it is what I want. I don't mean to be crying."

Michael led Susannah inside, his arms wrapped tight around her. "You cry all you want. Get it out of your system. Come tomorrow, you'll see it will all be okay."

Moira washed dinner dishes while Caitlyn and Conor finished their homework. While they took their baths, she folded the last of the laundry that Patrick had brought in earlier that day. As Patrick told them bedtime stories and sang them each a goodnight song, she read over the calendar they kept posted on the refrigerator, on which Patrick has just posted the newest bookings Mack had sent to the Macready's Bridge boys.

"Looks like you have quite a busy month ahead," she commented when he returned to the kitchen.

"I do. I'm looking forward to the shows, but Moira, will you and our kids be okay while I'm gone?"

"Aye, we'll be fine. Conor and Caitlyn are older now; they can help with more around the house."

Patrick pointed to the coats and boots they'd left strewn about near the doorway. "They're doing a fine job of that already, I can see."

Moira shrugged. "That? That's nothing. You know I see to that every night before bed."

"You shouldn't have to." Patrick shook his head as he put the coats and boots away in the closet where they belonged. "I'll talk to them both tomorrow."

"There's no need Pat. They're good kids; while you're gone they'll be on their best behaviour." Moira poured fresh tea for them both and settled herself on the sofa, raising her feet to rest on the ottoman. "Now, how about you play me some of the songs you and the boys have recorded."

As he played, Moira tried to focus on his music but found her mind wandering. Most days she was happy with the life she and Patrick had built, the twins they were already raising, and the picturesque cottage they shared. Tonight she wished they had more money, not a lot, just enough to afford a larger house, enough to assure herself they could afford the twins she now carried. She tried to convince herself they'd find room for two new cribs and next year they'd have money enough to expand their cottage, and all would fall into place. She had her doubts though, just as she had her doubts that the twinges she'd felt inside her all day, for two days in a row, were only the twins moving about, making themselves comfortable in her very small womb. A nagging thought at the back of her mind warned her something was wrong. She would not let on to Patrick though. He had a steady schedule of shows booked as the holiday season approached. She would not add to his stress. For now, she forced all the doubts and fears that crowded her mind to disperse,

and focused her attention back to the melodies
Patrick drew out of the fiddle in his hands.

11

Niall woke Sunday morning to the sound of rain tapping a light staccato rhythm on his window. He rose, looked outside, found the grounds closest to the house and barns puddled, and feared Pauline would cancel their plans. All through Mass he found it hard to focus on the homily and prayers; visions of Pauline's face and figure pressed in on his mind. After Mass he checked his mobile phone a half dozen times to see if she'd called to reschedule and debated more than that whether he should call her. He was just about to do so when her car pulled into the drive.

Stepping out in bright yellow Wellies and a raincoat to match, Pauline called out, "Fine weather for ducks! You do have ducks, don't ye?"

Niall sheltered her with his father's large green umbrella. "No ducks, but our sheep's wool is washed nice and clean!" He directed her into the barn, the closest shelter he could provide. "I was afraid the rain would keep you away."

"It could have if you weren't on the other end of the drive." She slipped her arm around his. "Go on, show me your sheep."

Niall obliged, grateful the barn was not well lit and Pauline would not see the scarlet shades he knew his cheeks were turning. "The sheep are all out to pasture except Milo here, he's old and not up to the weather so we keep him inside on days like this.

These are just some of the pitchforks, cutters and tools we use, and bits of wire and such."

They reached the end of the barn. Niall turned to head back, but Pauline stopped him with a hand on his arm and a forceful, lingering kiss. "I've wanted to do that since you first entered The Harp." She confessed when she broke the kiss off. "Sorry, I just couldn't wait any longer."

Niall locked gazes with Pauline's deep green eyes and found the same desire in them he knew filled his own. "I couldn't either," he admitted. He kissed her again, long and hard, one hand sliding down her back, resting just below her hip, the other hand caressing her arm, gripping her shoulder, holding her in place. They kissed again, a quick kiss shortened by the sound of a door opening and a voice calling, "Niall? Are you out here?"

"My mam," he whispered, then called back, "Here Mam. We'll be right in."

"Landed yourself in it now, haven't ye?" Pauline laughed at Niall's grimace. "There's no getting around introducing me to your parents."

Niall shook his head. "Best just get it over with!" He led Pauline inside where he found his parents seated at the kitchen table, sharing fresh tea and scones, and introduced, "Mam, Da, this is my friend Pauline."

"His girlfriend, I'm thinking." Pauline corrected with a gleam in her eyes as she shook Niall's parents' hands. "I'm glad to know ye. I work at The Harp just a bit down the road; if ye stop in sometime I'll see to it ye both get free pints."

"We don't get out much," Mr. Donoghue admitted, "but with a wee lass as lovely as yerself to greet us we might just take you up on that."

Mrs. Donoghue set out two clean sets of cups and plates. "You're welcome to join us for tea, although my guess is our Niall has something else planned."

"I did think I'd drive you around a few places," Niall admitted, "show you more of the farm, and one or two of my favorite spots. If you'd rather stop here that's fine."

Pauline smiled at Niall's parents. "Another time, if Niall invites me, I'd love to have tea; but I'm looking forward to the ride now if you don't mind."

"You're quite the charmer," Niall teased as he and Pauline stepped back outside. "I can see I'll have to keep an eye on you."

"Your parents seem nice." Pauline handed Niall her car keys. "Here, you can drive mine if you want. Do you have any brothers and sisters?"

"No. You?"

"Four brothers, two sisters. I'm in the middle. And if ye hurt me at all my brothers will come looking for you."

Niall might have been scared off by the thought of four brothers watching his every move, but the light in Pauline's eyes, the slight upturn of her nose and the magic of her smile had captured him. Hurting her was far beyond anything he would ever do.

Niall drove Pauline to the pastures where his family's sheep grazed despite the steady rain falling on them. "This is where our farm ends. The property runs from here to our house and back to the lough behind us." For now, he kept to himself the question of who in truth the land belonged to.

"Who owns that massive house on the other side?" Pauline asked.

"Aidan does." Niall pushed aside the flash of anger that sprang up inside him. "You know, my friend you've seen at the pub with me."

"Is that so?" Pauline flashed a teasing smile at Niall. "I think I've picked the wrong punter to take up with!"

Niall called her bluff. "You can go after him, but you might as well know he's no richer than I am."

Pauline made a show of considering the estate house across the way, then shifted closer to Niall behind the wheel of her car. "No, it's you I want."

Niall caught the scent of her perfume, thought it smelled like sunshine and spice, and thought her arm resting against his with the slightest amount of pressure was the most satisfying thing he'd felt in years. He thought Pauline's voice, always tinged with a hint of laughter behind her words, was sweeter than any lark's song he'd ever heard floating on the air.

"There's something I want you to see." Niall suggested as he drove her car beyond where the farm ended. He turned left on a dirt road then followed the road up the tallest hill in back of their farm, hoping when he reached the top her reaction would be worth the rough ride. At the top of the hill he pulled her car to a stop along the side of the road. "Here you go. Best view in all the county."

Pauline took in the landscape spread before them, valley of soft green fields, trees and farms sprinkled across the green, the small lough that separated Niall's farm from Aidan's estate, a larger lough in the distance. "Niall this is beautiful." She whispered, awed by the scenery below them.

"It is, isn't it?" Niall's voice was hushed as well. "This is my favorite spot. I don't share it with everyone, just very special people."

"I feel honored you've included me in that group." Pauline leaned her head on Niall's shoulder, eyes fixed on the pastoral scene before her.

"I had to show you," he teased. "You're my girlfriend!" He turned her face to his and kissed her again.

Alternating between practicing songs for the upcoming gigs Mack had booked for Macready's Bridge and squeezing more work in on his house, Aidan set about painting his bedroom, next on his list of rooms to sort out before the band's hectic schedule kicked in. For his room he'd chosen the deep blue of the ocean at calm, planning to introduce various other shades of ocean blue as accents. As he worked he recalled a conversation the band had had months earlier at Niagara Falls, as their spring tour was drawing to a close. "The ocean, she's calling me something fierce," he had said back then.

Funny how things change, he thought now as his paint brush and roller transformed faded, dirt-marred green walls to the blue he'd imagined ever since moving in. He'd chosen an inland house rather than one by the ocean. He'd been too busy, since moving, to spend time on her shores or to even miss her. Perhaps when he'd made more progress on the house he'd take time off to visit her. He'd take Niall with him; maybe they could rent a boat and fish like he'd done with Michael on Lough Erne.

At the thought of Niall, Aidan realized it had been days since he'd spoken to his friend, and even longer since he'd had a meal with the Donoghues. With a sudden pang he realized how much he missed them, how much he missed a sense of family around him. He set the roller down, wiped his hands clean, and dialled Niall's number.

His call went straight to voicemail. Guessing Niall to be off taking care of the sheep, Aidan rang the Donoghues' house.

"I'm sorry love, he's off with a girl." Mrs. Donoghue replied when he asked if Niall were home. "Pauline from The Harp. I'm surprised he didn't tell you."

"I'm sure it just slipped his mind. When Pauline's involved he does tend to forget everything else."

Mrs. Donoghue chuckled, "I can see why. Would you like me to have him call you later?"

"No thanks. I'll catch him another time."

Aidan set his phone aside, crushed. Ever since they'd started working together, he and Niall had shared almost everything with each other. He would have been the first person Niall would have told about an outing with Pauline. Aidan couldn't imagine why Niall had chosen not to. For the past couple of weeks, he'd had a feeling something was wrong between Niall and himself, Now, he was sure. What it was though, and how he would resolve it, he hadn't a clue.

Aidan returned to his practicing and painting but found his attempts at both futile, his mind too distracted to concentrate. So, Niall and Pauline were out on a date were they? Aidan smiled at the thought. No matter what issues he was having with Niall at the moment, Niall was a good bloke. Any girl would be lucky to have him fall for her.

He wondered where they'd go. Knowing Niall, he'd no doubt introduce her to his sheep first. From there Aidan couldn't say, but imagined Niall and

Pauline off in the wilds somewhere, perhaps climbing some hill or strolling some quiet country lane.

How good it would feel to walk a country lane with a girl, he thought. The idea caught him off guard. He found Fionna drifting in and out of his mind. He saw her again walking the beach or painting with her easel set in the sand. He saw her again at the Marble Arch in Dublin with a boyfriend beside her. They'd never had a relationship, she owed him nothing; but now, at the thought of Niall seeing Pauline, Aidan wished he'd stayed in touch with Fionna. Time to move on, he told himself, although telling didn't make it any easier to do.

He pushed on painting until midnight, fell into bed exhausted, yet lie awake trying to solve the riddle of what barrier existed between Niall and himself and trying not to think any more of Fionna.

"I'm heading into Belfast for a bit." Niall informed his parents at breakfast the next morning. "Is there anything you need?"

Will and Anna Donoghue exchanged surprised glances. "And what would you be going all the way to Belfast today for?" Will asked. "Couldn't it wait until my appointment next week?"

"No." Niall debated how much he should tell them. At last he said, "I need to check the public records to confirm our farm's status."

Still feeling guilt that he'd let his son down by not straightening the missing title issue out years earlier, Mr. Donoghue asked, "Would you like me to come with you?"

Niall watched his parents, both looking concerned now, both appearing to him a bit more worn and fragile than he'd seen before his father's illness. No matter what he thought or felt at the moment concerning Aidan, his primary job at this time was to look out for them. Sure he'd love their company on the trip ahead. He'd love to make a day of it for the three of them, a bit of research, a bit of sightseeing and a fine meal to cap it all off. If the research proved what he thought it would though, the trip would cease to be fun. No, better to let them relax at home and let him do the leg work. They could deal with the outcome when he returned.

"Da, I'd love to have you with me, but I doubt you're up to the trip yet. I'll be fine. I'll be home in time for dinner."

The Public Records Office of Northern Ireland, PRONI, stood in the Titanic Quarter in Belfast. Even though Niall had researched as much as he could online and thought he knew how to find what he needed here, standing in front of the building now kicked his nerves into high gear. He wondered if the whole trip had even been necessary. Maybe he and his parents should just continue paying the bank and leave things as they were. Maybe no harm would come of that. Deep in his heart though, he knew the land ownership issue had to be confronted so they could sort out which steps to take to ensure at least his parents' security as they approached the next phase of their lives.

He stepped inside, followed signs and arrows and at last reached the room where his farm's records would be held. With the help of PRONI staff he located the catalog relevant to what he wanted, and after searching through the catalog, at last isolated the documents he thought he needed. He submitted a request to see the relevant documents; in short time they were brought to him in the reading room.

He read them three times over and made careful notes of numbers, dates and names on a small pad of paper he carried. The records were crystal clear. The maps, recitation of names and details of property history all confirmed what he had already known. Aidan owned his family's farm.

On his way home, Niall stopped off at the market in town and bought a bouquet of fall flowers for his mother and his father's favorite sticky buns. Reaching home, he pulled the special brandy, reserved for holidays and celebrations, from its cupboard in the living room and set that, along with the flowers and buns, on the kitchen table.

"Mam, Da," he called. "Come in here. I have some news."

"Looks to be good news," his mother guessed, pointing to the brandy. "Oh, and aren't the flowers lovely! Whatever did you buy them for?"

"You should have something beautiful to cheer you, Mam." He answered.

"And sticky buns?" his father asked. "What's with all this spoiling of us?"

"Sit down." He motioned to chairs for them both and joined them. "I treated you both because you work hard and you deserve a reward." He poured three small glasses of brandy and passed them around. "Here, let's toast the farm and all you've done to preserve it over the years."

After they each took a drink he told them, "I've done some research online, and confirmed in Belfast today who the owner of the farm is."

They waited on him. He waited until he was ready. Then he told them, "Aidan owns the farm. When he bought the estate house the farm was part of the land included in the sale."

Mrs. Donoghue stated, "Well that's alright then. Sure Aidan would never kick us off our farm."

"His farm," Niall corrected. "And I'm not so sure he wouldn't."

"Why would ye say that lad?" Mr. Donoghue asked. "You've been off Aidan a few weeks now. What aren't you telling us?"

"He's located some ancient writings, ogham stones and such. Sure they're a great draw for tourists. He still has a fair amount of repair work to do on his house. The money tourists would bring in would help him out, not to mention what historians will want to do with the land. I wouldn't be surprised if archaeological digs were set out on our farm. No, Aidan will want to take the farm over for his own use. We best start planning what we'll do when that happens."

Mrs. Donoghue shook her head. "No, I can't believe that. Our Aidan wouldn't do that to us."

"'Your man' has already distanced himself from us." Niall could no longer keep anger out of his voice. "When's the last time he stopped by? No, he has no loyalty here. In the end he'll choose his way with no regard to how it affects us."

"You've quite a low opinion of your friend there, boy." Mr. Donoghue remarked. "I'm with your mam. I can't believe Aidan would treat us that way. The best thing would be for all of us to sit down with him and talk this out."

Niall drained the brandy in his glass and poured himself another, which he downed in one shot. "Da, I heard him on the phone. He's already making his plans. Go ahead, invite him over if you want. I wouldn't trust a thing he says though."

After Niall retreated to his room upstairs Anna turned to Will and asked, "Aidan wouldn't put us off the land, would he?"

Will shook his head. "I don't think so. I am surprised he hasn't said anything to us though."

The next morning, Mrs. Donoghue picked up the phone to try and resolve matters in her own way. "Aidan, we haven't seen you for a bit. How are you?"

Niall frowned at his mother, motioning for her to not be so pleasant on the phone. She waved him off and asked, "We were wondering, would you like to join us for lunch today? I've fresh potato soup, and soda bread just out of the oven."

"Did you have to invite him for a meal?" Niall demanded when she'd hung up the phone. "It's meant to be a business meeting, not a social call."

"Would it hurt to be kind to him?" Mrs. Donoghue retorted. "He's not our enemy after all."

"He just happens to own our land." Niall reminded her.

"Aye, and if we carry on good relations with him sure it will work in our favor." Mr. Donoghue cautioned his son, "It wouldn't hurt for you to set aside your anger and remember Aidan's been your best friend until now. We might be able to save our farm if we're fair with him."

Aidan appeared a short while later, bearing the peach pie he'd bought at market the night before. "I'm sure it doesn't compare to yours, Mrs. Donoghue, but I didn't want to show up empty handed."

Mrs. Donoghue set the pie in the middle of their kitchen table, now set for four. "That was very thoughtful of you."

As Aidan hung his coat up on a hook by their back door and took a seat at the table he apologized, "I'm sorry I haven't been over for a bit. I didn't want to intrude while you were all dealing with Mr. Donoghue's illness." He gave Niall's father a concerned look. "I'm glad you're feeling better."

"Thank you, lad," Mr. Donoghue told him. "You never have to stay away though. You can stop over any time."

As they ate they talked of the Macready's Bridge recording and schedule, Aidan's work on the house, and the forecast for storms moving in by week's end. Halfway through the meal, Niall lost patience with the small talk.

"Will ye get on with it!" He demanded of his father. "Let's cut straight through to the reason Aidan's here."

Mrs. Donoghue turned silent and stared at her plate.

Aidan glanced from Niall's father to his mother, then to Niall, then back to Mr. Donoghue, wondering what was going on.

Mr. Donoghue pushed his plate away, flashed a warning look at Niall, cleared his throat and started in. "Aidan we have missed seeing you, but that's not the only reason you're here. The long and short of it is, with my illness we've tried to clear some paperwork up and, well, title to our land is one of the things we've needed to sort out."

Aidan sat back, relieved. "I think I can answer that."

Niall blurted out, "I'm sure you can."

"I found some papers in the attic." Aidan told them. "I've had it checked out and somehow your farm is part of the land I bought with the house."

"When did you think you would tell us?" Niall demanded. "How long were you going to keep it a secret? Until all your plans are sorted and there's no turning back?"

"What plans?" Aidan asked, astonished at Niall's angry outburst. "I don't know what you're talking about."

"Ogham stones! Architectural finds! Plans to open this area up for tourists!"

"How did you know about the stones?"

"I heard you on the phone."

Aidan shook his head. "You've got it wrong. I don't know what you heard, but I don't have any plans to turn either of our places into a tourist attraction. Truth be told I don't know what I'm going to do, but I'd never hurt you and your family."

"We appreciate that." Mr. Donoghue spoke, hoping to calm his son down. "I guess you know how important the farm is to us."

"Of course I do." Aidan looked straight at Niall. "I can't believe you'd even think I would do something to disrupt your place here."

Niall could not be convinced or calmed. "You have house repairs. Tourists would bring good money your way. Of course you're going to exploit what you've found."

"You're wrong." Aidan pushed his chair back and stood up. To Mrs. Donoghue he said, "Thank you for lunch, it was delicious." With that he grabbed his coat and left.

"Why did you go on like that?" Mr. Donoghue demanded of Niall. "We were meant to work out an arrangement with Aidan. Now I doubt he'll show us any kindness at all."

"Da, don't be so naive. He was never going to show us kindness. He's sitting on a treasure here and he knows it."

"I think you're wrong." Mrs. Donoghue started to clear dishes away. "Sure we'll never know now."

Aidan slammed the door closed behind him as he stormed into his house. How the hell could Niall get it so wrong? How could he think Aidan would treat him and his family with so little regard? Aidan remembered a conversation with Allan at the studio, was that the one Niall had overheard? It couldn't have been. Niall had been in the kitchen with the others, nowhere near where Aidan and Allan had talked. Still he'd heard something and had held his anger in for days without saying a word. Aidan was furious. Niall should have known him better. He spent the next two hours casting the brunt of his anger on the drawers and doors he threw closed with a vengeance, on the tools he flung into their storage bin, on the nails he pounded into place to hold new shelves in the pantry.

Two hours later, his anger spent, Aidan fell into the recliner in his study worn out from his emotions. He glanced at the Donoghue farm across the lough from his place. Niall and his father, bundled against the rising wind, surveyed their house's roof, Niall pointing to one of the peaks. After a short discussion they returned inside.

Aidan wondered, how would I feel if I was in their place? If I'd found out someone else owned what I thought was mine? If the only home I'd ever known was threatened?

He knew he would act the same way Niall had.

Hoping he could clear the air between them, Aidan rang Niall's number. He half expected his call would end up in voicemail. To his surprise, Niall answered the phone. "What do you want?"

"Listen, lunch didn't go well. I'm sorry. I'd like to resolve all of this with you if I can."

"There's nothing to resolve. Just do what you want. I'll look after my parents." With that, Niall hung up.

Niall listened to the wind blowing harder outside, buffeting the windows when strong gusts blew. He turned to his father sitting across the kitchen table from him and asked, "Are you sure the roof will hold? That edge we looked at earlier today was looser than I thought. Should we have called someone?"

"The roof will hold fine. It's been through worse."

"Alright. You remember I'm off to Dublin tomorrow for a show with the boys."

"I do. How will you get along with Aidan?"

Niall shook his head. "I don't know."

Mr. Donoghue advised, "You know you're going to have to sort this with him. You can't leave it the way it is now."

This time Niall kept his anger in check. "It's not up to me to fix, Da. He's the one scheming to pull our land out from under us. I can't resolve that."

"He's not the scheming type. If you talk to him, I think you can work things out in our favor. You at least have to try."

Niall listened to his father as he always did, not sure this time he could do as his father asked. Before bed that night, Niall looked across the lough to Aidan's house, the lone light shining upstairs hinting that Aidan, as well, was turning in for the night. Niall watched a long time, past when Aidan's light went out, past when he heard his parents settle themselves into bed, past when the wind had blown itself out and calm had returned to the countryside.

He saw again Aidan coming to the farm months ago after the accident that had claimed his family, how lost and ill Aidan had been, how time with Niall's family had helped him turn his life around. He thought of the closeness that had developed between Aidan and his family, Aidan as much as one of them now. Niall tried to reconcile that image with the conversation he'd overheard. Perhaps his father was right. Aidan could not possibly have in mind anything that would harm Niall or his family. Still, he knew what he'd heard. His ears didn't lie.

12

Fionna stepped off the bus, not sure why she'd agreed to meet Hugh at the pub. She wished she'd stuck to her original plan of staying back at the apartment and working on her oil painting which would be due in a week. She was frustrated by the abstract of St. Patrick's Cathedral she'd started, a style she still struggled with despite the several conversations and exhibits she and Hugh had gone through on the topic. She should scrap it all and start over, she thought. Instead she'd given in and agreed to the night out.

She found Hugh and her friends at a table near the rear of a very crowded pub. "Looks like everyone else had the same idea," she commented as she draped her coat across the back of the lone empty chair at their table. "I'm sorry I'm late; I missed the earlier bus."

"I knew I should have picked you up." Hugh berated himself. "Next time I won't let you talk me out of it."

"Nor will I," Fionna agreed.

High picked up her hand. "Hmmm, grey, beige, white paint. Let me guess: the abstract again?"

"I hate how it looks! I hate abstract!"

Gwen laughed, "I should do your abstract and let you do my realism. I just can't get the landscape I'm working on to come out right."

Paul disagreed with them both. "You're just painting what you see. I'm trying to build feckin' St. Patrick's in a feckin' abstract out of feckin' wire. Give that a try sometime!"

"Try converting it to a green design." Hugh countered. "All that open space, high ceilings, stained glass windows. I have to design a model that would conserve energy on a budget at that place. Sound like fun?"

Amid their laughter, ordering wine, ordering meals, competing with each other to see who had the harder task, Fionna took no notice of the band taking the stage at the other end of the pub. As the conversation shifted from the challenges of design and art to current displays at various galleries in town and what methods they'd like to try next, the band started to play. Halfway through the set, Fionna thought she recognized one of the singer's voices. Turning her head so she could see the band better, she caught sight of the blond singer in the center and froze.

Aidan! Here! After months of dreaming and hoping, after weeks of trying to move beyond his memory, here he was in the flesh, as real as the food she ate and the friends who shared her table.

Mesmerized, Fionna forgot her surroundings and focused on Aidan through two more songs, until Hugh leaned forward and cut into her line of view.

"Someone you know?"

Fionna felt her face grow red hot. "I'm sorry," she apologized to Hugh. "Yes, I used to know him."

Gwen asked, "Isn't that the boy you've painted a number of times?"

Boy sounded so immature, Fionna thought, not at all like the very mature man who had made love to her. Memories of his touch, his passion,

194

crowded her mind and lit a fire inside her. She brushed both aside before they could overwhelm her. "Yes," she confirmed. "That's him."

She caught Hugh studying her, trying to figure where he stood now that a shadow from the past, and a significant one if he'd appeared in some of her artwork, had all of a sudden reappeared. Placing her hand over his she apologized again, "I didn't mean to be rude. I'm sorry." The rest of the evening she forced herself to stay focused on Hugh, to keep her eyes turned away from the stage, to force Aidan out of her mind although, truth be told, half of her caught every word Aidan sang while the other half chatted with Hugh. She did manage to catch the name of Aidan's band, Macready's Bridge, as people at the next table over were talking, but couldn't overhear any more details.

When Hugh offered to take her home at the end of their evening Fionna had no choice but to comply, although she suspected his motive was to keep her from staying behind and reconnecting with Aidan. He got out of the cab with her when they reached her apartment building and followed her to her door.

"Would you do me one favor?" he asked as she pulled her key from her handbag.

"If I can. What is it?"

"If you're going to get back together with your musician friend, let me know now. Don't let me think there's something between us if there's not."

She wanted to tell him what he wanted to hear, that Aidan meant nothing to her now, that she would choose Hugh over Aidan any time. She found she couldn't give him that assurance. All she could promise was, "If I ever decided to see anyone else I'd let you know."

Michael, Patrick and Aidan each basked in the glory of performing again, the teasing and chemistry between them onstage, the occasional stories in between songs that even they, having heard the stories many times over, enjoyed, how each song resonated in their hearts and the euphoria of applause from the audience after each song was through. They felt alive in ways nothing else they did could stir.

Niall shared little of their joy. While he loved performing, tonight his passion for music was overshadowed by his anger. He did his best to mask it by focusing on the songs he played, blocking out as much of his onstage surroundings as possible. He'd never played such a difficult show. By the time it was over he knew he never wanted to suffer through one like it again.

"Have you got a minute?" He asked Mack when their gig was over.

"Sure." Mack motioned to the others to go ahead to the bar for their pints. "What's bothering you tonight?"

Niall didn't try to deny he had something on his mind. "Does it show?"

"To me, yes. You seemed disconnected from the others. I doubt everyone saw it, but I did and I'd guess the other boys did as well."

"I'm sorry. Mack, I have to tell you I'm leaving the band."

"What?" Mack hadn't seen this coming at all. "Why would you quit? Is it your father? I thought he was doing better."

"It's not my father." Niall hesitated, not wanting to go into details about the break in friendship he and Aidan had suffered. "I just feel the need to step away. Can we leave it at that?"

Mack shook his head. "Niall, this is a critical decision. It changes your life and impacts the whole group. Can't you tell me any more about what's behind it?"

"It's personal, Mack. I'm fine, my parents are fine, but I need to do this."

With no understanding of the reasons behind Niall's decision, Mack was at a loss for any way to counter it. "Your timing's not the best, you realize. You've seen the list of gigs I've booked between now and Christmas, haven't you?" When Niall replied yes, Mack continued, "We've a full schedule the next few weeks. It would be bad business to back out of that many commitments, and you know the boys couldn't continue on without you. There's no time to find a replacement."

"I don't mean to put you and the group in a bad spot. I know my timing is lousy but it can't be helped."

Mack tried to identify the emotion he heard behind Niall's voice: Anger? Bitterness? Both were so unlike Niall that Mack could not make sense of them or of Niall's request. Still, the piper seemed hell bent on his decision. Mack's task was to find a way to delay him until whatever was wrong could be set right, or at the very least until they could find a replacement for the future.

"Niall, I understand you're in the midst of a problem of some sort. I won't force you to talk about it if you're not ready. I would like to ask you one thing, though. Given our commitments, could you stay with the band until the end of the year? If you still feel you need to leave come January, I won't try to talk you out of it."

Niall stared at the hardwood floor of the stage. He noticed how the grains of wood varied and blended, each one different, together forming a cohesive unit. He thought how Macready's Bridge was the same. One board taken out of the stage floor would leave a gap that would mar the floor's beauty and durability. One gap in the band would leave a hole that couldn't be mended. His leaving would put the rest of Macready's Bridge in a bad spot, and the band could not cancel gigs Mack had worked so hard to book for them. He tried to imagine working side by side with Aidan. It seemed impossible; nor did he know of a way to end the stalemate with his former friend. His father and mother both counseled confronting Aidan, listening to his side of the story, but Niall had no interest in or use for anything Aidan might say. Working with him would be uncomfortable, sure. Still Niall knew he owed Mack, Patrick and Michael loyalty enough to work with them until the end of the year. He would just stay clear of Aidan as much as he could.

"Alright, Mack. I can't make any promises, but I'll try."

"Thank you. And Niall, if you ever do want to talk you can call me anytime."

Mack watched Niall leave the pub without saying goodbye to the others. In his mind he sifted through every issue he could think of that might force Niall to make such a drastic decision. Coming up blank, he motioned Aidan over to him.

"Aren't you ready for your pint yet? Hey, where's Niall?"

Mack nodded toward the door. "He just left."

Aidan didn't seem surprised. Mack asked, "Did he say anything to you today?"

"About what?"

"He told me he's leaving the band. I've talked him into trying to stay on the next few weeks; I'm not sure he will, though."

"Leave the band?"

Aidan hadn't looked surprised at the news. Sure Aidan was covering something, Mack asked, "Do you know what's bothering him?"

"I think so. Mack, can you leave it with me? I'll try to sort something out."

"Alright. Let me know how you get on."

The day after seeing Aidan at the pub, Fionna visited the coffee bar near her apartment where she could access the internet and research Macready's Bridge. The band's website listed members Michael Sullivan, Patrick Leahy, Niall Donoghue and Aidan O'Connell. So that's your last name, she thought. She memorized the pictures Aidan appeared in, then went on to read his biography. On the news and notes page, the website mentioned the recent loss of Aidan's family. More curious than ever, she researched Aidan O'Connell himself and came across several articles that described in depth the car accident that had claimed the lives of his father, sister and grandmother. Fionna remembered Aidan saying he was dealing with a personal problem of sorts. No wonder he had been so aloof at the beach, so withdrawn. She reread the articles, then reviewed the upcoming dates and places where Macready's Bridge was scheduled to perform. Fionna wrote the information down, not sure which shows she could attend but determined to find a way to at least one.

Aidan sat at the large desk in his study, his father's desk he'd had moved here from the auto shop. While some days the memory of his father working at the same desk was painful, tonight he found the desk comforting, as if some of his father's wisdom would pass on to him through its wood surface, worn smooth in places from his father's own hands.

He stared at the ogham stone pictures and at the map and papers he'd found so many weeks ago. When he'd first found them, the map and papers had just been mysterious items that had aroused his sense of curiosity. Now they were tangible evidence of the history of the land his house stood on, and the land around his including the farm his den window looked out on. He stared at the farm now, saw the kitchen light on and pictured Niall and his family finishing dinner there, watched Niall walk out of the house and across the yard to the barn, imagined Niall working or playing his pipes to the sheep inside the barn where a light had now been switched on.

Ogham stones, as he knew from Allan and Jack and general knowledge he'd gained on his own over the years, could be quite profitable if displayed to the public in the right way. He looked at his bank account statements and the list of repairs he knew his house would need next. He knew Allan would welcome the chance to write a paper on his discovery or present information of it to his contacts. Aidan had no doubt that spreading word of their existence and location would bring him more than enough money for the repairs still to be done.

Then he recalled the recent episode at the Donoghue's house, how his cordial visit had turned so wrong, how furious Niall had been. He thought of Niall choosing to leave the band he'd loved so much. He remembered so many times in recent months he and Niall had spent on the boat on the lough between them, or enjoyed tea and biscuits as they sat at water's edge, sharing the easy friendship they had both formed over the past couple of years. The thought that their friendship now was a source of discomfort so great Niall felt he had to step away cut Aidan to the core.

As he looked out over his property, Aidan spotted the unmistakable ghostlike figure of Timothy McCabe leaning against the outside of the carriage house, cap in hand, gazing out over the lough and farm behind Aidan's house. Aidan recalled the messages Timothy had given him, how they'd led to his discovery of the map and writings and the ancient stones. Wondering whether the discoveries had been good given his falling out with Niall, Aidan rose, slipped on his jacket and strode out to confront him.

"Storm's coming," Timothy announced as Aidan approached. "Three days I give it, then the howling winds will set in. Best make sure you've got everything tied down, and warn your friend over there." Timothy pointed his thumb toward the Donoghues' farm.

"He's not my friend right now. You've seen to that."

"Aye, I've heard the falling out you've had." Timothy ignored Aidan's surprised look. "Why are ye laying that at my doorstep?"

"The stones and the writings. You told me to find them. What good has finding them done?"

Timothy eyed the young man before him while he sucked on the stem of a pipe he held in his hand. At last he replied, "That's for you to work out."

"No. You're driving me in the direction of all these discoveries. You've got a plan behind it all. Tell me the plan."

Timothy shook his head. "Laddie, when I was a school master my job was to impart knowledge, provide information to my charges. I never told them what to think or do with what they learned; that was their choice."

Aidan joined Timothy's gaze over the lough and beyond. As he studied the scene he recalled Timothy's earlier words, and asked about them now. "You mentioned a fire once. Tell me about it."

Sadness clouded Timothy's face. "There was always a farmhouse across the field there where the one stands now. Back then two families shared the one house, and always more coming and going. Oh, the struggles we had back then, poverty, hunger, persecution if anyone dared follow the Faith; but hard workers the people were, strong and proud. They'd find a way through any hard time. Loads of children there always were as well, all of them laughing and playing even in their work. Their mammies and daddies were always so glad to see a hedge master come through and give the wee'ans a bit of learning.

"Two families living there, with a dozen children between them and a few more staying over for their lessons. There had been trouble in town the week before, rumors of priests and hedge masters in the region. The landowners were all up in arms.

"Now I'm not saying what started the fire, but we'd been not long in bed when it erupted, me sleeping in the carriage house here, the older kiddies and some of the men sleeping in the barn. Midsummer it was, air dry and warm for a change. The word was we'd be celebrating Mass in the morning. Next thing we knew, the barn was on fire. With everything dry it went up like a blade of hay, consumed in the blink of an eye. Several of us rushed in to try to save them that were sleeping in the barn, but the fire raged out of control; we couldn't save a soul. Three men and seven children were lost that night. Oh, the wailing all the next day was dreadful, those mammies so heartbroken for their babies. No one ever investigated. The landowners gave all the workers a day off to bury their dead, then it was back to work as usual."

Aidan let Timothy's story sink in. "Did you move on after that? You couldn't continue teaching if the authorities suspected you were still around."

Timothy was silent several long minutes before answering, "I died in the fire, boy."

Lost for words, Aidan could only stare at the figure before him, fading a bit as his story was told. "I've stayed on all these years," Timothy continued, "witnessed all the comings and goings of the people that crossed this land. I'm tied to the people here until things can be made right."

Before Aidan could ask what he meant, Timothy had faded into the dark night sky.

13

All morning Moira had felt something was wrong inside her. She'd grown used to the ever-present twinges and pains that arced across her abdomen while she cooked meals, hung laundry and cleaned the cottage. For days, as they'd increased, she had convinced herself they were nothing more than the stretching and changing of her insides as the babies she carried grew. She'd been careful to drink plenty of water and rest on the sofa as often as she could, although she had to admit to herself she could always use more rest.

Today though, the pains seemed different, a little lower and stronger accompanied by an unsettled, almost nauseous feeling. She managed to prepare oatmeal for Conor and Caitlyn's breakfast and pack their lunch sandwiches before Patrick drove them to school. While he took their car in for brake work, she stepped outside to hang the sheets and towels she'd washed out on the line to dry.

Moira had pegged two sheets and bent down to pick up a third when a pain sharper than any she'd known tore across her stomach. She straightened, but the pain remained. Forgetting the laundry, she eased her way back to the house, praying the car's brakes would be done in short order and Patrick would soon be home. By the time Moira reached the sofa, her legs were trembling and perspiration glistened across her face.

Relieved to hear his car pull into their driveway, as soon as he walked into their house she called out, "Pat, call the doctor! I think something's wrong!"

Alarmed at how pale she looked and the fear in her eyes that had always reflected such calm, Patrick tried to keep panic out of his voice as he told her, "I'm sure everything's fine, you've no doubt been pushing yourself too hard. Still, I'll call for the first appointment we can get."

Grateful for a doctor who understood Moira's pregnancy risk, an hour later they were in the clinic for a scan. Moira and Patrick followed the images on the screen as Dr. McAfee conducted the sonogram. "There," she pointed out, "Baby A's heartbeat is nice and strong." She traced slow circles over Moira's abdomen. "Baby B, there's your wee heartbeat as well." She pointed out four tiny hands and four small feet. If a shadow crossed her face, Patrick brushed it off as a change in light reflecting off the screen and nothing more.

With the scan completed, Dr. McAfee wheeled the equipment away and faced Moira and Patrick. "Your babies are fine, but I am concerned about the pains you've been having. I'd like you to have two weeks' complete bed rest. If you can't get that at home, I can arrange a hospital stay."

"I'll see to it she gets her rest." Patrick shook Dr. McAfee's hand. "Thank you for easing our fears."

Dr. McAfee placed a reassuring hand on Moira's shoulder. "If you have any more concerns, let me know. If I'm off duty have the hospital call me."

"I wonder why she said that." Moira commented as they left the hospital. "Have them call her if she's off duty. Do you think she's hiding anything from us?"

"Not at all. She's just a caring doctor, one of the things you've always liked about her. She said that to make you feel better. If she had any real concerns, we'd be checking you into hospital now."

As they turned from the parking lot onto the main road for home Moira asked, "What if bed rest doesn't work? I've been resting the past week and I'm still having cramps."

"You've only rested in bits since I've been home. You still want to run everything around the house. No more of that, ye wee stubborn woman! I'm in charge now."

Moira laughed in spite of her fears. "And how will ye run things when you're next away with the boys?"

"Easy. Your mother will stay with you then."

"You never like having my mother stay at our house."

Patrick grinned. "That's why she'll only be there while I'm away."

Moira studied the grey clouds moving over the ocean, how they seemed to be growing darker and sweeping in faster. To her they mirrored her fears, an approaching storm gathering strength, blowing closer. Was it some problem with her babies, she wondered, or some other crisis she could not yet imagine? Whatever it was, she hoped she and Pat could withstand what came their way. Turning to Pat she said, "You do know at some point you're going to have to get on better with my mother."

"I do." Patrick agreed. "We're going to need her help more than ever once the babies are born."

"Maybe we could have her out for dinner this Sunday? Only you'd have to make dinner."

"Friday," he corrected as he pulled into their driveway. "We'll have to have her out Friday. I'm meant to be off to Galway for a show with the boys Saturday night. I'll work it all out with her. You get yourself into bed now while I gather the laundry in." He waved off her protest. "And if you give me any lip I'll not be bringing you any tea when I'm done."

"Where do you want to hang these?" Michael handed Susannah a string of fairy lights out of the bag of Christmas decorations she'd brought home from her shopping excursion with Diane.

"I thought by the front windows." She held the lights up next to a strand of synthetic holly. "I thought I could intertwine them with this."

"That's a good idea." He pulled more lights out and a box of red and green glass ball ornaments. "Do we need to get a tree to go with these?"

"I'm going to put them in that clear crystal vase." She pointed to a large empty vase on the dining room table. "I thought that would be pretty if we have company over for dinner." Susannah ran her eyes around their apartment, imagining dinners and Christmas festivities, carols playing in the background, laughter and chatter around a crowded dining room table. Then she stopped her imagination short and dropped the garland and lights to the floor. "Oh Michael, who am I kidding? We won't be having any dinner company, or any other company for that matter. Christmas will come and go and we'll not have had anyone over."

He set the box aside. "By anyone I take it you mean family?"

A heavy sigh escaped her lips. "Yes. I tried calling my parents yesterday, left them a message and I still haven't heard back from them. I don't suppose . . ." She hesitated. "I don't suppose you've been in touch with your parents."

"No. I could call my mother, but she'll never go against anything my father chooses so what's the point?"

"Michael, I just don't know if I can take this. I know they won't be at our wedding, whatever date we go with now we've lost our booking. But Christmas? I just don't know how to do that without our family around. Is this how it's going to be the rest of our lives?"

"No. They'll come around someday. I promise. This Christmas though, let's go somewhere for the night. Book a hotel, something grand, something so special we won't even care who is or isn't around us."

Susannah crossed the room and hugged Michael. "Thank you. We can't afford that but it's a lovely thought."

"Then let's have friends over. Diane, and a date for her; maybe I can get Niall or Aidan and a couple of girls as well. We can have a party."

"Diane was right about you."

Michael frowned. "In what way?"

"You are a good man." She kissed him, then returned to her decorations. "Alright. We'll spruce the place up here and have a grand party. Maybe I can cook a roast duck. Or salmon. Or a good crown roast; they always look so festive."

Susannah called out plans, started lists, and gave Michael directions on where decorations should be set. He went along with all her ideas, happy to see the glow return to her eyes and cheeks. She hadn't lit up like that in weeks, Michael realized. All her dreams had become stuck between two stubborn old men. He also realized it was up to him to unstick things. He'd start tomorrow. Just then, another idea struck.

"Suze, let's set this all aside and take a drive. Look, the rain has eased up and all the Christmas lights are going on. Go grab your coat."

"Now? Can't it wait for another time? I've all this planning and decorating to do."

"No, I want to show you something. Go! Get your coat."

Wondering what Michael could be up to, Susannah hurried into the bedroom, ran a brush through her hair, checked her makeup and retrieved her coat. As she did, Michael grabbed cheese and crackers from the kitchen and the half empty wine bottle from dinner the night before.

He drove them south of Dublin, towards the Wicklow Mountains. As he drove he checked the rear view mirror a number of times. When he reached the spot he wanted he turned the car around, pulled over to the side of the road and shut the car's engine off.

Dublin's lights shone like a field of diamonds spread before them. Away from all of the noise and crowds, the scene looked as magical as a vast fairyland.

"I've never seen this view before." Susannah's voice was hushed, entranced by the city spread below them.

"I discovered it driving home one night. I've always remembered it." Michael opened the wine and poured cups for each of them. "Here." He handed a cup to her, and the open container of cheese and crackers. "What do you think?"

"Michael, it's beautiful."

"You know, with all our focus on the wedding and all that's gone on around that we've never discussed long term plans." Michael pointed to the view before them. "Where would you like to live when we've outgrown our apartment?"

Susannah recalled her words to Michael weeks earlier when she told him she'd be happy living anywhere as long as they were together. Now, considering the region below them and admitting what she knew was honest within her she told Michael, "I'd like to live outside the city, not too far out though. I'd like a nice house with an open floor plan and a beautiful view."

"No roadside cottage for you then?" Michael teased, fearing in his heart the house she had in mind was large and expensive like his parents' house, like hers.

"Not unless you can tear it down and rebuild it into what I want." Susannah teased back.

"Are you talking posh neighborhoods then?"

Susannah shook her head. "No. I know we can't afford that. It doesn't have to be fancy, just pretty."

"What do you mean by pretty?" He asked, hoping at least on this matter their ideas would match. "Corinthian leather and Waterford crystal?"

Susannah knew she deserved that. "No. The wedding was one thing, I wanted to pull out all the stops on that. I don't want a cramped cottage for our house, and I don't want second hand furniture. Beyond that I swear to you I don't want a museum house, I won't be after trying to impress the world."

Michael released an inward sigh of relief. For all her fuss over wedding plans and dreams, he was thankful her sights for where they would live were set on more practical housing, not impossible ideas. "Then we agree." He clasped Susannah's hand in his and they admired the scene below them until fresh rain set in and they were forced to drive back home.

Patrick rose from the dinner table and asked Conor and Caitlyn, "Will you two clean the table and start on the dishes while I check on your mum?"

"We will Daddy." Caitlyn promised for them both. "Come on Conor, you have to help."

Conor hurried to the sink and grabbed the dish cloth. "I'll wash dishes and you can clean the table."

"I want to wash." Caitlyn pouted.

"Stop it." Patrick ordered them both before a fight broke out. "Conor you can wash tonight, tomorrow it will be Caitlyn's turn. Now get things cleared here; when I return I'll help you with your homework."

Patrick brought fresh water and a slice of lemon pie back to Moira. "Here, I thought this might cheer you."

Moira frowned. "I could be on the sofa, you know. I don't have to be stuck way back here apart from you all."

"I've got one pouty child out front," Patrick ordered with mock solemnity. "I don't need another one back here. On the sofa you'd get no rest, you'd be up trying to get your hands into everything that needs doing."

"Who's pouting?" Moira asked, sliding over so Patrick could lie on the bed next to her.

"Caitlyn this time. Tomorrow sure it will be Conor. Nothing for you to worry over; I've got them well under control."

Moira laughed. "They'll keep you running in circles, those two. Did you call my mother yet?"

"No, I waited until now. You can have a wee chat with her while I go back out to the kitchen." He pulled his phone out. "Here, ring her up."

"Hi mum. I hope I'm not catching you in the middle of eating." Moira said when her mother answered the phone. "I have a favour to ask if I can." She listened as her mother spoke, then took her next turn. "Patrick and I were hoping you could come out for a bit. I've been placed on bedrest and Patrick has to go out of town for a few days." Moira listened again, her face giving way to surprise. "When did you do that and why are you only telling me now?"

Patrick jerked his head around to look at her. "Problem?" he mouthed, knowing the answer would be yes.

Moira waved him off. "Mum, I'm so sorry I can't be there to help. Please tell your friends I'm grateful to them." She listened a few more minutes, then rang off and handed the phone back to Patrick. "My mum's broken her leg. She can't come out."

"You're joking. That's her then, horrible timing and all."

"Pat I don't know what we'll do. I can try calling church, maybe someone there can help us out."

Patrick rose from the bed, leaned over to kiss Moira's cheek, and fixed the pillows and blankets around her. "Don't you give it a thought, love. I'll work things out. You get rest now. I'll send the kids back when their homework is done so you can chat with them before they turn in for the night."

All while Patrick helped the kids with their homework, his mind searched for solutions to their dilemma. For all the people in church or town that they knew, he could think of no one able to help overnight if he was away. In the end only one decision seemed right. He waited until Conor and Caitlyn had bathed, spent some time with Moira and then gone to bed, and Moira herself had drifted to sleep over the book in her hands, then placed his call.

Mack had spent the afternoon picking up branches and debris around his property, securing windows in the house and barn and rechecking their supply of turf and heating oil. Winter was upon them now, Christmas just a couple of weeks away, and before that a full slate of Macready's Bridge shows. He wanted things well sorted before he left so Kate wouldn't have to worry about anything.

He'd just finished securing the patio furnishings against the cold Atlantic wind when Kate knocked on the window between them and held up his phone, motioning for him to come inside.

"Mack, I have a problem with the tour." Patrick informed him from the other end of the phone. "Moira's on bed rest the next two weeks, at least. Her mother was going to stay here while I was away but she's fallen and broken her leg. She'll need care herself and won't be able to look after Moira or our kids. I don't dare leave Moira alone. I don't see how I'll be able to make our gigs."

Mack rolled his eyes heavenward and shook his head. First Niall, now Patrick. What would be next? "Pat, I'm so sorry. Don't cancel yet though. We may be able to come up with a solution."

Kate set a cup of tea before Mack to warm him after his outside work. As she turned to retrieve her own tea and a plate of biscotti, an idea struck Mack.

"Pat, I might have something. Can I call you back in a few minutes?"

Kate returned and sat across from him at their dining room table. "Why does Pat want to cancel?"

213

Mack relayed the story of Moira's mother and Patrick's concerns, then eyed Kate. "I wonder, would you help Patrick and Moira out for a couple weeks? They can't afford to have him miss out on work right now and it would give you a taste of having kids around."

"I suppose Deirdre could manage the store while I was away." Kate thought out loud. "She could always reach me by phone if she had any questions."

"Patrick's house is small," Mack cautioned. "Would you be comfortable there?"

"I'd be fine. Or Moira and the twins could come here, although I doubt Moira would want them to miss school and sure she'd want to be near her doctor. No, best if I go there as long as she doesn't fuss over things on my account."

"Can I tell Patrick then?"

Kate nodded, "Go ahead. I'll call Deirdre as well."

The next morning Michael drove to the countryside with two goals in mind. First he drove to his parents' house and, when his mother opened the door, asked to speak with his father.

"I'm in between conference calls," his father growled, not pleased with Michael's interruption. "What do you want?"

Michael sat down in the chair across from his father's desk, refusing to be rushed. "Susannah and I want you to be at our wedding. We've postponed it once but we won't postpone it again. Her dream is to have our families with us when we get married. I want to give her what she's dreamed of for so long."

His father opened his mouth to speak, but Michael cut him off. "I know you don't approve of me. You never have. I'm not here to argue that. I'm not here to ask for any money either. We know our parents aren't going to contribute to the wedding; we've worked that out on our own. All we want is our parents there to share in our day. I know you're too busy to set aside any time for me as a rule; this one event is all I'm asking for and I won't ask for anything more."

Mr. Sullivan's phone rang. Michael thought his father looked the slightest bit conflicted, torn between his son and his business, before he turned to answer it. "Must just be my imagination." He told himself, returning to his car sure his father would take little note of what he had said.

Michael's second stop was farther out and forty minutes south of his parents' home. He'd located the address in Susannah's wedding invitation list, and called first to make sure her father would be home.

Turning onto the lane that led to the Tierney's house, Michael pulled his car off to the side and sat there a full five minutes, awed by the view ahead of him. Secured behind a heavy wrought iron gate built into a tall stone wall that surrounded the property, Susannah's family home was twice as large as his own. Beyond the gate a massive fountain cascaded water into a large circular pool. As Michael drove closer he discovered two large arboretums, one on either side of the house, with paths leading past each to sculpted gardens protected by lower walls. Michael counted eight chimneys rising from the gabled roof of the large grey stone house.

Part of Michael was humbled that Susannah came from more riches than he'd ever guessed, and understood on a deeper level why her father would think him so unworthy a choice as her husband. A larger part of him was furious that her father, with so much money behind him, could deny his only daughter any amount of funds towards her wedding, an amount her father would no doubt not miss at all. Hanging on to his anger, brushing his sense of inferiority aside, Michael rang through to the house from the security speaker at the gate, gave his name and his reason for calling, was buzzed through and pulled up to the house where a uniformed guard met him.

"Park here sir, and go straight up to the house."

Another uniformed man met Michael at the heavy wooden front door. "This way, please." Michael followed him through an arched-ceilinged, marble-floored hallway to a library with high shelves filled with books, a thick steel blue carpet his feet fairly sank into, and Susannah's father ensconced behind a large mahogany desk.

"Welcome, Michael." Mr. Tierney rose and extended his hand. He pressed a buzzer and the same uniformed man who'd led Michael to the library reappeared, carrying a silver tray with coffee and biscuits which he placed on a corner of the desk before retreating.

"Coffee?" Mr. Tierney offered. After pouring steaming cups for them both, Mr. Tierney sat back behind the desk. "Now what can I do for you?"

Hard to hang onto his anger surrounded by such elegance and hospitality, Michael hesitated a second before recovering his will. "I came to speak to you about the wedding."

Mr. Tierney set his coffee down, examined Michael head to toe, then nodded. "Go on."

"I know you feel I'm below the standards you set for your daughter. I'm a musician. That's what I've chosen and, God willing, that's what I'll spend my life at. I've already had this out with my father and I don't intend to change."

Impressed by the young man's resolve, Mr. Tierney nodded again. "I see."

"It's not me I've come to see you about. It's your daughter. Susannah has her heart set on the wedding of her dreams. We're not asking for money," Michael was quick to point out as he saw a shadow of resistance flicker across Mr. Tierney's face. "We've worked our plans out to fit what we can afford without any help from our families. What I can't arrange though, what I can't help Susannah with, is you."

Mr. Tierney leaned back against his leather chair. He had to give the lad credit, throwing himself into the cavern between a distanced father and daughter.

Michael continued, "Susannah has her heart set on you being at her wedding, walking her down the aisle and being a part of what should be the happiest day of her life. I can't give her a lifestyle to match what she was raised on. I can't even give her everything she's dreamed of by way of her wedding. I can though try one last time to give her what she wants most. I've come to ask you to reconsider and be there for her, for our, wedding. We won't ask for anything else."

The lad was eloquent, Mr. Tierney thought, a fighter with a respectful, clever use of the tongue. Too bad the lad had his head stuck on music; he would make a good negotiator.

"Michael, you have to understand. I've only the one daughter. I love Susannah with all my heart. I do, however, know a bit more of the ways of the world than the pair of you do. Dreams are wonderful things in their place. They don't always pay the bills.

They don't always provide for the crises that insert themselves into our lives. Now I've heard your music and I must say you're good, you and your band. You know I like you as a general matter. That being said, I can't help wanting the very best for my only daughter. I want someone who will always be able to provide for her no matter what life throws her way. I doubt you can do that on a musician's pay."

"Agreed, sir. But love, doesn't that count for more than money?"

Mr. Tierney recalled his own beginnings, how he and Lillian had had so little between them, how hard he had worked to amass the fortune he now controlled and in so doing provide an elegant lifestyle for his wife and daughter.

"Michael, it does count a great deal to lovers. I'm a father though, and my own standards are quite a bit higher. However, I do appreciate your coming here and speaking your piece."

Michael drove back to Dublin proud that he'd tried his best for Susannah, but sure he'd accomplished nothing at all. He stepped into their apartment to find Susannah bursting with excitement.

"Michael, Markree Castle just called! They've had a cancellation and want to know if we'd like the date."

"What date do they have?"

"The Saturday between Christmas and New Year."

"That's just two weeks away."

"I know. Just think, we could start the new year off as husband and wife!"

Michael wished he could share her excitement, yet he was still unsure and asked her one more time, "What if our fathers haven't changed their minds? Forget my father, what if yours hasn't? Are you sure this time you'd still go ahead with the wedding?"

He had every right to ask, she knew. She'd let him down once before. She would not put him through that again. "Let's take the Markree date," she pleaded. "If my father can't accept our marriage by then, so be it."

"I don't know." Moira told Patrick after the kids had gone to school and he had outlined for her Mack and Kate's plan. "She's used to Mack's beautiful house. What if she couldn't stand our place?"

"Kate's not like that. She's got a good heart, and I think you two would get along well. I think you'd enjoy her company."

"I'm not sure I could stand to have a stranger cleaning my house and looking after my children."

"We don't have any other choice." Patrick hadn't wanted to be so blunt with Moira, but there was no other way. "There's no one else we can call on. If Kate doesn't come out here I'll have to leave the band."

Moira felt a twinge of pain in her stomach, a reminder of why she'd been driven to bed rest. She could see in Patrick's eyes the pressure he was under, the enormity of the decision he had to make. She recalled every time she'd seen him play his fiddle, how deep his passion for music ran, how much a part of him it was. He could no more cut music out of his life than he could stop eating or breathing. She would not be the cause of him leaving a band he so loved.

"Ah, Patrick, take no mind of me. I'm all hormonal and touchy these days. I'm sorry. Please tell Kate her offer is very much appreciated and we'd love to have her come help us out."

Patrick studied her. "Are you sure? You won't feel the need to get up while my back is turned and help her out?"

"Aye I'm sure. You go off and work with the boys. Kate and I will be fine while you're gone."

14

Aidan was halfway through cooking eggs and potatoes for breakfast when a loud zap and snap cut through the air and his stove went cold.

"Damn!" He muttered. He hadn't slept well, he was hungry, and now this!

He tried two kitchen light switches and found both unresponsive. The dining room and living room lights remained dark when he tested them. Upstairs, none of the switches he tried provided light or power.

At the power box in his house's utility room Aidan found the same old wires he'd seen when inspecting the house before buying, but saw nothing out of the ordinary. He returned to the kitchen wondering who he should call. Jack would have a good electrician's name, he knew, but all his connections would be in Derry. Aidan preferred to work with someone local. He thought of calling Barry Patterson, hoping the roofer would have an electrician among his contacts in the building industry.

Then he looked across the way to the Donoghues' farm. Mr. Donoghue would no doubt know a good electrician. Would he share his knowledge though? Or had Niall convinced his parents to have nothing to do with Aidan? He debated a few minutes then picked up his phone. His electricity wouldn't fix itself; he needed help.

"Mr. Donoghue? I've lost power at my house. You wouldn't know an electrician I could call would you?"

"The whole house, Aidan?" Will Donoghue held up a hand to stop whatever angry comment Niall was about to make at the mention of Aidan's name. "Aye it sounds as if you've got quite a problem there. I'd call Tommy Clancy out. He's been in business a good long while; he'll see you sorted."

Aidan wrote down the phone number Mr. Donoghue gave him. "Thanks. I'll give him a try."

No matter the situation between his son and the lad across the way at the moment, Mr. Donoghue felt sorry for the boy. "Is there anything you need? I can have our Niall bring over some hot tea water and soup in a bit. And you can stay the night here if your power's not back on by then."

Aidan pictured how happy Niall would be at that prospect. "Thanks, Mr. Donoghue, but I've got a fireplace and good supply of turf; I'll have heat enough to keep me warm and to boil water or cook over. I should be fine."

"What was that all about?" Niall demanded after his father ended the call.

"Aidan's lost power at his house."

Niall slammed his hand down on the kitchen table so hard his father and mother both jumped. "There you go then! You know what's coming next don't you?"

Mrs. Donoghue shook her head. Mr. Donoghue, suspecting what was coming next, challenged Niall. "No, what?"

"In that old house if the power's out ten to one he'll need a full rewiring. How much do you think that will cost?" Without waiting for his parents to answer, he went on. "A fair pound I'll guess. Where do you think he'll be getting that money? He doesn't have a bottomless bank account, you know."

His parents both remained silent, starting to see where Niall was headed, neither willing to entertain the thought.

"Aidan's sitting on a gold mine. He'll work a deal soon enough with some agency or other and soon our land will be overrun with historians and tourists. There's no other way he can keep paying for what his house needs."

"I think you're wrong." Mrs. Donoghue protested, although her eyes held no certainty in them and her voice was unsure.

Mr. Donoghue shook his head. "I still don't see Aidan treating us that way. Still he will need a fair amount of money and he's not got many options for that, I'll credit you."

Tommy Clancy's first reaction to the condition of the wiring in the former Gallagher estate house was, "You're that lucky you haven't had a fire before now."

"That bad is it?" Aidan asked, peering over the electrician's shoulder to the frayed wiring he'd pulled out of the wall.

"Aye, look here. Your wiring's all exposed. You've a definite fire hazard here. The whole house will need rewiring."

"You couldn't just replace the bad sections?"

"No." Tommy pointed to the walls all around him. "No way of knowing what's good and bad behind all that plaster. You'd have to pull out a section at a time in order to see, and for all that work you might as well just put new wiring back. This wiring here, I'd say it goes back to the 1940's, 50's at best. You're long overdue for an update."

"I see. How much do you think that will cost?" He cringed inside waiting for the answer.

Tommy surveyed the rooms around them. "A place this large? You're looking at three thousand quid easy."

He watched the lad draw a sharp breath. There was something about the young man he liked, his polite nature, his acceptance of whatever Tommy said. He wasn't like a lot of young men he'd dealt with the past few years, young couples with money out to restore old properties, full of fancy, outlandish dreams they wanted at dirt cheap cost. No, Aidan seemed down to earth, facing a monumental task in a common sense way. "You know," he told Aidan, "my wife's always had a keen affection for this place. I'll cut my price down to two thousand plus change if you'll give her a tour someday when your work here is done."

Aidan's face brightened. "That would be fine. When can you start?"

"I'll start straight off. You're looking at several days to complete the job, though."

While Tommy Clancy worked, Aidan called Mr. Donoghue back. "Thanks for the recommendation. He's starting in now. I wondered, though, if you could help with one more thing."

"If I can, of course."

"The repairs will take a few days. I'm meant to be off with the band starting tomorrow and I'll need someone to keep an eye on things here. I hate to ask but . . ."

"Consider it done," Mr. Donoghue assured before Aidan could finish. "Anna and I will watch over your place."

"Thank you," Aidan responded, relieved. Then he remembered Mack's request. "Is Niall there? Can I speak with him?"

Mr. Donoghue handed the phone over, but Niall refused to take it.

"You have to speak to him." The elder Donoghue ordered.

Niall glared at his father but gave in. "Make it fast." he growled into the phone.

Aidan ignored Niall's tone. "Mack tells me you want to leave the band. Is that true?"

"Yes." One word was the best Niall could manage.

"You can't do that. We need you."

"I told Mack I'll stay on until we break for Christmas. Then I'm done."

Aidan's heart fell like a rock dropped into the lough that separated their lands. "I wish you wouldn't. We could talk things out if you'd give me a chance."

Niall shook his head, an involuntary action he knew Aidan couldn't see. "There's nothing to talk about." Then, because he wanted to hurt Aidan and could think of no other way he added, "I wish you'd never bought that house."

Angry himself, Aidan shot back, "Sometimes I wish that too!"

The day had started so well, he thought. Sun had cut through the three days of rain they'd just suffered, and he was packed and ready for a week's worth of gigs. How fast a good day can change, he though now. He'd have to drain his bank account to pay for the electric work, and his best friend wanted nothing to do with him. He gazed at the living room walls around him. Perhaps he should cut his losses now, sell up and move back to Derry. Or out to the abandoned cottage he remembered seeing by Patrick's house. Or chuck everything in and become a recluse in some hidden cove where the ocean and he could be reunited.

Aidan pictured his house and Niall's family farm, the peaceful fields dotted with Donoghue sheep, and the shining blue lough between them. He thought of the ogham stones and Timothy McCabe's story and the history that tied them all together. He remembered the feeling of family and belonging he'd experienced when he first moved into his new house, and felt fresh pain at the impasse between himself and Niall now.

After considering all of his options he called his solicitor, James Maloney and asked, "Have you had time to go over the material I sent you?"

"Yes Aidan, I have. It's quite interesting."

"The property boundaries, do you know if they're correct?"

Mr. Maloney pulled a folder out of the stack on his desk, opened it and reviewed its maps and writings again. "They are."

"And the title? Were you able to confirm anything on who owns which parcels of land?"

"I was indeed. The information you provided me is correct. It's all your land."

They talked over the implications of the discovery, the cost of refurbishing the house, and multiple options for handling it all.

"You know what I want, right?" Aidan asked after they'd debated the pros and cons of each idea. "Can you work that all out?"

Mr. Maloney nodded. "I do indeed. I should have this sorted for you before Christmas."

Niall glanced across the field to Aidan's house. It felt so odd packing the car to drive to Galway for a gig without Aidan sharing the journey. A fleeting thought flashed across his mind: he could call Aidan and try to set things right between them. He let the thought vanish as fast as it had appeared. There could be no reconciliation without protection for his family.

Mrs. Donoghue brought a thermos of hot tea and a bag of fresh biscuits out to Niall. "Here's a wee treat for you to enjoy along the way."

"Thanks Mam. Are you sure you and Da will be okay while I'm gone? The effects of his chemo seem to be easing up, but he's still pretty weak."

"Aye, son, we'll be fine. I'll make sure he gets his rest and doesn't overdo."

"I'll be glad when this chemo is done." Niall surveyed the land around him. "The sheep shouldn't give you any bother today, but if you need help you have the list of neighbors to call, right?"

"I do." Mrs. Donoghue watched her son finish loading his car. "I wish you weren't driving alone. You could always call across the way; I'm sure you could share the ride."

He saw the direction she pointed to. "No Mam. I'm only going to Galway. It's not that far; I'll be fine driving alone now I have your snack to keep me going."

As he drove away he watched the farm grow smaller and smaller in his rear view mirror until it was a mere dot and then gone. He prayed God would watch over his parents while he was away.

Fionna smoothed the front of the new dress she'd bought, hunter green to match her eyes and show off her copper-colored hair. She wondered once again if she was overdressed, wondered how many others would be dressed in jeans instead, and wished the butterflies in her stomach would take the night off. No, others might be fine with jeans; but she had a plan, she was sure the dress was the right choice. She checked her hair again, ran a brush through it for the seventh time and added a fresh touch to her makeup. Satisfied she'd done everything she could to look her best, she turned away from the mirror in the Galway bed and breakfast she had booked for the night, stepped out, hailed a cab and was soon at Monroe's, where Macready's Bridge would be playing that night.

As the Macready's Bridge boys gathered in the small backstage dressing room to prepare for their show, Mack drew Niall aside.

"I've been reading some of the social media posts we've received over the past several days. People are asking what's wrong between you and Aidan."

Niall averted his eyes from Mack to the wall behind him. "What makes them think anything's wrong?"

"You're different onstage with Aidan than you are with the others. You don't tease each other like you used to and you don't exchange any smiles with him anymore. Can you let go of whatever's bothering you for the rest of the tour and treat him like you do Michael and Pat?"

Niall felt his face burn, embarrassed that he'd been called out on this. Mack was right, he knew. He'd have to pretend everything was fine for the sake of the band. One more week, he could handle that, then he'd be through with the band and with Aidan.

"Alright Mack. I'll do what I can."

Fionna had arrived early at Monroe's and spotted an empty table in the second row just off to the left, the same side where Aidan's guitars had been placed. He would have to notice her at some point during the show. She prayed he would remember her the way she recalled him.

The band was into its fourth song when Aidan caught sight of her. He lost two beats of guitar notes, then scrambled to catch up to the others. His eyes kept returning to her though, and twice more he misplayed notes in the song.

Remembering his promise to Mack, Niall leaned over when the song was finished and whispered to Aidan, "You played that one well!"

Surprised that Niall spoke to him at all Aidan laughed and whispered back, "Wait till you see what I do with the next one."

He fought to keep control of his music throughout the rest of the show, his mind juggling memory of the notes and chords he needed to play with those of the girl seated before him now and the beach where they had first met. Patrick, Michael, Mack and Niall each noted his distraction. At the end of the show, in the small backstage dressing room, they teased him.

"Young Conor could play better than that!"

"Seamus and Kellan could play better than that!"

"We'd stand a better chance if we blindfolded you from now on!"

"I don't know who the lass is, but ten to one she's waiting for you out there." This last was from Michael and, guessing he was right, Aidan didn't know if he should rush out to see her or run in the opposite direction.

Mack glanced at his watch. "Not to rush romance or anything, but we have to leave soon. If you're going to chat with her at all you best do it now."

Fionna was still seated at the same table watching the people around her file out, looking nervous as if unsure whether she should stay or go. When Aidan stepped into the room, she smiled.

"I can't believe I've found you."

"I can't believe you're here." Aidan sat down across from her. "Where's your boyfriend tonight?"

Fionna frowned, confused. "What boyfriend?"

"The one I saw you with at Marble Arch a few weeks ago."

Stunned, Fionna asked, "You were at Marble Arch? Why didn't you stop by and say hi?"

"You looked busy that night."

Aidan looked for all the world like a jealous lover. Fionna would have laughed if she hadn't been so concerned about making a good impression. "Oh Aidan he's not my boyfriend, just a mate I've met along the way. I'm at the art school in Dublin now. He's been quite helpful to me."

"Art school?" Aidan covered her hand with his own to congratulate her. "Well done, you! Did you have to put up much of a fight?"

Fionna nodded, her copper hair shining in the pub's low lights the same way Aidan remembered it shimmering in his camper. "Aye a bit, but not as bad as I feared. And you? I didn't know you had a band going. You're quite good."

"Only quite?" Aidan feigned injury.

Fionna laughed. "Yes, quite. The more I see of you the higher my opinion might go." Then she turned serious. "I read about your family. Aidan, I'm so sorry."

"It's okay. I'm finding my way around it all."

"I'm glad." Behind Aidan, Fionna could see the rest of the band enter the room, their coats on and instrument cases in hand, and glance Aidan's way. "I think your friends are ready to leave. I don't want to hold you up."

Aidan watched Mack and the rest of the band walk towards the exit door then stop and wait. "I guess they are. We have to leave in a minute; we're headed to Kerry next."

Fionna rose. "Will I see you again?"

"Sure. We're on tour another week, then off for the holidays. Will you be going home for Christmas?"

"Yes." She slipped a piece of paper into his hand. "Here's my number. If you want, you can call me. If you don't, I understand." She didn't, but it felt like the right thing to say.

"I will call." Aidan promised. "In January. We'll see each other soon." He lingered a moment longer then heard Mack clear his throat several feet away, a signal the time clock was running. Before turning to leave Aidan hugged Fionna and kissed her cheek, then hurried to catch up with Mack and the boys.

Fionna waited several minutes, not wanting to step away and break the spell Aidan's presence had cast over her. Then she walked out into the night, called for a cab and returned to the bed and breakfast.

Mack had been tempted to stay the night in Galway, but having suffered enough mechanical breakdowns and unexpected weather over the years chose to drive straight to Kerry after their show. He and the boys arrived at the small hotel Mack had booked at one-fifteen in the morning and crept up to their rooms and into their beds with as little noise as they could manage. Before he fell asleep Mack texted Kate, knowing she would not rest until she heard from him. "Show a success," he texted. "At Kerry now. Hope you and Patrick's family are all well."

Two minutes later he received a text back from Kate, "Glad you're okay. Moira resting, twins a great help. Love staying with them. Moira will be glad when Patrick's home."

"Sleep well," Mack texted back. "Hugs. Love you."

"Love you too," Kate replied. "Xxoo."

Aidan found himself unable to sleep, still keyed up from the events of the Galway show. Despite the hour, he rang Fionna's number. "I hope I didn't wake you." He apologized when she answered. "I had to call just so you'd know I won't be forgetting you."

Fionna turned her room's light on low. "I wasn't asleep yet. I still can't believe we met again after so many months."

"I hope I can see your artwork someday."

"You will," Fionna promised. "In January when we see each other next."

"Great. I better ring off now before I wake anyone here."

"Good night Aidan." Fionna ended the call before she could add I love you, fearing that would be a terrible mistake.

Over breakfast the next morning, Patrick called Moira. "Just checking in to see how you're feeling. You're still obeying bed rest aren't you?"

"I am." Moira accepted the cup of tea Kate had brought her. "It's quite boring though. Not sure how much more of this I can take."

"You'll take all you have to, lady. Are you getting on well with Kate?"

"She's a dream, Pat. She won't let me raise a finger, does all the cooking and cleaning and the twins are crazy about her."

"I don't know what we would have done if Mack and Kate hadn't offered their help." Patrick turned to Mack across the table from him and gave him a thumb's up. "We'll have to do something nice for them when this is all through."

"We could name the babies after them." Moira suggested.

"I'm not that grateful!" Patrick teased, although the idea wasn't a bad one.

Moira laughed as well. "We'll think of something."

After their call ended Moira turned to Kate, who was washing breakfast dishes in the kitchen within earshot of Moira's sofa position where Kate had allowed her to stay during the day. "We truly are grateful. We'd have been lost without your help."

Kate dried her hands and moved to the chair opposite Moira. "You have no idea what it means to me to be here. The dress shop was getting a bit boring, and I love spending time with you and your kiddies. It seems to me we're both helping each other out."

"I hope you don't mind me taking over your bed here each day."

Kate brushed Moira's worries off. "It's your sofa not mine, and it's right where you need to be by day. Much better than being cooped up in your bedroom twenty-four seven, don't you agree?" Moira nodded. "Right then, what would you like for lunch? I've got a delicious squash soup I could make, or some individual pizzas to try."

"You do too much, Kate." Moira protested. "Why don't we just have sandwiches. They're easy to make. We could save the pizzas for dinner; the kids would love them. You need to put your feet up a bit and watch a good movie with me."

Niall was cordial to Aidan for the week that remained of their tour. During their free time he kept his distance, calling home to check on his parents, relieved that each day his father grew stronger, or spending time poking around whatever shops each town had to offer. While they worked he kept his promise to Mack and treated Aidan the same as he treated Patrick and Michael, although perhaps with less frequent teasing and chatter.

"You've all been brilliant this tour." Mack congratulated each of them after their last show. "Enjoy your Christmas, and we'll all see each other at Michael's wedding."

As they all departed each other's company, Mack drew Niall aside once more. "Thank you for staying to see us through these shows. Will you be at Michael's wedding?"

"Aye, I'll be there."

"And beyond?"

Niall tried to imagine working with anyone else. Mack had been more than a manager; he'd guided them all so well and had treated each of them with so much patience and grace. He was a friend and confidant as well as a boss. Still the two weeks had been difficult, holding his tongue when he so often wanted to lash out at Aidan, the strain of trying to keep peace between himself and Aidan for the sake of the others wearing him out. No, some things were best left behind.

"Mack, I don't think anything's changed. Let's get through the holidays and the wedding and then I'll give you my answer; but don't count on me." He thought this the easiest way he could break things off.

Mack had no choice but to agree. "Fair enough. I have to tell you, though, I'm still praying you'll have a change of heart."

Niall thought his family's farm had never looked more beautiful as he pulled into the driveway. His father must have indeed been feeling better; Niall noted how the farm had remained cleaned and well-tended in his absence, supplies stored away in their proper sheds, no foul messes littering the grounds.

"I hope that's ham dinner I'm smelling." He called out as he stepped into the kitchen.

Anna Donoghue hurried to greet him. "You're early! I didn't think you'd be home for hours yet."

"I could go back out and return later if you'd like."

"Don't you dare!" Anna hugged her son tight. "Sit yourself down; I'll call your father in for tea and you can give us all the news of your shows."

As they talked, Niall looked around the kitchen he'd grown up in and tried to not think of how much he would miss it when Aidan took over their farm. He had no idea where they'd go and hated the thought of uprooting his parents at this stage in their lives, but there was no way he'd stay here once strangers invaded their land.

That night after his parents had retired, Niall bundled his coat around him and slipped out to the patio behind his house. In back of him the outline of Aidan's grand home was visible in the half moonlight.

Aidan's bedroom light was still on. Niall thought back to the summer they'd just gone through, Aidan's time at their farm when he'd been so devastated, so lost, the fun they'd had boating and swimming in the lough between them, even the patio where he stood now which he and Aidan had helped his father set up for his mother. He recalled how excited they'd all been when Aidan had chosen to move to the house behind them. He wished now Aidan had never laid eyes on the house. Nothing he could change on that, he knew. They'd get through Christmas, the last one they'd spend on their farm. Come January he'd help his parents build a new life somewhere else.

15

"I've missed you." Pauline set a pint before Niall and set her hand over his to stop him from paying. "This one's on me. How have your shows gone?"

"Very well." Niall ignored his conscience kicking at him for lying. "I've missed you and all."

"Too bad we don't have room for a band here." Pauline wiped the bar with a clean towel as she talked. "I'd love to hear you play."

"Someday you will."

"Your friend's been invisible these past few weeks. Is he okay?"

Niall shrugged. "He's had a lot on his plate." Then he stopped. "No, that's not it. Truth is, we've had a falling out."

"I thought as much." Pauline pulled pints and poured fresh wine for other patrons then returned to Niall. "What are you going to do about it?"

"Me?" Niall cried out so loud all eyes in The Harp turned to him. He felt his face turn red hot. "I'm sorry, but why should I be the one to work things out? You don't know what Aidan's done."

Pauline sent him a flirty smile. "Because I'll love you that much more for taking the high road."

God, she had gorgeous green eyes. Unless he'd misread her signals, the light in her eyes carried an invitation as well. And she'd used the word love. A corner of Niall's heart he'd thought so frozen it would never thaw began to melt.

"Alright. I'll try, although it might take some time. Now where am I taking you during Christmas?"

Pauline's smile faded. "I'm leaving to visit my sister in Chicago tomorrow. I'll be away until after New Year."

Niall forced himself to hide his disappointment. "You'll have a grand time with her. Will you go out with me once you're back home?"

"Try and stop me!" Pauline laughed and poured him another pint.

Two days before Christmas, Aidan walked through his house and noted for the first time the absence of decorations, carols and other seasonal music filling the house, of aromas of cookies, cakes and breads emanating from the kitchen. This would be his first Christmas without his family and he hated the feel of it, emptiness overwhelming him like it overwhelmed a field with a solitary tree standing weathered and forlorn in its center. He had counted on joining Niall and his family for the holiday; now that seemed out of the question. He hoped the envelope in his hands would straighten things out. If it didn't, well, there was always Jack and Rita's invitation to join them for Christmas dinner.

He waited until he saw Niall drive away in his car, no doubt on some Christmas errand or other, then hurried over to Niall's house where he found Mr. Donoghue in the barn just as he'd hoped.

"Aidan, good to see you. We've missed you around here."

Aidan shook Mr. Donoghue's outstretched hand. "Good to see you, sir. You're looking well."

An uncomfortable expression flickered across Mr. Donoghue's face. "About the last time you were here, what Niall said, I'm sorry. Niall's mother and I don't share his anger."

"You've no need to apologize." Aidan handed the envelope he carried over to Niall's father. "Could you give Niall this? Don't tell him it's from me; just say you found it in with the mail."

"Aye, I will." Mr. Donoghue wiped his hands on his overalls then took the envelope from Aidan. "Niall's gone out for an hour or so. Would you like to come in for tea? I know our Anna would love to see you."

Aidan was tempted. The thought of Mrs. Donoghue's bread and butter or jam, and the warm company of the two people who had become a second family to him would no doubt ease the loneliness building up like a pressure cooker inside him. With his luck though, Niall would come back early, catch him on their land, and another argument would erupt. Best not to take that chance, he thought.

"I'd love to but I have a lot of things to sort out at my house after being away. I just wanted to run this over to you."

Mr. Donoghue watched the young man return to his house. The air of sadness the lad carried lingered with him until a breeze chased it away. Then he took the envelope inside and set it on the table with the rest of the mail they'd received that day.

Aidan thought while he was out he should buy a Christmas tree, or a wreath, or at the very least a string of lights or a candle to set in his window. He had no Christmas spirit though, and returned to his house, grabbed a can of stout and turned the television on, selecting a sports channel where any game going would be better than the sentimental holiday overload most channels were full of these days.

Kate placed the last ornament on the tree Mack had brought in earlier that morning, adjusted two gold bows so they hung straighter, then joined Mack on the sofa to study her finished work.

"Looks nice." Mack told her, giving her a peck on the cheek and handing her a glass of eggnog, the non-alcoholic kind she'd mixed while he was out selecting their tree. He'd mix up a batch of the good stuff later.

"You found a perfect tree." Kate tasted the eggnog, then settled into Mack's arm stretched out along the back of their sofa. "I can't believe we're celebrating Christmas together again. There's something missing though."

Mack surveyed the kitchen with its draped evergreen garland and fairy lights, the dining room graced with gold candles, red-berried holly boughs in tall gold vases and gold glass ornaments hung from the chandelier, and the living room where a huge red-bowed wreath hung on the front door and multicolored ornaments hung from grapevine strands along the top of the window drapes, fairy lights twinkled at the windows and on the tree, and stockings for Kate and himself hung empty from the mantle waiting to be filled.

"You've thought of everything." He told her. "What more could you want?"

"Children dashing about the house laughing, even fighting. Christmas is made for children." Kate caught Mack's wary look. "I'm not talking adoption right now. I was just thinking, Conor and Caitlyn would love playing with Seamus and Kellan, and Patrick and Moira won't be going to her mother's house now her mother's caught a stomach bug on top of her broken leg. Moira told me once how much she loves this house, and I know she's bored being flat on her back all day, and ..."

Mack's laughter interrupted her. "My God, woman, you do run on and on!"

Kate gave Mack's arm a playful slap. "Stop laughing and tell me what you think. Could we have them here for Christmas? We could take them back home when we go to Michael's wedding. Oh sure they've got their own tree by now, and they'll want to be spending Christmas in their own house. It was a daft idea." She sank back, dejected.

Mack smiled and shook his head. "Not a daft idea at all, my love. In fact, I think it's grand. Shall I call them or would you like to?"

Niall studied the envelope his father handed him. It was odd to receive a letter with no return address or postmark. He wasn't waiting on anything, nor were his parents or they'd have opened the envelope already. The whole thing was strange.

"Are ye going to study that envelope all evening?" Mr. Donoghue asked. "Some of us are more curious about what's inside the thing than what it looks like on the outside."

"I'll open it. You found it just stuck in with the mail, did you say?"

"I did." His father considered a lie in this case not a terrible thing. "Just sitting there it were, with your name on it and all. Now hurry and open the thing up."

Niall slit the top of the envelope with one of his mother's knives, peered inside it and withdrew a bundle of papers. The first thing he noticed was Aidan's name at the bottom of the cover page.

"It's from him across the way." Niall threw the papers down on the table, not caring what they contained. "Plans for how he's going to use our land no doubt. Or maybe our eviction notice."

"Niall!" Mrs. Donoghue's sharp tongue cut through him. "You were brought up to be kinder than that. He's got a name and you know it. And you could at least look at the papers to see what they are instead of thinking you know all the answers."

Subdued, Niall nodded. "Yes Mam. I'm sorry." He slid the papers toward him and read the top page. His eyes grew wide as he read, turning subsequent pages faster and faster, then rereading them all once more.

Stunned, he looked up at his father and mother. "It's a deed and title to our land, all in our name. He's gone and set our place back in our name. There's an agreement as well that neither Aidan nor we will advertise or give public access to the ogham stones without one another's permission."

A broad smile spread across Mr. Donoghue's face. "Isn't that something now? All these years I worried about sorting this out, and here Aidan's gone and done it for us."

Mrs. Donoghue thought back to the last time Aidan had come to their home, and how he'd been sent away in such a shameful fashion. "Niall, you best be bringing that boy over here! Right now! I'll have an extra place for dinner set by the time you get back with him. Hurry!"

Aidan was still watching sports when someone knocked on his door. Not in a social mood, he ignored the knock hoping whoever it was would leave him alone. The knocking grew louder, followed by Niall's shout, "Aidan I know you're home. Open up!"

Aidan rose, turned the television off and opened the door. "What do you want?"

"What I want is to tell you I'm a daft fool and a rubbish friend, and I don't know why you should forgive me but I'm asking you to."

"Come in." Aidan held the door open but offered no chair once Niall was inside.

"I'm sorry." Niall repeated. "I was wrong. Please forgive me."

Aidan avoided eye contact with him. "You hurt me deep. You never gave me a chance to explain."

"You're right."

"If you'd listened to the whole phone conversation or asked about it later you'd know I never had any intention to ever hurt you and your family." He turned his eyes to Niall. "I can't believe you'd think I would ever do otherwise."

Niall had no defense. "I was horrible to you."

All of the hurt and anger of the last few weeks swept over Aidan again. This time he chose to let the flood flow out, washing away with it all residue of hurt. "It's over." He told Niall. "It's all behind us. But please, don't ever do that to me again."

"I won't. Now I best get you back to my house for dinner or my mother will be running across the field to drag us home herself."

They returned to find Mrs. Donoghue had reset their table with her lace tablecloth and best dishes. She had just set her best tureen, filled with piping hot stew, on the table when Niall and Aidan entered.

She hugged Aidan tight. "I'm sorry we've let you stay away for so long. Please forgive us."

"There's nothing to forgive." He hugged her back. "It's all behind us now."

As they ate Mr. Donoghue commented, "What I don't understand is how you knew we didn't have title to the farm."

"I told you about the papers I found in the attic while I was clearing through some things," Aidan explained. "I did some research on them, and the stones corroborated what I'd found. When I learned the papers indicated I owned your land I just couldn't let that be. It didn't seem right, so I had it corrected."

He looked at each of the faces around him. "Of course I sorted this all out before Christmas for a selfish reason. I'm hoping you'll let me spend some part of Christmas with all of you. Otherwise I'm afraid it's going to be a rough day."

Mr. Donoghue spoke for them all. "You'll come right over as soon as you're up in the morning. We'll hold breakfast for you, you can stay the whole day."

Patrick pulled a ceramic holly and candle centerpiece from the box of Christmas decorations Moira had asked him to retrieve from their entryway closet and set it on their kitchen table.

"Not there." Moira directed from the sofa that had become her daytime resting place. "Put it here on the coffee table."

Patrick obeyed. Next, he lifted out the pine garland and started to drape it along the fireplace mantle as she did every year.

"Not like that Patrick," she corrected. "You've got it all uneven and twisted."

He looked where she pointed. It wasn't twisted. Uneven maybe, but he had been going to correct that without her telling him to. He sighed under his breath, turned his back to her so she wouldn't see his impatience, and straightened the garland so she'd be happy.

"Could you set the candles in the windows next?" Moira asked.

Patrick gathered the candlesticks and holders from the box and started to place one in each window of their house.

"No, Pat! You're doing it wrong. Fix each of the holders with ribbon, the way I always do, then add the candle, then place them in the windows, and make sure they're centered. You've got them all over the place!"

Patrick collected the candles he'd set out so far, threw all of the candles and holders in the box and dropped down onto the chair by the fireplace. "Do it yourself woman, or let me do it my way."

"You know I can't do it."

"Then leave me to it. For God's sake Moira, nothing about this Christmas is normal. Will it matter where the flaming candles are, or if the garland's crooked or where I place the flaming centerpiece?"

Patrick almost never lost his patience like that. Angry at herself for being so critical of his attempts to help, Moira held her tongue until, a minute later, Patrick apologized.

"It's not your fault." She responded. "I know I'm a right pain these days. I'm just so frustrated. I hate being stuck on the sofa all day. I haven't done any Christmas baking and I've no idea how I'll manage Christmas dinner. Oh Pat, I'm a terrible wife and mother!" With that she burst into tears.

"You're not a terrible anything." Patrick rose to comfort her, but the phone rang just then. He hesitated, not sure which needed his attention first.

"Go on, answer it. I'm okay."

Patrick hesitated another second then picked his phone up. "Hello?"

"Pat, it's Mack. Kate and I were doing a bit of decorating around our house and we just wondered how you were all getting on. I suppose with your kids there you've got your tree up already?"

"No, as a matter of fact we don't. Moira and I were just talking about that."

"Good. Kate and I were wondering if you'd like to come spend Christmas with us."

"Oh Mack, I don't know. Four of us invading your peaceful home, you wouldn't know what hit you."

"We'd enjoy it." Mack assured him. "Kate would love having your twins around, and with Moira laid up my guess is you won't be having much of a Christmas dinner."

Patrick protested, "I was going to make them my special tuna crisp sandwiches."

"So Kate's Christmas turkey can't tempt you?"

"Not even close!"

Mack had to laugh as he pictured Patrick serving sandwiches on disposable plates to his family. "Pat, I'm sure Conor and Caitlyn would be happy with anything you served them. Still they'd have fun here with Kate and our dogs, and my guess is you and Moira could use a break. I could pick you up when the kids are home from school, and bring you back home when we drive down for Michael's wedding."

"Hold on a minute, Mack. Let me talk to Moira." Pat covered the phone with his hand and turned to her.

"I heard." Moira told him before he could say a word. "I don't know, what do you think?"

"It would give you a change of scenery, and you did say you loved Kate's company."

"We'd be such a burden on them though, or at least I would be."

"You'd be no burden at all. I think we should accept."

Moira glanced at the sparse decorations they'd just now started to put up and the bare kitchen with no baked goods on the counters. Not much fun for the kids, she thought. "I agree."

In the end Aidan decided to join Niall and his family for Christmas Eve Mass, then spend the night at their house. "Sure you could stay at yours," Mrs. Donoghue noted, "but there's not much fun in waking up all alone Christmas morning and we'd love to have you here."

She was right. The thought of an empty house at Christmas, this Christmas, was too painful. During Mass Aidan thought of all the Christmas Eves he'd spent with his family. Time for new traditions, he realized and pushed memories away, although they lingered on the periphery of his mind. After Mass they sat around the fire in the Donoghue's living room, he and Niall playing carols on guitar and pipes, Mrs. Donoghue singing along while Mr. Donoghue rested in the recliner. Aidan tried to forget all the times he and his father played their guitars at Christmas while his granny and Jeannie sang along.

After a half dozen songs Aidan stood, stretched and stated, "That's me done for the night.

Niall, wake me up when you're ready to see what Father Christmas brought!"

Upstairs, Aidan gazed out the Donoghue's guest room window to the farm on which their house sat. Peaceful in the dark of night, few shadows showing in the weak moonlight, Aidan thought of the papers he'd had drawn up releasing the land back to them the way he'd wanted, the way it always should have been. No doubt about it, he'd made the right decision. He could not have stood seeing another family in this house or on this land, nor a steady stream of strangers disturbing this haven.

In the distance his own house stood, a dim block of dark against the night sky. His heart danced with excitement as it always did when he thought of the plans he had for the place he now called home; tonight though, he was glad to be here in the guest room where he'd first started his recovery after the loss of his family. As he slipped into bed and drew the familiar warm blankets around him, he whispered "Happy Christmas" to his father, his sister and grandmother, and even his mother with whom they now dwelt.

Mr. Donoghue rose from his recliner and drew his wife to her feet. "Anna, time for bed for us both." He hugged Niall, who was packing his pipes away in their cases. "Goodnight, son."

"Night, Da." He stopped his mother from heading to the kitchen and took the cups, saucers and plates she carried away from her. "Go on, Mam. I'll take care of these."

Mrs. Donoghue resisted, but Niall held firm. "I've got the kitchen, it's part of my Christmas present to you. You can have it back in the morning."

He listened as his parents climbed the stairs a little slower than they used to. A few minutes later he heard their bed creak as they settled in for the night.

He washed their few dishes and set them in the rack to dry, then sat in his father's recliner and watched the last of the fire's embers die down. The house settled around him, odd creaks here and there, noises as familiar to him as his own deep breaths. He thought how close they'd come to losing the only home he had known, the farm he'd always planned to work with his father and someday with his own son. What a lesson he'd learned, jumping to conclusions over the phone call he'd overheard. How much energy he'd wasted on anger towards his best friend, when the whole mix up could have been resolved if he'd given Aidan a chance to explain. He hoped he'd remember the lesson the rest of his life.

"Aunt Kate, can we take the dogs outside to play again?"

Kate smiled and nodded, "Yes Caitlyn, you and Conor can go play with them, just remember what Uncle Mack said about staying close to the house." She watched them dash outside, rust red fur flying after blue coats and black boots, a mixture of barking and cheering ringing through the air, then turned to Moira seated in the cushioned chair Mack had moved into the archway between the dining room and kitchen.

"Are you sure you and Patrick don't mind them calling us aunt and uncle?"

"I love it, truth be told." Moira shifted in her chair, trying to find a comfortable position, which was becoming harder and harder to do. "The twins don't have any aunts or uncles nearby, only Patrick's brother and his wife and they're down in Australia."

"I'm so glad you and your family joined us for Christmas. You've made Mack's and my holiday that much more special."

"Kate, I don't know how we would have managed if you and Mack hadn't called."

"Moira, I know you would have given those two a lovely Christmas without us."

"They would have had no Christmas sweets." Moira turned serious. "I'm so sorry they broke your mother's mixing bowl. We'll find something special to replace it."

"You'll do no such thing." Kate placed a hand on Moira's arm. "It was an old dish. I've got plenty of others. I'll cherish the memory of the fun we had baking far more than I'll ever miss what we lost in the process."

In the living room, Patrick and Mack played backgammon in front of a crackling fire. After suffering his fourth loss in a row, Patrick threw his hands up. "Damn! That's some tough strategy you've got."

"Do you give up?"

"Never! Set the board up again."

Mack stacked black and white chips in alternating rows on the backgammon board between them. "Kate's rubbish at this game. I'm glad to have someone to challenge me."

Patrick leaned back in his chair, watched Moira and Kate chat in the dining room and peered out the window to his children playing with Mack's dogs. "I can't tell you how grateful I am for your invitation to spend Christmas here."

"It's been our pleasure. Kate loved having your kids help her with dinner today."

"That was a delicious dinner. Much better than my tuna crisp sandwiches would have been. It's been wonderful for Moira to have Kate to talk to as well, and Conor and Caitlyn adore your dogs. We can't have a dog at our house, at least not right now."

"How are you going to manage two more children in your wee cottage?" Mack wondered, then added, "If you don't mind me asking."

"At the start the babies will sleep in our room. We may have to move Conor into Caitlyn's room at some point; we should be able to set bunk beds up there, then the babies will have Conor's room. That should get us through the first year or two anyway." Patrick grinned, "Unless you and Kate want to trade houses with us!"

Mack pointed to the backgammon board, set and waiting for action. "Beat me three games in a row and we'll discuss it!"

16

Susannah woke at four-thirty in the morning and could not fall back to sleep. At five o'clock she gave up trying and slipped out of bed, careful not to wake Michael. She tiptoed out to the living room, powered up her laptop and opened the file named "wedding".

All of the details had been listed, checked and rechecked. The guest list, abbreviated by finances and by the last minute change in their dates, had been matched to her seating chart for the tables at their reception. Her clothes had been packed and she'd supervised Michael's packing as well. She'd printed a map to Markree Castle along with their reservation details and guest list and placed them in a folder, which she now double checked to confirm she had placed in her suitcase.

Satisfied she'd done everything she could to ensure their wedding would be perfect, Susannah leaned back in her chair and thought of the one detail she could not control.

Neither she nor Michael had heard anything from their parents. Not since she'd called and left messages for each of them with the date they'd been able to book at Markree. Not for Christmas Eve or Christmas Day. She'd been tempted to call each of them again, but Michael had held her back.

"They've gotten your messages and they know what holiday this is. If they can't be bothered to pick up the phone, just let them go."

He'd been right, of course. Still, all through Christmas she'd thought of her parents, missed their traditional Christmas Eve banquet and the champagne and orange juice start to the morning after, missed reminiscing with her mother over Christmases past and missed her father's egg and bacon breakfast, the one meal of the year when he took over the kitchen. She wondered what traditions Michael's family followed, and imagined the traditions she and Michael and their family would someday build.

Too early to call her father now, and knowing Michael would be angry if she did, Susannah held the dream of her father walking her down the aisle and of their wedding dance together a moment longer, then packed the dream away in her mind and turned back to the photos of Markree Castle she had saved on her desktop. Some of her dreams had been sacrificed but Markree was a fairy tale place of its own, and at the end of the day she would be Mrs. Michael Sullivan.

Moira had slept very little and could not get comfortable in Mack and Kate's car as they drove her and her family home. She headed straight for the sofa while Patrick and their kids carried overnight bags and Christmas presents into the house.

"Are you sorry you're missing Michael's wedding?" She asked Patrick after Mack and Kate had left.

Patrick gazed at her as if she were the most beautiful woman in the world, so far from what she felt in her huge, clumsy condition. "Not for a moment. I can see their pictures any time. I'm not going anywhere without you right now."

An hour later, shooting pains arced across her stomach. Moira broke out in a sweat, called for Patrick, looked around the house when he didn't answer and realized he was outside playing tag with their twins. She struggled to stand, bending over when the next round of pain hit, and called out louder, "Pat! Hurry! Come here!"

This time Patrick heard her and ran in to find her clutching a kitchen chair, panic etched across her face.

"They're coming, Pat!" Tears rose in Moira's eyes and spilled down her cheeks. "They're too early! I don't know what to do!"

Patrick took charge just as Moira had known he would. "Here." He pulled a kitchen chair out for her. "Sit down, just for a minute. It will all be okay."

With no time to call in help from any of their neighbors or friends, Patrick had no choice in what Conor and Caitlyn would need to do. He called them in, both children running at the urgency in his voice. He sat them on the sofa and forced assurance into his voice. "I need you both to help your mum and me. Your mother's going to have the babies, isn't that grand? I'm going to take her to the hospital right now. I need you both to stay here. You can watch television and make yourselves sandwiches for tea. I'll call you in just a while to let you know how things are going. Will you both be on your best behavior and not get into any fights while we're gone?"

Wide-eyed, Caitlyn asked, "Is our mum going to be okay?"

Conor, trying to fill the role of man of the house, nodded. "Yes Da, we'll be good. We promise."

"Lock the door behind me and keep it locked. And don't worry, your mum will be fine and soon you'll have brothers or sisters to help her look after."

Michael wondered how he was able to drive so straight on narrow winding roads given the nerves that ran roughshod over him, flipping his stomach in huge somersaults and causing his hands to shake whenever he pulled them away from the steering wheel. This was it! He was about to marry the most beautiful woman in the world. He still had no clue why Susannah had chosen him over the dozen or so handsome, wealthy, upward-driven men she'd dated before him. He only hoped he could make her happy, that she wouldn't regret her choice in the years to come.

At the end of the small lane he pulled their car onto, Markree Castle rose, an imposing grey stone structure both grand and mysterious. Susannah squealed with delight when she saw it. He hoped they hadn't entered some Alfred Hitchcock style alter-world.

His concern evaporated as they walked up Markree's entryway, its gleaming white vaulted ceiling, walls and stone steps ushering them into a world of elegance far exceeding anything Markree's photos had promised. The stairway brought them up to a formal reception area with massive stone fireplace, carved wood staircase and magnificent stained glass window depicting the family tree of the Cooper family, the castle's original owners.

Susannah's eyes sparkled with delight. "It's even more grand than I dreamed! Michael, I believe I have indeed stepped into a fairy tale world."

The receptionist checked them in, then pointed to a lounge area beyond double doors. "You have some guests waiting for you."

They followed where she had pointed. At the end of the next hall, to the left, sitting in chairs next to tall, red draped windows, sat Michael's parents.

Stunned, Michael stared from his father to his mother, and back to his father. "What are you doing here?"

"I'm sure you didn't mean that the way it sounds." Susannah spoke with a nervous laugh. "They're here for our wedding."

"She's right." Mr. Sullivan pulled a chair out for Susannah. "Here, sit down, both of you."

Wary of what his father might be up to, Michael sat across from him.

"I know I've surprised you," Mr. Sullivan started. "I should have told you earlier we would be here. I also know you and I haven't agreed on many things."

Michael held his tongue. He would not argue, not on this most special day.

Mr. Sullivan continued. "I still can't say I agree with your career choice, but Michael, I do have to say I'm impressed by your independence and resolve to carve out your own path through this world. Your mother reminded me you're a lot like me in that regard." Mr. Sullivan paused and smiled at his wife, such an uncharacteristic movement Michael was glad he was sitting down for fear of falling over from shock.

"I have one son." Mr. Sullivan finished. "I hope you'll only be married the once. I don't want to regret years from now that I missed this."

Michael recovered his voice at last. "Thank you Dad. I'm glad, we're glad you're here."

Michael was given a temporary alcove room to prepare in, while Susannah had full use of the luxurious bridal suite. With Diane's assistance she dressed, reapplied her makeup, and touched up her hair with a curling iron. Checking her image in the room's full length mirror she asked Diane, "Is it okay? Did I make the right choice on my dress? I should wear my hair different, shouldn't I? An upsweep? Do I have time for that?"

"Stop panicking." Diane told her. "You're driving yourself 'round the bend. You look lovely."

Susannah searched for truth in her friend's eyes. "Honest?"

Diane smiled, reached out to adjust a corner of Susannah's veil, and stepped back. "Honest. You look brilliant."

A knock on the door interrupted them. Susannah rushed into the bathroom. "If that's Michael, tell him he can't see me yet!"

"I'm sorry we're late." Mr. Tierney apologized as Diane opened the door. "We missed the last couple of turns."

Susannah stepped out from her hiding place, disbelief written across her face.

Her mother eyed her head to toe. "Susannah my dear, you look beautiful."

"Be right back. I have to check on the flowers." Diane excused herself, allowing Susannah and her parents some private time.

Susannah stared at them both, not quite sure whether they were a figment of her imagination. "Dad, I thought you said you wouldn't be here."

"I did." Mr. Tierney admitted as he stepped inside and closed the door behind them. "I was wrong. Your Michael helped me see that."

Susannah gave her parents a blank look. "Michael did?"

"Yes. He had a talk with me, helped me see things in a different light. He's a wise one, your Michael. You'd do best to keep him."

Susannah hugged her father and mother. "I plan to. Now you're both here, my day will be perfect."

Michael stood at the front of the small chapel to the side of Markree's grand entranceway and watched people file in and take the seats Niall and Aidan ushered them to. He admired how Susannah's choice of simple altar flowers of white chrysanthemums and lilies, offset by red bows that matched the red bows adorning the end of each pew, lent an air of classic elegance to the chapel. Mack stepped up to Michael, informed him Patrick was on his way to the hospital with Moira, then stood in the best man position next to Michael. Michael nodded twice to his parents seated in the front row, still stunned but pleased by their unexpected presence.

When the harpist who sat in a corner of the chapel started playing the traditional wedding song, Michael joined the rest of the guests in looking towards the chapel's entryway. Susannah stood there in elegant white with a red rose bouquet mirroring the colors of the chapel's decorations. Her slim satin dress accentuated her trim figure, while the seed pearls and sequins scattered across the neckline, sleeves and hemline of her dress reflected light in every direction. Two things above these caught Michael's eyes, though. One was the gentleman on Susannah's arm; Michael was elated to see her father had made it to his daughter's wedding after all. The other was the bright light in Susannah's green eyes, radiating every hope and joy she had for the future she and Michael were about to embark on. Susannah locked eyes with Michael. He almost forgot the nerves that had consumed him all day as he held her gaze while she walked up the aisle to join him.

Patrick sped to the hospital, focusing on the road as best he could while at the same time feeling every pain that doubled Moira over and hearing every panicked cry she could not stifle. Praying all the way, Patrick almost collapsed with relief as they reached the hospital.

The registration attendant rushed them through the admission process and soon they were in the examination room. Nurses and assistants measured blood pressure, heart rate, space of time between contractions, and checked the babies' positions before confirming what he and Moira already knew: labor had started, the babies would be three months premature.

"This is it!" He squeezed Moira's hand and gave her a reassuring smile. "Today we'll get to meet our new wee babies." He kept up a steady line of chatter aimed at encouraging her, all while he was terrified inside. Three months early; what problems would they run into? What if the babies weren't healthy? Dear God, we've done the best we could. Please let everything be okay.

He entered the delivery room with Moira and was relieved to see Dr. McAfee had arrived in time. He kept one eye on Moira and the other on the doctor and nurses as they draped sheets over Moira's abdomen and legs, positioned her for the birth of their twins and set instruments out to perform the deliveries. He tried to ignore the monitors beeping around him and the concerned looks on the doctor's and nurses' faces.

"Remember how nervous we were when Conor and Caitlyn were born?" Patrick spoke in a quiet tone, forcing Moira to concentrate on him instead of the bustling around them and the pains that indicated the babies' appearances were imminent. Moira managed a smile and nod in response. "Look at them now," Patrick continued. "Look how grand they are. You'll be just as grand a mum to our new babies."

A sudden sharper pain tore through Moira's abdomen, she turned white as the sheets that covered her body, the monitors surrounding them screamed in rapid succession and Patrick was forced out of the room.

"I'm sorry, Mr. Leahy." The guiding attendant apologized. "We need to have you wait out here. I'm sure everything will be fine. We'll let you know as soon as we can."

"It's all over now for you." Aidan teased Michael, lifting a glass of champagne in celebration. "You're an old married man! No more fun to be had."

Michael laughed and glanced over to Susannah, chatting on the other side of the dining room Markree Castle had set their reception in. "Aidan, you have no idea. The fun is just starting."

"Pretty soon you'll be changing nappies and burping babies." Niall joined in their fun. "Hey, I wonder how Patrick's getting on. Maybe he'll have new babies the same day you're married. Now that would be a celebration!"

Aidan nodded towards Michael's parents conversing with Susannah's at a table nearby and remembered the conversation he and Michael had exchanged on the boat that summer. "Looks like there's been a break in the impasse between you and your father. Well done, my friend."

Michael remembered the conversation as well. "It's a start."

Mr. Tierney joined them then. "I'm sorry for the interruption. Michael, if we could, your parents and Susannah's mother and I would like to talk with you both."

"Of course." He agreed, shoving aside his sudden fear that their perfect day was about to be ruined. He made his way over to where Susannah was chatting and led her back to the table where their parents sat.

Mr. Tierney started, "First, we all want to congratulate you both on a lovely wedding. I know we haven't made it easy for you and we're sorry for that. You've both proved to all of us though that you're ready to take on married life, and someday children as well." He turned to his daughter. "I don't think I've ever been more proud of you than I am right now."

Before Susannah could respond, Mr. Sullivan spoke. "Michael, we know you and your lovely bride had to cancel your honeymoon. The Tierneys and your mother and I have something for you we hope will make up for that."

Michael stared a moment at the letter sized box he'd been handed, then gave it over to Susannah. "Here, you can open it."

Susannah slid the white embossed paper open and withdrew a small silver box, with a piece of paper and a photo inside. The photo showed a thatched-roofed, open-aired cottage surrounded by palm trees, a pristine beach and turquoise waters. She read to Michael the words on the note attached to the photo, "We hope you enjoy your honeymoon. Love, your parents."

"Look under the photo." Mr. Tierney instructed. Michael lifted the picture and found airline tickets and money. "Your flight leaves at noon tomorrow." Mr. Tierney explained. "You won't have much time to pack; the money is for you to buy whatever you need once you reach Bimini."

Patrick tried to pray while he waited in the hospital anteroom but found praying hard, his mind and heart consumed with fears for Moira and the twins being delivered behind the door that separated them. It seemed an eternity had passed before the door opened and Dr. McAfee stepped out.

"Patrick, I'm sorry we had to make you leave. In the midst of a hard delivery we find it best to get our new fathers out of the way."

"Never mind that. Moira, is she okay? And the babies? Are they alright?"

In the space of the few seconds Dr. McAfee hesitated before answering, Patrick's heart fell to the floor. "Moira's had a hard time of it. The pain she felt was internal hemorrhaging. She's lot a lot of blood. I have every faith she'll recover, but I'm afraid we'll have to keep her here a few days."

"She will be okay though?" Patrick begged a clearer answer.

Dr. McAfee nodded. "Aye, she will."

"The babies." Patrick demanded. "Tell me about our babies."

"You have a new daughter and son. Ten fingers and ten toes on each."

Patrick sensed Dr. McAfee withheld something. "What aren't you telling me?"

"You know they're premature. Their lungs are not fully developed yet, and their wee hearts aren't at full scale. I'm sure they'll be fine," she hurried to add, reading the fear spread across Patrick's face. "We will need to keep them here a while though, in our preemie unit, to make sure they're healthy."

Patrick let the doctor's words sink in. "When can I see my wife and my babies?"

"Give me a couple of minutes to clean up. I'll escort you myself."

17

Patrick held Moira's hand and watched her sleep, her steady breaths rising and falling like silent, visible heartbeats. She looked better, he thought. Maybe tomorrow she could come home.

Moira stirred, her eyes flickered open, closed again, then reopened. She saw Patrick seated beside her hospital bed and smiled. "How long have I slept this time?"

"Since three o'clock. It's eight at night now."

"I'm so sorry. Not much company for you these days, am I?"

Patrick smoothed back the stray hairs that had fallen across her forehead. "You're fine. You've been through a lot; you need your sleep."

"How are the babies? When did you see them last?"

"Two hours ago."

"Oh Pat, how hard for you to have to split your time between my room and theirs. Not the way we wanted any of this to go, is it?" Tears rose in Moira's eyes, a combination of fear, tiredness and regret that her husband had to bear the brunt of things alone.

Patrick hugged her. "Now don't you be crying. I'm fine, and if you're a good girl I'll give you a ride over to see our babies yourself."

In the room where premature babies were cared for, Patrick and Moira hovered over two cribs, one holding a girl and one a boy, each of them sleeping, the boy with fists closed tight, the girl with fingers relaxed, spread over the blanket that covered her.

"They're so small." Moira whispered, afraid to wake them up. "Why are there tubes in their noses?"

"Remember we told you that yesterday? It's oxygen, helping them breathe until their lungs are a wee bit stronger."

"They will get stronger though, right? They'll be okay?"

"Yes love, they will. Soon they'll be home and you'll not be getting a minute's rest."

Moira watched them sleep, eyes closed to the world, both babies looking so peaceful, so sweet. "I know what names I want for them. Would you like to hear?"

"You bet. I'm getting tired of calling them Baby Boy and Baby Girl!"

"Eamon and Eileen." She watched for Patrick's reaction. "Do you like those names?"

"I do." Patrick tested the names over each baby's crib; they fit, they felt and sounded right. "They're perfect names. What made you think of them?"

"Eamon is Mack's middle name, Eileen is Kate's. They've done so much for us Pat, having us over for Christmas, staying with Conor and Caitlyn now while we're here. I wanted to do something special to let them know how much we appreciate all they've done. Is that okay?"

Patrick placed an arm around Moira's shoulders. "Moira, it's more than okay. Mack and Kate will be so pleased."

They said good night to the babies and the nurses attending them, and returned to Moira's room. After she was settled in bed Patrick pulled a surprise out of his coat pocket, a small champagne bottle and two plastic cups.

Moira teased, "Thinking of getting me drunk and having your way with me?"

Patrick returned her laughter. "It wouldn't take more than this, would it? No, it's New Year's Eve, or have you forgotten?"

"With all that's gone on, yes I did. I'm so glad you remembered."

"Aunt Kate, can we make a welcome home sign for our mum? She's still coming home tomorrow isn't she?"

Kate saw the hint of worry behind Conor's enthusiasm. "We hope so, Conor. Your father will know by morning."

"But not the babies yet, right?" Caitlyn turned downcast eyes Kate's way.

Kate rubbed the back of Caitlyn's head. "No they won't be home tomorrow, but soon. I think the sign for your mother's a wonderful idea. Maybe Uncle Mack can help you find paper for it while I finish preparing dinner."

Mack located a pad of paper and a roll of tape. He drew big hollow letters on separate pages which Conor and Caitlyn colored in. After dinner, while Kate washed and dried dishes, he helped them tape the pieces of paper together to form a big, bright banner. They found balloons and string in a drawer which he promised to help them blow up in the morning.

"We should have got flowers." Caitlyn announced, crestfallen. "Our mum loves flowers."

"Your father's already bought her a big bouquet." Mack reminded her; yet his heart softened. He had to make her feel better. "We can go to market tomorrow though, if you'd like, and buy her some more."

"Thanks Uncle Mack." Caitlyn hugged him, then bounded down the hall for the bubble bath Kate had run for her.

After Conor's bath they all played one more game of cards and had ice cream sundaes as a special treat.

"Do you have to go?" Caitlyn asked as Kate tucked her into bed.

Kate sat on the edge of the little girl's bed. "Yes, dear, once your mum is home Uncle Mack and I will have to get back to Seamus and Kellan. Our neighbors have been watching them, remember?"

Caitlyn nodded. "Can I come play with them sometime?"

"Of course you can. Now, you close your eyes and dream sweet dreams about your new brother and sister, okay?"

Mack saw Conor tucked into bed then reminded him, "When your mum comes home you'll have to help her out a bit. She'll still need a few days of resting. Will you do that for your dad and for me?"

Conor gave a solemn nod. "Yes, Uncle Mack. She will be okay though, won't she?"

Mack read the boy's worries. "She will indeed. You'll help out when your new brother and sister come home as well, won't you?"

"Yes. Daddy and I talked about that. I might have to share my room with Caitlyn when the babies come home."

"Will you be okay with that? You won't fight with Caitlyn will you?"

Conor shook his head. "No, I promise I'll be good."

Mack rustled the boy's head, then reached over to turn his bedside lamp off. "You're a good lad Conor. Sleep well."

"Goodnight Uncle Mack." The boy called after him as he stepped into the hall.

On the coffee table in front of the sofa Kate had laid out cheese and crackers, two glasses and a bottle of champagne. Mack looked at her, puzzled.

"New Year's Eve," she reminded him.

"Good heavens, Kate! Clear out of my mind it's gone."

"Good thing I remembered then."

Mack poured a glass of champagne for each of them, then they snuggled in front of the fire, both of them tired in a contented way. The quiet cottage and quiet countryside left them each alone with their thoughts. After a long stretch of silence Kate asked, "Do you think Pat and Moira will be able to cope with such a large family in this tiny cottage?"

"They'll make do." Mack assured her. "He's very capable at providing whatever his family needs."

"What about when you go out on tour in the spring?" Kate wondered. "How will Moira handle all four kiddies alone?"

Mack knew Moira's mother could be called on and had no doubt other help existed, but sensed Kate had some idea brewing on her mind. "What would you suggest?"

Kate felt Mack's arm around her, strong and secure. She prayed it would stay there when she revealed her plan.

"They could always move in with us."

Mack withdrew his arm, sat up and stared at her. "What?"

Kate sat up as well. "Think about it. We have more than enough room. The kids could go to school by us, and there's a hospital close by in Derry if the babies needed anything. When you and Pat are away, I could be there to help Moira with the children."

Mack considered her plan. "What if we don't all get along? A visit over the holidays is one thing, two families sharing a house quite another."

"We could convert your barn into a love nest for us and let them have the big house. They could rent out their cottage here and build a bit of savings up for their future, or come here on vacations when they want a break from us. Oh Mack, please say yes. It's such a grand idea."

"They might not want it, or haven't you thought of that?" Mack pointed out. "Patrick's quite independent. He will want to take care of his family."

"Can we at least make the offer to them?"

Mack recalled again Kate's desire for children. He'd seen first-hand how much Conor and Caitlyn enjoyed her and how well she and Moira got on. It would be an adjustment, no doubt; yet when he thought on it Kate's idea wasn't half bad. He poured fresh champagne for them both, sat back on the sofa and motioned for her to join him. As the clock struck twelve and a new year rolled in, he thought how wonderful it was to have Kate back in his life. He would pursue any idea she had if it made her happy.

Michael watched Susannah dress and style her hair. New Year's Eve on Bimini, they were lucky to reserve a table for dinner. After that they would join other beach goers seeing the new year in with champagne under the stars.

"I still can't believe our parents set this honeymoon up for us."

Susannah checked her makeup in the bathroom mirror. "I had no idea you had gone to talk with my father. What did you say to convince him to be at our wedding?"

"I pointed out he had one daughter and he didn't want to miss out on her one special day."

She turned the bathroom light off and joined Michael in the bedroom. A soft breeze stirred the gauze curtains at the window; outside, the ocean's hushed waves rolled in to shore and back out in steady succession.

"Michael, can you believe it? We're married at last and starting the new year together. I don't know when I've ever been happier."

"Me either." He agreed and kissed her. She kissed him back, their passion grew hotter, and soon they were making love on the bed's satin sheets, their dinner reservation forgotten.

Niall celebrated New Year's Eve with his parents with the same traditions they'd followed as long as he could remember. Next year, with any luck, he'd be celebrating with Pauline. The day after tomorrow she'd return from her holidays, and he had already formulated several ideas of how to deepen their relationship.

Tonight though belonged to his parents, to shrimp cocktail appetizers, steaks cooked over the grill, his mother's cheesy potatoes and the gingerbread she'd prepared for after. They would play cards and drink brandy, the one night in the year his father and mother allowed themselves to ignore limits and risk intoxication. Classic hits would play on the radio in the background; at midnight his father and mother would dance to Frank Sinatra, then they'd all go to bed and in the morning another year would start.

Tonight, as they danced, he imagined dancing with Pauline, imagined the traditions they would someday build of their own. He wondered if she liked Frank Sinatra or who she would rather dance to. He wondered if she would mind living in a cottage he would build on his father's land, if his father would allow it. Always his favorite night of the year to dream and build new plans for the future, Niall settled in bed with his mind swirling with visions of Pauline, and dinners and dances, and moonlight drives down quiet country roads.

Aidan watched moonlight reflect off the lough in back of his house. Hard to believe another year was over, he thought. This year, more than any other, had brought so much change to his life. He remembered other New Year's Eves when he and his father would play music and sing songs with whatever friends stopped by, when his grandmother would lay out a spread of ham and turkey slices, vegetables and fruits, breads, pastries and cakes, and everyone who stopped by would fill a plate and share in the celebration. Jeannie would have a few friends stay over; in the morning they would all have sore heads, save his granny who would cook a quiet breakfast and tiptoe around the house until noon.

There would be no sore heads tomorrow for him; yet he wasn't as sad as he thought he would be. The year was almost behind him. Macready's Bridge had a new album coming out, they would tour again and continue to find new ways to build their following. He had plans for the house he'd moved into; he would finish plaster repairs and painting walls, and one step at a time would restore the old estate home into a place of grandeur. He would furnish his home studio with the best equipment he could afford, and someday Roisin Studios would thrive.

As he looked out at the carriage house turned studio, a familiar figure appeared. Aidan grabbed his father's coat and dashed out.

"Best of the season to ye, young Aidan!" Timothy McCabe called out. "Sure it's a grand time of year."

"To you as well." Aidan replied, not sure if it was appropriate to wish a ghost a good holiday but afraid to not do so.

"You've been gone these past weeks."

"We were on tour, then I was busy with Christmas celebrations."

Timothy nodded. "I see you and your friend have sorted your problems out."

"We have." Aidan confirmed, not quite sure how Timothy knew. "How did you know they didn't have title to their land, that I held the keys to getting that sorted?"

"I told you lad, I've watched over this land all these long years." Timothy fell silent a moment, surveying Niall's farm and Aidan's property, an air of resignation tinged with sadness surrounding him. "Now it's all sorted, I'll be moving on."

"What do you mean moving on?" Aidan asked, all of a sudden afraid. "Where will you go?"

"I've done what I came here to do. I worked other farms as well, you know. It's time I moved on to the next place; they have even bigger problems to sort out."

"Will I ever see you again?"

Timothy shook his head. "No young Aidan, but any time you hear wind chimes and no breeze to move them, you'll know I'm around keeping an eye out to make sure you're alright."

Timothy McCabe's form faded from view by degrees, growing fainter and fainter until he had mixed with and disappeared into the stars. Aidan stood by the carriage house several long minutes wondering if Timothy would return. When he didn't, and when a chill started to settle in his bones despite the jacket he wore, Aidan stepped back into his house.

The ogham stone pictures caught his eye from the kitchen table where he'd last left them. He glanced through the kitchen window to the farm behind him, glad all the turmoil between himself and Niall had been settled. Catching sight of Niall's light still on, an idea struck him. He picked up his phone.

"Niall, grab your coat and meet me out back."

"It's past midnight. What do you want?"

"You'll see. Dress warm."

Aidan searched his refrigerator and found the bottle of champagne he'd tucked into it months ago when he'd first moved into the house. He grabbed that and two coffee mugs, slipped his coat on and met Niall out by the lough between their houses.

"Couldn't this wait until morning?" Niall asked, wondering what could be so important it had to be taken care of right now.

"No." Aidan produced the champagne. "I remembered, we haven't celebrated your title being resolved."

"We did that at dinner a few nights ago, didn't we?"

"Not proper, not with champagne."

"Ye daft fool!" Niall laughed. "Alright then, let's crack open that bottle."

Aidan poured the bubbly liquid into coffee mugs, handed one to Niall and walked over to the rowboat, now turned over and resting upside down for winter. "Here, have a seat."

"Dear Jaysus, I've a crazy neighbor on my hands!" Niall joked. "I think my family and I should move after all."

"You'll do no such thing. You're tied to that land over there." Aidan raised his mug in a toast. "Here's to home, and family and friends, and all that matters in this world."

Niall raised his mug to join Aidan's, then leaned back against the boat. "Look how clear the stars are tonight."

"Indeed. Did you pick one to wish upon?"

"Aye." They were silent a minute, then Niall asked, "What did you wish for?"

"Fionna."

"The girl at the show in Galway? Is she the same one you met at the beach?"

"She is. I have her number; I'll call her tomorrow."

"She's a stunner," Niall had to admit, "but her smile's nowhere near as bright as Pauline's."

"I hear you've struck up quite a friendship with her. Think you'll be up to The Harp as often as I may be going to Dublin?"

"Could be."

Aidan refilled their coffee mugs. "Maybe next year the four of us will be drinking champagne out by our lough."

"Only if it's a bit warmer. I can't imagine Pauline and Fionna dressed to the nines, out here freezing to death!"

"What can you imagine?" Aidan asked.

Niall thought a while then told him, "Pauline and myself, you and Fionna, raising families side by side, as giddy with love as Michael and Susannah are, as settled as Mack and Kate, as full of laughter and love as Patrick and Moira and their brood are, as secure as my dad and mam are."

Aidan let the image settle around them both, then drained the bottle into their mugs and raised one last toast. "To the future, and good friends to share it with."

Acknowledgements

In writing this book, I am once again thankful to Ann Crisafulli for her editing work, and to Beth Bales Ostrowski for her brilliant artwork in Crossing The Lough Between's cover. Larry Meister's assistance with a number of computer and technical issues that arose as I worked on this book was invaluable. To Mark and Jill at No Frills Buffalo, it is a pleasure, as always, to work with you. To Bob and Joyce Grinewich and Ed and Kim Krajewski, thank you, as always, for being such wonderful companions on the road of faith and life. To my mother Cora, sisters Laurie, Maureen and Roberta, Uncle Bill and Aunt Ann, thank you as always for your support. Finally, I am indebted to Beth, Sue, Charlene, Deb, Joan, Stacey, Jennifer, Lisa, Tanya and Kelley: what an amazing ride life has been since our friendships were formed!

About the Author

Sinéad Tyrone is a Western New York writer. She has written one prior novel, *Walking Through The Mist*, as well as a poetry collection, *Fragility*. In addition to writing, she is an avid photographer and reader, and is also studying the Irish Gaelic language.

Visit Sinéad's website at www.sineadtyrone.com.

www.ingramcontent.com/pod-product-compliance
Lightning Source LLC
Chambersburg PA
CBHW070324260626
47160CB00003B/938